Faceless Killers

HENNING MANKELL

Faceless Killers

A MYSTERY

TRANSLATED FROM THE SWEDISH

BY STEVEN T. MURRAY

THE NEW PRESS NEW YORK

LIBRARY OF CONGRESS CATALOGING-IN-PUBLICATION DATA
Mankell, Henning, 1948–
    [Mördare utan ansikte. English]
    Faceless killers: a mystery / Henning Mankell;
    translated from the Swedish by Steven T. Murray.
        p.   cm.
    ISBN 1-56584-341-X (hc.)
    ISBN 1-56584-605-2 (pbk.)
    I. Murray, Steven T. II. Title.
PT9876.23.A49M6713 1997
839.7'374—dc20   96–26260

Originally published in Sweden as *Mördare utan ansikte* by Ordfronts Förlag.
Published in the United States by The New Press, New York
Distributed by W. W. Norton & Company, Inc., New York

The New Press was established in 1990 as a not-for-profit alternative to the large,
commercial publishing houses currently dominating the book publishing industry.
The New Press operates in the public interest rather than for private gain,
and is committed to publishing, in innovative ways, works of educational, cultural,
and community value that are often deemed insufficiently profitable.

The New Press is deeply grateful to the Swedish Institute for its generous support.

Book design by BAD

www.thenewpress.com

Printed in the United States of America

9 8 7 6 5 4 3 2 1

Faceless Killers

Chapter One

He has forgotten something, he knows that for sure when he wakes up. Something he dreamed during the night. Something he ought to remember.

He tries to remember. But sleep is like a black hole. A well that reveals nothing of its contents.

At least I didn't dream about the bulls, he thinks. Then I would have been all sweaty, as if I had suffered through a fever during the night. This time the bulls left me in peace.

He lies still in the darkness and listens. His wife's breathing at his side is so faint that he can hardly hear it.

One of these mornings she'll be lying dead beside me and I won't even notice, he thinks. Or maybe it'll be me. One of us will die before the other. Daybreak will reveal that one of us has been left all alone.

He looks at the clock on the table next to the bed. The hands glow and point at quarter to five.

Why did I wake up? he thinks. I usually sleep till five thirty. I've done that for over forty years. Why am I waking up now?

He listens to the darkness and suddenly he is wide awake.

Something is different. Something is no longer the way it usually is.

Carefully he gropes with one hand until he touches his wife's face. With his fingertips he can feel that she's warm. So she's not the one who died. Neither of them has been left alone yet.

He listens to the darkness.

The horse, he thinks. She's not neighing. That's why I woke up. The mare usually whinnies at night. I hear it without waking up, and in my subconscious I know that I can keep on sleeping.

Carefully he gets out of the creaky bed. For forty years they've owned it. It was the only piece of furniture they bought when they got married. It's also the only bed they'll ever have in their lives.

He can feel his left knee aching as he walks across the wooden floor to the window.

I'm old, he thinks. Old and used up. Every morning when I wake up I'm surprised all over again that I'm seventy years old.

He looks out into the winter night. It's the eighth of January, 1990, and no snow has fallen in Skåne this winter. The lamp outside the kitchen door casts its glow across the yard, the bare chestnut tree, and the fields beyond. He squints his eyes toward the neighboring farm where the Lövgrens live. The long, low white house is dark. The stable in the corner against the farmhouse has a pale yellow lamp above the black stable door. That's where the mare stands in her stall, and that's where she suddenly whinnies uneasily at night.

He listens to the darkness.

The bed creaks behind him.

"What are you doing?" mutters his wife.

"Go back to sleep," he replies. "I'm just stretching my legs."

"Is your knee hurting again?"

"No."

"Then come back to bed. Don't stand there freezing, you'll catch cold."

He hears her turn over onto her side.

Once we loved each other, he thinks. But he shields himself from his own thought. That's too noble a word. Love. It's not for the likes of us. Someone who has been a farmer for over forty years, who has stood bowed over the heavy Scanian clay, and does not use the word "love" when he talks about his wife. In our lives, love has always been something totally different.

He looks at the neighbor's house, squinting, trying to penetrate the darkness of the winter night.

Whinny, he thinks. Whinny in your stall so I know that every-thing's normal. So I can lie down under the quilt for a little while longer. A retired crippled farmer's day is long and dreary enough as it is.

Suddenly he realizes that he's looking at the kitchen window of the neighbor's house. Something is different. All these years he has cast an occasional glance at his neighbor's window. Now something suddenly looks different. Or is it just the darkness that's confusing him? He blinks and counts to twenty to rest his eyes. Then he looks at the window again, and now he's sure that it's open. A window that has always been closed at night is suddenly open. And the mare hasn't whinnied at all.

The mare hasn't whinnied because Lövgren hasn't taken his usual nightly walk to the stable when his prostate acts up and drives him out of his warm bed.

I'm just imagining things, he says to himself. My eyes are cloudy. Everything is the same as usual. After all, what could happen here? In the little town of Lenarp, just north of Kade Lake, on the way to beautiful Krageholm Lake, right in the heart of Skåne? Nothing ever happens here. Time stands still in this little town where life flows along like a creek with no vigor or intent. The only people who live here are a few old farmers who have sold or leased out their land to someone else. We live here and wait for the inevitable.

He looks at the kitchen window again, and he thinks that neither Maria nor Johannes Lövgren would forget to close it. With age a sense of dread comes sneaking in; there are more and more locks, and no one forgets to close a window before nightfall. To grow old is to live in fear. The dread of something menacing that you felt when you were a child returns when you get old.

I could get dressed and go out, he thinks. Hobble through the yard with the winter wind on my face, up to the fence that divides our property. I could see with my own eyes that I'm just imagining things.

But he decides to stay put. Soon Johannes will be getting out of bed to make coffee. First he'll turn on the light in the bathroom, then the light in the kitchen. Everything will be the way it always is.

He stands by the window and realizes that he's freezing. The cold of old age that comes creeping in, even in the warmest room. He thinks about Maria and Johannes. We've had a marriage with them too, he thinks, as neighbors and as farmers. We've helped each other, shared the hardships and the bad years. But we've shared the good times too. Together we've celebrated Midsummer and eaten Christmas dinner. Our children ran back and forth between the two farms as if they belonged to both. And now we're sharing the long-drawn-out years of old age.

Without knowing why, he opens the window, carefully so as not to wake Hanna. He holds on tight to the latch so that the gusty winter wind won't tear it out of his hand. But the night is completely calm, and he recalls that the weather report on the radio had said nothing about any storm approaching over the Scanian plain.

The starry sky is clear, and it is very cold. He is just about to close the window again when he thinks he hears a sound. He listens and turns, with his left ear toward the open window. His good ear, not his bad right ear that was injured by all the time he spent cooped up in stuffy, rumbling tractors.

A bird, he thinks. A night bird calling.

Suddenly he is afraid. Out of nowhere the fear appears and seizes him.

It sounds like somebody shouting. In despair, trying to make someone else hear.

A voice that knows it has to penetrate through thick stone walls to catch the attention of the neighbors.

I'm imagining things, he thinks again. There's nobody shouting. Who would it be?

He closes the window so hard that it makes a flowerpot jump, and Hanna wakes up.

"What are you doing?" she says, and he can hear that she's annoyed.

As he replies, he suddenly feels sure.

The terror is real.

"The mare isn't whinnying," he says, sitting down on the edge of the bed. "And the Lövgrens' kitchen window is wide open.

And someone is shouting."

She sits up in bed.

"What did you say?"

He doesn't want to answer, but now he's sure that it wasn't a bird he heard.

"It's Johannes or Maria," he says. "One of them is calling for help."

She gets out of bed and goes over to the window. Big and wide, she stands there in her white nightgown and looks out into the dark.

"The kitchen window isn't open," she whispers. "It's smashed."

He goes over to her, and now he's so cold that he's shaking.

"There's someone shouting for help," she says, and her voice quavers.

"What should we do?"

"Go over there," she says. "Hurry up!"

"But what if it's dangerous?"

"Aren't we going to help our best friends if something has happened?"

He dresses quickly, takes the flashlight from the kitchen cupboard next to the corks and coffee cans.

The clay outside is frozen under his feet. When he turns around he catches a glimpse of Hanna in the window.

Up by the fence he stops. Everything is quiet. Now he can see that the kitchen window is broken. Cautiously he climbs over the low fence and approaches the white house. But no voice calls to him.

I'm just imagining things, he thinks again. I'm an old man who can't figure out what's really happening anymore. Maybe I even dreamed about the bulls last night. The old dream about the bulls charging toward me when I was a boy and making me realize that someday I would die.

Then he hears the cry again. It's weak, like a moan. It's Maria.

He goes over to the bedroom window and peeks in cautiously through the gap between the curtain and the window frame.

Suddenly he knows that Johannes is dead. He shines his flashlight inside and blinks hard before he forces himself to look.

Maria is crumpled up on the floor, tied to a chair. Her face is bloody and her false teeth lie broken on her spattered nightgown.

Then he sees one of Johannes's feet. All he can see is his foot. The rest of his body is hidden by the curtain.

He limps back and climbs over the fence again. His knee aches as he desperately stumbles across the frozen clay.

First he calls the police.

Then he takes his crowbar out of a closet that smells like mothballs.

"Wait here," he tells Hanna. "You don't need to see this."

"What happened?" she asks with tears of fear in her eyes.

"I don't know," he says. "But I woke up because the mare wasn't neighing in the night. I know that for sure."

It is the eighth of January, 1990.

Not yet dawn.

Chapter Two

The incoming telephone call was recorded by the Ystad police at 5:13 AM. It was taken by an exhausted officer who had been on duty almost without a break since New Year's Eve. He had listened to the stammering voice on the phone and thought that it was just some deranged senior citizen. But something had sparked his attention nevertheless. He started asking questions. When the conversation was over, he hesitated for just a moment before lifting the receiver again and dialing a number he knew by heart.

Kurt Wallander was asleep. He had stayed up far too long the night before, listening to recordings of Maria Callas that a good friend had sent him from Bulgaria. Again and again he had returned to her *Traviata,* and it was close to two AM before he finally went to bed. By the time the ring of the telephone roused him from sleep, he was deep in an intense erotic dream. As if to assure himself that he had only been dreaming, he reached out and felt the covers next to him. But he was alone in the bed. Neither his wife, who had left him three months earlier, nor the black woman with whom he had just been making fierce love in his dream, was present.

He looked at the clock as he reached for the phone. A car crash, he thought instantly. Treacherous ice and someone driving too fast and then spinning off E14. Or trouble with refugees arriving on the morning ferry from Poland.

He scooted up in bed and pressed the receiver to his cheek, feeling the sting of his unshaven skin.

"Wallander."

"I hope I didn't wake you."

"No, damn it. I'm awake."

Why do I lie? he thought. Why don't I just say it like it is? That all I want is to go back to sleep and recapture a fleeting dream in the form of a naked woman.

"I thought I should call you."

"Traffic accident?"

"No, not exactly. An old farmer called and said his name was Nyström. Lives in Lenarp. He claimed that the woman next door was tied up on the floor and that someone was dead."

Wallander thought quickly about where Lenarp was located. Not so far from Marsvinsholm, in a region that was unusually hilly for Skåne.

"It sounded serious. I thought it best to call you at home."

"Who have you got at the station right now?"

"Peters and Norén are out looking for someone who broke a window at the Continental. Shall I call them?"

"Tell them to drive out to the crossroads between Kade Lake and Katslösa and wait there till I show up. Give them the address. When did the call come in?"

"A few minutes ago."

"Sure it wasn't just some drunk calling?"

"Didn't sound like it."

"Huh. All right then."

Wallander dressed quickly without showering, poured himself a cup of the lukewarm coffee that was still in the thermos, and looked out the window. He lived on Mariagatan in central Ystad, and the façade of the building across from him was cracked and gray. He wondered fleetingly whether there would be any snow in Skåne this winter. He hoped not. Scanian snowstorms always brought periods of uninterrupted drudgery. Car wrecks, snowbound women going into labor, isolated old people, and downed power lines. With the snowstorms came chaos, and he felt ill equipped to meet the chaos this winter. The anxiety of his wife leaving him still burned inside him.

He drove down Regementsgatan until he came out on Österleden. At Dragongatan he was stopped by a red light, and he turned on the car radio to listen to the news. An excited voice was talking about a plane that had crashed on some far-off continent.

A time to live and a time to die, he thought as he rubbed the sleep from his eyes. He had adopted this incantation many years ago. Back then he was a young policeman cruising the streets in his home town of Malmö. A drunk had suddenly pulled out a big butcher knife as he and his partner were trying to take him away in the squad car from Pildamm Park. Wallander was stabbed deep, right next to his heart. A few millimeters were all that saved him from an unexpected death. He had been twenty-three then, suddenly profoundly aware of what it meant to be a cop. The incantation was his way of fending off the memories.

He drove out of the city, passing the newly built furniture warehouse at the edge of town, and caught a glimpse of the sea in the distance. It was gray but oddly quiet for the middle of the Scanian winter. Far off toward the horizon there was the silhouette of a ship heading east.

The snowstorms are on their way, he thought.

Sooner or later they'll be upon us.

He shut off the car radio and tried to concentrate on what was in store for him.

What did he know, really?

An old woman, tied up on the floor? A man who claimed he saw her through a window? Wallander sped up after he passed the turnoff to Bjäre Lake and thought that it was undoubtedly an old man who was struck by a sudden flare-up of senility. In his many years on the force he had seen more than once how old, isolated people would call the police as a desperate cry for help.

The squad car was waiting for him at the side road toward Kade Lake. Peters had climbed out and was watching a hare bounding back and forth out in a field.

When he saw Wallander approaching in his blue Peugeot, he raised his hand in greeting and got in behind the wheel.

The frozen gravel crunched under the car tires. Kurt Wallander followed the police car. They passed the turnoff toward Trunnerup and continued up some steep hills until they came to Lenarp. They

swung onto a narrow dirt road that was hardly more than a tractor rut. After a kilometer they were there. Two farms next to each
other, two whitewashed farmhouses, and carefully tended gardens.

An elderly man came hurrying toward them. Wallander saw
that he was limping, as if one knee was bothering him.

When Wallander got out of the car he noticed that the wind
had started to blow. Maybe the snow was on the way after all.

As soon as he saw the old man he knew that something truly
unpleasant awaited him. In the man's eyes shone a horror that
could not be imaginary.

"I broke open the door," he repeated feverishly, over and over.
"I broke open the door because I had to see. But she'll be dead soon
too."

They went in through the broken door. Wallander was met by
a pungent old-man smell. The wallpaper was old-fashioned, and
he was forced to squint to be able to see anything in the dim light.

"So what happened here?" he asked.

"In there," replied the old man.

Then he started to cry.

The three policemen looked at each other.

Wallander pushed open the door with one foot.

It was worse than he had imagined. Much worse. Later he
would say that it was the worst he had ever seen. And he had
seen plenty.

The old couple's bedroom was soaked in blood. It had even
splashed onto the porcelain lamp hanging from the ceiling. Prostrate
across the bed lay an old man with no shirt on and his long underwear pulled down. His face was crushed beyond recognition. It
looked as though someone had tried to cut off his nose. His hands
were tied behind his back and his left thigh was shattered. The
white bone shone against all that red.

"Oh shit," he heard Norén moan behind him, and Wallander
felt nauseated himself.

"Ambulance," he said, swallowing. "Hurry up."

Then they bent over the woman, half-lying on the floor, tied
to a chair. Whoever tied her up had rigged a noose around her

scrawny neck. She was breathing feebly, and Wallander yelled at Peters to find a knife. They cut off the thin rope that was digging deep into her wrists and neck, and laid her gently on the floor. Wallander held her head on his knee.

He looked at Peters and realized that they were both thinking the same thing. Who could have been cruel enough to do this? Tying a noose on a helpless old woman.

"Wait outside," said Wallander to the sobbing old man standing in the doorway. "Wait outside and don't touch anything."

He could hear that his voice sounded like a roar.

I'm yelling because I'm scared, he thought. What kind of world are we living in?

Almost twenty minutes passed before the ambulance arrived. The woman's breathing grew more and more irregular, and Wallander was starting to worry that it might come too late.

He recognized the ambulance driver, who was named Antonson.

His assistant was a young man he had never seen before.

"Hi," said Wallander. "He's dead. But the woman here is alive. Try to keep her that way."

"What happened?" asked Antonson.

"I hope she'll be able to tell us, if she makes it. Hurry up now!"

When the ambulance had vanished down the gravel road, Wallander and Peters went outside. Norén was wiping his face with a handkerchief. The dawn was slowly approaching. Wallander looked at his wristwatch. Seven twenty-eight.

"It's a slaughterhouse in there," said Peters.

"Worse," replied Wallander. "Call in and request a full team. Tell Norén to seal off the area. I'm going to talk to the old man."

Just as he said that, he heard something that sounded like a scream. He jumped, and then the scream came again.

It was a horse whinnying.

They went over to the stable and opened the door. Inside in the dark a horse was rustling in its stall. The place smelled of warm manure and urine.

"Give the horse some water and hay," said Wallander. "Maybe there are other animals here too."

When he emerged from the stable he gave a shudder. Black birds were screeching in a lone tree far out in a field. He sucked the cold air into his throat and noticed that the wind was picking up.

"Your name is Nyström," he said to the man, who by now had stopped weeping. "You have to tell me what happened here. If I understand correctly, you live in the house next door."

The man nodded. "What happened here?" he asked in a quavering voice.

"That's what I'm hoping you can tell me," said Wallander. "Maybe we could go into your house."

In the kitchen a woman in an old-fashioned dressing gown sat slumped on a chair crying. But as soon as Wallander introduced himself she got up and started to make coffee. The men sat down at the kitchen table. Wallander saw the Christmas decorations still hanging in the window. An old cat lay on the windowsill, staring at him without blinking. He reached out his hand to pet it.

"He bites," said Nyström. "He's not much used to people. Except for Hanna and me."

Kurt Wallander thought of his wife who had left him and wondered where to begin. A bestial murder, he thought. And if we're really unlucky, it'll soon be a double murder.

Suddenly he had an idea. He knocked on the kitchen window to get Norén's attention.

"Excuse me for a moment," he said, getting up.

"The horse had both water and hay," said Norén. "There weren't any other animals."

"See that someone goes over to the hospital," said Wallander. "In case she wakes up and says something. She must have seen everything."

Norén nodded.

"Send somebody with good ears," said Wallander. "Preferably someone who can read lips."

When he came back into the kitchen he took off his overcoat and laid it on the kitchen sofa.

"Now tell me," he said. "Tell me, and don't leave anything out. Take your time."

After two cups of weak coffee he could see that neither Nyström nor his wife had anything significant to tell. He got some of the chronology and the life story of the couple who had been attacked.

He had two questions left.

"Do you know if they kept any large sums of money in the house?" he asked.

"No," said Nyström. "They put everything in the bank. Their pensions too. And they weren't rich. When they sold off the fields and the animals and the machinery, they gave the money to their children."

The second question seemed meaningless to him. But he asked it anyway. In this situation he had no choice.

"Do you know if they had any enemies?" he asked.

"Enemies?"

"Anybody who could have possibly done this?"

They didn't seem to understand his question.

He repeated it.

The two old people looked at each other, uncomprehending.

"People like us don't have any enemies," the man replied. Wallander noticed that he sounded offended. "Sometimes we quarrel with each other. About maintaining a wagon path or the location of the pasture boundaries. But we don't kill each other."

Wallander nodded.

"I'll be in touch again soon," he said, getting up with his coat in his hand. "If you think of anything else, don't hesitate to call the police. Ask for me, Inspector Wallander."

"What if they come back...?" asked the old woman.

Wallander shook his head.

"They won't be back," he said. "It was most likely robbers. They never come back. There's nothing for you to worry about."

He thought that he ought to say something more to reassure them. But what? What security could he offer to people who had just seen their closest neighbor brutally murdered? Who had to wait and see whether a second person was going to die?

"The horse," he said. "Who will give it hay?"

"We will," replied the old man. "We'll see that she gets what she needs."

Wallander went outside into the cold dawn. The wind had increased, and he hunched his shoulders as he walked toward his car. Actually he ought to stay here and give the crime-scene technicians a hand. But he was freezing and feeling lousy and didn't want to stay any longer than necessary. Besides, he saw through the window that it was Rydberg who had come with the team's car. That meant that the techs wouldn't finish their work until they had turned over and inspected every lump of clay at the crime scene. Rydberg, who was supposed to retire in a couple of years, was a passionate policeman. Although he might appear pedantic and slow, his presence was a guarantee that a crime scene would be treated the way it should be.

Rydberg had rheumatism and used a cane. Now he came limping across the yard toward Wallander.

"It's not pretty," Rydberg said. "It looks like a slaughterhouse in there."

"You're not the first one to say that," said Wallander.

Rydberg looked serious. "Have we got any leads?"

Wallander shook his head.

"Nothing at all?" There was something of an entreaty in Rydberg's voice.

"The neighbors didn't hear or see anything. I think it's ordinary robbers."

"You call this insane brutality ordinary?"

Rydberg was upset, and Wallander regretted his choice of words. "I meant, of course, that it was some particularly fiendish individuals who were at it last night. The type who make their living picking out farms in solitary locations where lonely old people live."

"We've got to catch these guys," said Rydberg. "Before they strike again."

"You're right," said Wallander. "If we don't catch anyone else this year, we've got to catch these guys."

He got into his car and drove off. On the narrow farm road he almost collided with a car coming around a curve toward him at high speed. He recognized the man driving. It was a reporter who worked for one of the big national papers and always showed up whenever something of more than local interest happened in the Ystad area.

Wallander drove back and forth through Lenarp a few times. There were lights in the windows, but no one was outside.

What are they going to think when they find out? he wondered to himself.

He was feeling uneasy. The discovery of the old woman with the noose around her neck had shaken him. The cruelty of it was incomprehensible. Who would do something like that? Why not hit her over the head with an axe so it would all be over in an instant? Why torture her?

He tried to plan the investigation in his head as he drove slowly through the little town. At the crossroads toward Blentarp he stopped, turned up the heat in the car because he was cold, and then sat completely still, gazing off toward the horizon.

He was the one who would have to lead the investigation, he knew that. No one else was even likely. After Rydberg, he was the criminal detective in Ystad who had the most experience, despite the fact that he was only forty-two years old.

Much of the investigative work would be routine. Crime scene examination, questioning people who lived in Lenarp and along the escape routes the robbers may have taken. Had anyone seen anything suspicious? Anything unusual? The questions were already echoing through his mind.

But Kurt Wallander knew from experience that farm robberies were often difficult to solve.

What he could hope for was that the old woman would survive. She had seen what happened. She knew.

But if she died, the double murder would be hard to solve.

He felt uneasy.

Under normal circumstances the uneasiness would have spurred him on to greater energy and activity. Since those were the prerequisites for all police work, he had imagined that he was a good cop. But right now he felt unsure of himself and tired.

He forced himself to shift into first gear. The car rolled a few meters. Then he stopped again.

It was as if he just now realized what he had witnessed on that frozen winter morning.

The meaninglessness and cruelty of the attack on the help-less old couple scared him.

Something had happened that shouldn't have happened here at all.

He looked out the car window. The wind was rushing and whistling around the car doors.

I have to get started, he thought.

It's just like Rydberg said.

We've got to catch whoever did this.

He drove straight to the hospital in Ystad and took the eleva-tor up to the intensive-care unit. In the corridor he noticed at once the young police cadet Martinson sitting on a chair outside a room.

Wallander could feel himself getting annoyed.

Was there really no one else available to send to the hospital but a young, inexperienced police cadet? And why was he sitting outside the door? Why wasn't he sitting at the bedside, ready to catch the slightest whisper from the brutalized woman?

"Hi," said Wallander, "how's it going?"

"She's unconscious," replied Martinson. "The doctors don't seem too hopeful."

"Why are you sitting out here? Why aren't you in the room?"

"They said they'd tell me if anything happened."

Wallander noticed that Martinson was starting to feel unsure of himself.

I sound like some grumpy old schoolteacher, he thought.

He carefully pushed open the door and looked in. Various machines were sucking and pumping in death's waiting room. Hoses undulated like transparent worms along the walls. A nurse was standing there reading a chart when he opened the door.

"You can't come in here," she said sharply.

"I'm a police inspector," replied Wallander feebly. "I just wanted to hear how she's doing."

"You've been asked to wait outside," said the nurse.

Before Wallander could answer, a doctor came rushing into the room. He thought the doctor looked surprisingly young.

"We would prefer not to have any unauthorized persons in here," said the young doctor when he caught sight of Wallander.

"I'm leaving. But I just wanted to hear how she's doing. My name is Wallander, and I'm a police inspector. Homicide," he added, unsure whether that made any difference. "I'm heading the investigation of the person or persons who did this. How is she?"

"It's amazing that she's still alive," said the doctor, nodding to Wallander to step over to the bed. "We can't tell yet the extent of the internal injuries she may have suffered. First we have to see whether she survives. But her windpipe has been severely traumatized. As if someone had tried to strangle her."

"That's exactly what happened," said Wallander, looking at the thin face visible among the sheets and hoses.

"She should have been dead," said the doctor.

"I hope she survives," said Wallander. "She's the only witness we've got."

"We hope all our patients survive," replied the doctor sternly, studying a monitor where green lines moved in uninterrupted waves.

Wallander left the room after the doctor insisted that he couldn't tell him anything. The prognosis was uncertain. Maria Lövgren might die without regaining consciousness. There was no way to know.

"Can you read lips?" Wallander asked the police cadet.

"No," Martinson replied in surprise.

"That's too bad," said Wallander and left.

From the hospital he drove straight to the brown police station that lay on the road out toward the east end of town.

He sat down at his desk and looked out the window, over at the old red water tower.

Maybe the times require another type of cop, he thought. Cops who don't react when they're forced to go into a human slaughter-house on an early January morning in the countryside of southern Sweden. Cops who don't suffer from my uncertainty and anguish.

His thoughts were interrupted by the telephone.

The hospital, he thought at once.

Now they're calling to say that Maria Lövgren is dead.

But did she manage to wake up? Did she say anything?

He stared at the ringing telephone.

Damn, he thought. Damn.

Anything but that.

But when he picked up the receiver, it was his daughter. He gave a start and almost dropped the phone on the floor.

"Papa," she said, and he heard the coin dropping into the pay phone.

"Hi," he said. "Where are you calling from?"

Just so it's not Lima, he thought. Or Katmandu. Or Kinshasa.

"I'm here in Ystad."

He was suddenly happy. That meant he'd get to see her.

"I came to visit you," she said. "But I've changed my plans. I'm at the train station. I'm leaving now. I just wanted to tell you that at least I thought about seeing you."

Then the conversation was cut off, and he was left sitting there with the receiver in his hand.

It was like holding something dead, something hacked off in his hand.

That damn kid, he thought. Why does she do things like this?

His daughter Linda was nineteen. Until she was fifteen their relationship had been good. She came to him rather than to her mother whenever she had a problem or when there was something she really wanted to do but didn't quite dare. He had seen her metamorphose from a chubby little girl to a young woman with a defiant beauty. Before she was fifteen, she never gave any hint that she was carrying around some secret demons that one day would drive her into a precarious and inscrutable landscape.

One spring day, soon after her fifteenth birthday, Linda had suddenly and without warning tried to commit suicide. It happened on a Saturday afternoon. Wallander had been fixing one of the garden chairs and his wife was washing the windows. He had put down his hammer and gone into the house, driven by a sudden uneasiness. Linda was lying on the bed in her room, and she had used a razor to cut both her wrists and her throat. Afterwards, when it was all over, the doctor told Wallander that she would have died if he hadn't come in when he did and had the presence of mind to apply pressure bandages.

He never got over the shock. All contact between him and Linda was broken. She pulled away, and he never managed to understand what had driven her to attempt suicide. When she finished school she took a string of odd jobs, and would abruptly disappear for long periods of time. Twice his wife had pressed him to report her missing. His colleagues had seen his pain when Linda became the object of his own investigation. But one day she would turn up again, and the only way he could follow her journeys was to go through her pockets and leaf through her passport on the sly.

Hell, he thought. Why didn't you stay? Why did you change your mind?

The telephone rang again and he snatched up the receiver.

"This is Papa," Wallander said without thinking.

"What do you mean?" said his father. "What do you mean by picking up the phone and saying Papa? I thought you were a cop."

"I don't have time to talk to you right now. Can I call you back later?"

"No, you can't. What's so important?"

"Something serious happened this morning. I'll call you later."

"So what happened?"

His elderly father called him almost every day. On several occasions Wallander had told the switchboard not to put through any calls from him. But then his father saw through his ruse and started making up phony identities and disguising his voice to fool the operators.

Wallander saw only one possibility of evading him.

"I'll come out and see you tonight," he said. "Then we can talk."

His father reluctantly let himself be persuaded. "Come at seven. I'll have time to see you then."

"I'll be there at seven. See you."

Wallander hung up and pushed the button to block incoming calls.

For a moment he considered taking the car and driving down to the train station to try and find his daughter. Talk to her, try to rekindle the contact that had been so mysteriously lost. But he knew that he wouldn't do it. He didn't want to risk her running away from him for good.

The door opened and Näslund stuck his head in.

"Hi," he said. "Should I show him in?"

"Show who in?"

Näslund looked at his watch.

"It's nine o'clock. You told me yesterday that you wanted Klas Månson here for interrogation at nine."

"Who's Klas Månson?"

Näslund looked at him quizzically. "The guy who robbed the store on Österleden. Did you forget about him?"

Then he remembered, and at the same time he realized that Näslund obviously hadn't heard about the murder that had been committed in the night.

"You take over Månson," he said. "We had a murder last night out in Lenarp. Maybe a double murder. An old couple. You can take over Månson. But put it off for a while. The first thing we have to do is plan the investigation at Lenarp."

"Månson's lawyer is already here," said Näslund. "If I send him away, he's going to raise hell."

"Do a preliminary questioning," said Wallander. "If the lawyer makes a fuss later, it can't be helped. Set up an investigation meeting in my office for ten o'clock. Make sure everyone comes."

Suddenly he was in motion. Now he was a cop again. The anguish about his daughter and his wife who had left him would have to wait. Right now he had to begin the arduous hunt for a murderer.

He moved the piles of paper off his desk, tore up a soccer lottery form he wouldn't get around to filling out anyway, and went out to the lunchroom and poured a cup of coffee.

At ten o'clock everyone gathered in his office. Rydberg had been called in from the crime scene and was sitting on a Windsor chair by the window. A total of seven police officers, sitting and standing, filled the room. Wallander phoned the hospital and managed to extract the information that the old woman's condition was still critical.

Then he told all of them what had happened.

"It was worse than you could imagine," he said. "Wouldn't you say so, Rydberg?"

"That's right," replied Rydberg. "Like an American movie. It even smelled like blood. It doesn't usually do that."

"We have to catch whoever did this," Wallander concluded his presentation. "We can't just let maniacs like this run around loose."

The whole room fell silent. Rydberg was drumming his fingertips on the arm of the chair. A woman was heard laughing in the corridor outside.

Kurt Wallander looked around. They were all his colleagues. None of them was his close friend. And yet they were a team.

"Well," he said, "what are we waiting for? Let's get started."

It was twenty minutes to eleven.

Chapter Three

At four in the afternoon Kurt Wallander discovered that he was hungry. He hadn't had a chance to eat lunch all day. After the investigation meeting that morning he had spent all his time organizing the hunt for the murderers in Lenarp. He kept thinking about the murderer in the plural. He had a hard time imagining that one person could have carried out that bloodbath.

It was dark outside when he sank into his chair behind his desk to try and put together a statement for the press. There was a stack of phone messages on his desk, left by one of the women from the switchboard. After searching in vain for his daughter's name among the slips, he put the whole pile in his in-box. To avoid subjecting himself to the unpleasantness of standing in front of the TV cameras of News South and telling them that at present the police had no leads regarding the criminal or criminals who had perpetrated the heinous murder of the old man, Wallander had appealed to Rydberg to take on that task. But he had to write the press release himself. He took a sheet of paper out of a desk drawer. But what would he write? The day's work had hardly involved more than collecting a large number of question marks.

It had been a day of waiting. In the intensive-care unit the old woman who had survived the noose was fighting for her life.

Would they ever find out what she had seen on that appalling night in the isolated farmhouse? Or would she die before she could tell them anything?

Wallander looked out the window, into the darkness.

Instead of a press release he started writing a summary of what had been done that day and what the police actually had to go on.

Nothing, he thought when he was finished. Two old people with no enemies, no hidden cash, were brutally attacked and tortured. The neighbors heard nothing. Not until the perpetrators were gone did they notice that a window had been smashed and hear the old woman's cry for help. Rydberg had not yet found any clues. That was it.

Old people on isolated farms have always been subjected to robbery. They have also been bound, beaten, and sometimes killed.

But this is something else, thought Wallander. A noose tells its gruesome story of viciousness and hate, maybe even revenge.

There was something about this attack that didn't make sense.

Now all they could do was hope. Several police patrols had been talking to the inhabitants of Lenarp all day long. Perhaps someone had seen something? When old people living in isolated locations were attacked, the perpetrators had often cased the place in advance. Maybe Rydberg would find some clues at the crime scene in spite of everything.

Wallander looked at the clock.

How long has it been since I last called the hospital? Forty-five minutes? An hour?

He decided to wait until after he had written his press release.

He put on the headphones of his Walkman and popped in a cassette of Jussi Björling. The scratchy sound of the '30s recordings could not detract from the magnificence of the music from *Rigoletto*.

The press release turned out to be eight lines long. Wallander took it to one of the clerks and asked her to type it up and then make copies. At the same time he was reading through a questionnaire that was supposed to be mailed out to everyone who lived in the area around Lenarp. Had anyone seen anything unusual? Anything that could be tied to the brutal attack? He didn't have much faith that the questionnaire would produce anything but inconvenience. He knew that the telephones would ring incessantly and two officers would have to be assigned full time to listen to useless reports.

Still, it has to be done, he thought. At least we can ascertain that no one saw anything.

He went back to his office and phoned the hospital again. But nothing had changed. The old woman was still fighting for her life.

Just as he put down the phone, Näslund came in.

"I was right," he said.

"About what?"

"Månson's lawyer hit the roof."

Wallander shrugged. "We'll just have to live with it."

Näslund scratched his forehead and asked how the investigation was going.

"Not a thing so far. We've gotten started. That's about it."

"I noticed that the preliminary forensic report came in."

Wallander raised an eyebrow. "Why didn't I get it?"

"It was in Hanson's office."

"Well, that's not where it's supposed to be, damn it!"

Wallander got up and went out in the hall. It was always the same, he thought. Papers didn't wind up where they were supposed to go. Even though more and more police work was recorded on computers, important papers had a tendency to get lost.

Hanson sat talking on the phone when Wallander knocked and went in. He saw that Hanson's desk was covered with poorly concealed betting slips and racing forms from various tracks around the country. At the police station it was common knowledge that Hanson spent the major part of his working day calling around to various trotting-horse trainers begging for stable tips. Then he spent his evenings figuring out innumerable betting systems that would guarantee him the greatest winnings. It was also rumored that Hanson had hit it big on one occasion. But no one knew for sure. And Hanson wasn't exactly living high on the hog.

When Wallander came in, Hanson put his hand over the mouthpiece.

"The forensic report," said Wallander. "Have you got it?"

Hanson pushed aside a racing form from Jägersrö.

"I was just about to take it over to you."

"Number four in the seventh race is a sure thing," said Wallander, taking the plastic folder from the desk.

"What do you mean by that?"

"I mean it's a sure thing."

Wallander walked out, leaving Hanson gaping behind him. He saw by the clock in the hall that there was half an hour left until the press conference. He went back to his office and carefully read through the doctor's report.

The brutal nature of the murder was thrown into even sharper relief, if possible, than when he had arrived in Lenarp that morning.

In the first preliminary examination of the body, the doctor was not able to pinpoint the actual cause of death.

There were just too many to choose from.

The body had received eight deep stab or chopping wounds with a sharp, serrated implement. The doctor suggested a compass saw. In addition, the right femur was broken, as were the left upper arm and wrist. The body showed signs of burn wounds, the scrotum was swollen up, and the forehead was bashed in. The actual cause of death could not yet be determined.

The doctor had made a note beside the official report. "An act of madness," he wrote. "This man was subjected to enough violence to kill four or five individuals."

Wallander put down the report.

He was feeling worse and worse.

Something didn't add up.

Robbers who attacked old people were hardly full of hate. They were after money.

Why this insane violence?

When Wallander realized that he couldn't come up with a satisfactory answer to the question, he again read through the summary he had written. Had he forgotten something? Had he overlooked some detail that would later turn out to be significant? Even though police work was largely a matter of patiently searching for facts that could be combined with each other, he had also learned from experience that the first impression of a crime scene was important. Especially when the officer was one of the first to arrive at a scene after the crime had been committed.

There was something in his summary that puzzled him. Had he left out some detail after all?

He sat for a long time without coming up with what it might be.

A woman opened the door and handed him the typed press release and the copies. On the way to the press conference he stepped into the men's room and looked in the mirror. He noticed that he needed a haircut. His brown hair was sticking out around his ears. And he ought to lose some weight too. In the three months since his wife had so unexpectedly left him, he had put on fifteen pounds. In his apathetic loneliness he had eaten nothing but fast food and pizza, greasy hamburgers, and donuts.

"You flabby piece of shit," he said out loud to himself. "Do you really want to look like a pitiful old man?"

He made a decision to change his eating habits at once. If it would help him lose weight, he might even consider taking up smoking again.

He wondered what the real reason was. Why almost every cop was divorced. Why the wives left their husbands. Sometimes, when he read a crime novel, he discovered with a sigh that it was just as bad in fiction.

Cops were divorced. That's all there was to it.

The room where the press conference was being held was full of people. He recognized most of the reporters. But there were a few unfamiliar faces too, and an adolescent girl with a pimply face was casting amorous glances at him as she adjusted her tape recorder.

Wallander passed out the brief press release and sat down on a little dais at one end of the room. Actually, the Ystad chief of police should have been there too, but he was on his winter vacation in Spain. If Rydberg managed to finish with the TV crews, he had promised to attend. But otherwise Kurt Wallander was on his own.

"You've received the press release," he began. "I don't have anything else to say at present."

"May we ask questions?" said a reporter Wallander recognized as the local stringer for *Labor News*.

"That's why I'm here," replied Wallander.

"If you don't mind my saying so, this is an unusually poor press release," said the reporter. "You must be able to tell us more than this."

"We have no leads to the perpetrators," said Wallander.

"So there were more than one?"

"Possibly."

"Why do you think so?"

"We think there were. But we don't know."

The reporter grimaced, and Wallander nodded to another reporter he recognized.

"How was he killed?"

"By external force."

"That can mean a lot of different things!"

"We don't know yet. The doctors aren't finished with the forensic examination. It'll take a couple of days."

The reporter had more questions, but he was interrupted by the pimply girl with the tape recorder. Wallander could see by the call letters on the lid that she was from the local radio station.

"What did the robbers take?"

"We don't know," replied Wallander. "We don't even know if it was a robbery."

"What else could it be?"

"We don't know."

"Is there anything that leads you to believe that it wasn't a robbery?"

"No."

Wallander could feel that he was sweating in the stuffy room. He remembered how as a young policeman he had dreamed of holding press conferences. But it had never been stuffy and sweaty in his dreams.

"I asked a question," he heard one of the reporters say from the back of the room.

"I didn't hear it," said Wallander.

"Do the police regard this as an important crime?" asked the reporter.

Wallander was surprised at the question.

"Naturally it's important that we solve this murder," he said. "Why shouldn't it be?"

"Will you be needing extra resources?"

"It's too early to comment on that. Of course we're hoping for a quick solution. I guess I still don't understand your question."

The very young reporter with the thick glasses pushed his way forward. Wallander had never seen him before.

"In my opinion, no one in Sweden cares about old people any longer."

"*We* do," replied Wallander. "We will do everything we can to apprehend the perpetrators. In Skåne there are many old people living alone on isolated farms. We would like to reassure them, above all, that we are doing everything we can."

He stood up. "We'll let you know when we have more to report," he said. "Thank you for coming."

The young woman from the local radio station blocked his path as he was leaving the room.

"I have nothing more to say," he told her.

"I know your daughter Linda," she said.

Wallander stopped. "You do? How?"

"We've met a few times. Here and there."

Wallander tried to think whether he knew her. Had the girls been schoolmates?

She shook her head as if reading his mind.

"We've never met," she said. "You don't know me. Linda and I ran into each other in Malmö."

"I see," said Wallander. "That's nice."

"I think she's great. Could I ask you some questions now?"

Wallander repeated into her microphone what he had said earlier. Most of all he wanted to talk about Linda, but he didn't have a chance.

"Say hi to her," she said, packing up her tape recorder. "Say hi from Cathrin. Or Cattis."

"I will," said Wallander. "I promise."

When he went back to his office he could feel a gnawing in his stomach. But was it hunger or anxiety?

I've got to stop this, he thought. I've got to realize that my wife has left me. I've got to admit that all I can do is wait for Linda to contact me herself. I've got to take life as it comes...

Just before six the investigative team gathered for another meeting. There was no news from the hospital. Wallander quickly drew up a shift schedule for the night.

"Is that necessary?" wondered Hanson. "Just put a tape recorder in the room, then any nurse can turn it on if the old lady wakes up."

"It *is* necessary," said Wallander. "I can take midnight to six myself. Any volunteers until midnight?"

Rydberg nodded. "I can sit at the hospital just as well as anywhere," he said.

Wallander looked around. Everyone seemed pale in the glare from the fluorescent lights on the ceiling.

"Did we get anywhere?" he asked.

"We've checked out Lenarp," said Peters, who had led the door-to-door inquiry. "Everybody says they didn't see a thing. But it usually takes a few days before people really think about it. People are pretty scared up there. It's damned unpleasant. Almost nothing but old folks. And a terrified young Polish family that is probably here illegally. But I didn't bother them. We'll have to keep trying tomorrow."

Wallander nodded and looked at Rydberg.

"There were plenty of fingerprints," he said. "Maybe that will produce something. But I doubt it. It's mostly the knot that interests me."

Wallander gave him a searching look. "What knot?"

"The knot on the noose."

"What about it?"

"It's unusual. I've never seen a knot like that before."

"Have you ever seen a noose before?" interrupted Hanson, who was standing in the doorway, wanting to leave.

"Yes, I have," replied Rydberg. "We'll see what this knot can tell us."

Wallander knew that Rydberg didn't want to say any more. But if the knot interested him, it might be important.

"I'm driving back out to see the neighbors tomorrow morning," said Wallander. "Has anyone tracked down the Lövgrens' children yet, by the way?"

"Martinson's working on it," said Hanson.

"I thought Martinson was at the hospital," said Wallander, surprised.

"He traded with Svedberg."

"So where the hell is he now?"

No one knew where Martinson was. Wallander called the switchboard and found out that Martinson had left an hour earlier.

"Call him at home," said Wallander.

Then he looked at his watch.

"We'll meet again in the morning at ten o'clock," he said. "Thanks for coming, see you then."

Everyone else had left by the time the switchboard connected him with Martinson.

"Sorry," said Martinson. "I forgot we had a meeting."

"How's it going with the children?"

"Damned if Rickard doesn't have chicken pox."

"I mean the Lövgrens' children. The two daughters."

Martinson sounded surprised when he answered. "Didn't you get my message?"

"I didn't get any message."

"I gave it to one of the girls at the switchboard."

"I'll take a look. But tell me first."

"One daughter, who's fifty years old, lives in Canada. Winnipeg, wherever that is. I completely forgot that it was the middle of the night over there when I called. She refused to believe what I was saying. Not until her husband came to the phone did it dawn on them what had happened. He's a cop, by the way. A real Canadian Mountie. I'm going to call them back tomorrow. But she's flying over, of course. The other daughter was harder to reach, even though she lives in Sweden. She's forty-seven, the manager of the buffet at the Ruby Hotel in Göteborg. Evidently she's training a handball team in Skien, in Norway. But they promised that they'd get word to her about what happened. I gave the switchboard a list of the Lövgrens' other relatives. There are lots of them. Most of them live in Skåne. Some of them will probably call tomorrow when they see the story in the papers."

"Good work," said Wallander. "Can you relieve me at the hospital tomorrow morning at six? If she doesn't die by then."

"I'll be there," said Martinson. "But is it such a good idea for you to take that shift?"

"Why not?"

"You're the one heading the investigation. You ought to get some sleep."

"I can handle it for one night," replied Wallander and hung up.

He sat completely still and stared into space.

Are we going to figure this one out? he thought. Or do they already have too much of a head start?

He put on his overcoat, turned off the desk lamp, and left his office. The corridor leading to the reception area was deserted. He stuck his head in the glass cubicle where the operator on duty sat leafing through a magazine. He noticed that it was a racing form. Is everyone playing the ponies these days? he thought.

"Martinson supposedly left some papers for me," he said.

The operator, who was named Ebba and had been with the police department for more than thirty years, gave a friendly nod and pointed at the counter.

"We have a girl here from the youth employment bureau," she said, smiling. "Sweet and nice but completely incompetent. Maybe she forgot to give them to you."

Wallander nodded.

"I'm leaving now," he said. "I'll probably be home in a couple of hours. If anything happens, call me at my father's place."

"You're thinking of that poor woman at the hospital," said Ebba.

Wallander nodded.

"What a terrible thing to happen."

"Yes, it is," said Wallander. "Sometimes I wonder what's happening to this country anyway."

When he went out through the glass doors of the police station the wind hit him in the face. It was cold and biting, and he hunched over as he hurried to the parking lot. As long as it doesn't snow, he thought. Not until we catch whoever it was who paid the visit in Lenarp.

He crawled into his car and spent a long time looking through the cassettes he kept in the glove compartment. Without really making a decision, he shoved Verdi's *Requiem* into the tape deck. He had expensive speakers in the car, and the magnificent tones surged against his eardrums. He drove off and turned right, down Dragongatan toward Österleden. A few leaves whirled across the road, and a bicyclist strained against the wind. The clock on the dashboard said it was six. Hunger was gnawing at him again, and he crossed the main road and turned in at OK's Cafeteria. I'll change my eating habits tomorrow, he thought. If I get to Dad's place a minute past seven, he'll accuse me of abandoning him.

He ate a hamburger special.

He ate so fast that it gave him diarrhea.

As he sat on the toilet he noticed that he ought to change his underwear.

Suddenly he realized how tired he was.

He didn't get up until someone banged on the door.

He filled the tank with gas and drove east, through Sandskogen, and turned off at the road toward Kåseberga. His father lived in a little house that seemed to have been flung onto a field between Löderup and the sea.

It was four minutes to seven when he swung onto the gravel driveway in front of the house.

That gravel driveway had been the cause of the latest and most lengthy of his quarrels with his father. Before, it had been a lovely cobblestone courtyard as old as the farmhouse where his father lived. Suddenly one day he got the idea of covering the courtyard with gravel. When Wallander had protested, his father was outraged.

"I don't need a guardian!" he had shouted.

"Why do you have to destroy the beautiful cobblestone court-yard?" Wallander had asked.

Then they had quarreled.

And now the courtyard was covered with gray gravel that crunched under the car's tires.

He could see that a light was on in the shed.

Next time it could be my father, he thought suddenly.

The moonlight killer who might pick him out as a suitable old man to rob, maybe even murder.

No one would hear him scream for help. Not in this wind, with five hundred meters to the nearest neighbor. Who was an old man himself.

He listened to the end of "Dies irae" before he climbed out of the car and stretched.

He went over to the shed, which was his father's studio. That's where he painted his pictures, as he had always done.

It was one of Wallander's earliest childhood memories. The way his father had always smelled of turpentine and oil. And the way he was always standing in front of his sticky easel in his dark-blue overalls and cut-off rubber boots.

Not until Kurt Wallander was five or six years old did he realize that his father wasn't working on the exact same painting year after year.

It was the motif that never changed.

He painted a melancholy autumn landscape, with a shiny mir-ror of a lake, a crooked tree with bare branches in the foreground, and, far off on the horizon, mountain ranges surrounded by clouds that shimmered in an improbably colorful setting sun.

Now and then he would add a wood grouse standing on a stump at the far left edge of the painting.

At regular intervals their home was visited by men in silk suits with heavy gold rings on their fingers. They came in rusty vans or shiny American gas-guzzlers, and they bought the paintings, with or without the grouse.

His father had been painting the same motif all his life.

The family had lived off his paintings, which were sold at fairs and auctions.

They had lived in Klagshamm outside Malmö, in an old converted smithy. Kurt Wallander had grown up there with his sister Kristina, and their childhood had always been wrapped in the intense smell of turpentine.

Not until his father was widowed did he sell the old smithy and move out to the country. Wallander had never really understood why, since his father was continually complaining about the loneliness.

He opened the door to the shed and saw that his father was working on a painting without the grouse. Just now he was painting the tree in the foreground. He muttered a greeting and continued dabbing with his brush.

Wallander poured a cup of coffee from a dirty pot that stood on a smoking spirit stove.

He looked at his father, who was almost eighty years old, short and stooped, but still radiating energy and strength of will.

Am I going to look like him when I get old? he thought.

As a boy I took after my mother. Now I look like my grandfather. Maybe I'll be like my father when I get old.

"Have a cup of coffee," said his father. "I'll be ready in a minute."

"I got one," said Wallander.

"Then have another," said his father.

He's in a bad mood, thought Wallander. He's a tyrant with his changeable moods. What does he want with me, anyway?

"I've got a lot to do," said Wallander. "Actually I have to work all night. I thought there was something you wanted."

"Why do you have to work all night?"

"I have to sit at the hospital."

"How come? Who's sick?"

Wallander sighed. Even though he had carried out hundreds of interrogations himself, he would never be able to match his father's persistence in questioning him. And his father didn't even give a damn about his career as a cop. Wallander knew that his father had been deeply disappointed when he had decided, at eighteen, to become a policeman. But he was never able to find out what sort of hopes his father had actually had for him.

He had tried to talk about it, but never with any success.

On the few occasions when he had spent time with his sister Kristina, who lived in Stockholm and owned a beauty salon, he had tried to ask her, since he knew that she and his father were on good terms. But even she had no idea.

He drank the lukewarm coffee and thought that maybe his father had wanted him to take over the brush one day and continue to paint the same motif for yet another generation.

Suddenly his father put down his brush and wiped his hands on a dirty rag. When he came over to him and poured a cup of coffee, Wallander could smell the stink of dirty clothes and his father's unwashed body.

How do you tell your father that he smells bad? he thought.

Maybe he has gotten so old that he can't take care of himself any longer.

And then what do I do?

I can't have him at my place, that would never work. We'd murder each other.

He watched his father rub his nose with one hand as he slurped his coffee.

"You haven't come out to see me in a long time," his father said reproachfully.

"I was here the day before yesterday, wasn't I?"

"For half an hour!"

"Well, I was here, anyway."

"Why don't you want to visit me?"

"I do! It's just that I have a lot to do sometimes."

His father sat down on an old rickety sled that creaked under his weight.

"I just wanted to tell you that your daughter came to visit me yesterday."

Wallander was astounded.

"You mean Linda was here?"

"Aren't you listening to what I'm saying?"

"Why did she come?"

"She wanted a painting."

"A painting?"

"Unlike you, she actually appreciates what I do."

Wallander had a hard time believing what he was hearing.

Linda had never shown any interest in her grandfather, except when she was very small.

"What did she want?"

"A painting, I told you! You're not listening!"

"I *am* listening! Where did she come from? Where was she going? How the hell did she get out here? Do I have to drag everything out of you?"

"She came in a car," said his father. "A young man with a black face drove her."

"What do mean by black?"

"Haven't you ever heard of Negroes? He was very polite and spoke excellent Swedish. I gave her the painting and then they left. I thought you'd like to know, since you have such poor contact with each other."

"Where did they go?"

"How should I know?"

Wallander realized that neither of them knew where Linda actually lived. Occasionally she slept at her mother's house. But then she would quickly disappear again, off on her own mysterious paths.

I've got to talk to Mona, he thought. Separated or not, we have to talk to each other. I can't stand this anymore.

"Do you want a drink?" his father asked.

The last thing Wallander wanted was a drink. But he knew that it was useless to say no.

"All right, thanks," he said.

A path connected the shed with the house, which was low-ceilinged and sparsely furnished. Wallander noticed at once that it was messy and dirty.

He doesn't even see the mess, he thought. And why didn't I notice it before?

I've got to talk to Kristina about it. He can't keep living alone like this.

At that instant the telephone rang.

His father picked it up.

"It's for you," he said, making no attempt to hide his annoyance.

Linda, he thought. It's got to be her.

It was Rydberg calling from the hospital.

"She's dead," he said.

"Did she wake up?"

"As a matter of fact, she did. For ten minutes. The doctors thought the crisis was over. Then she died."

"Did she say anything?"

Rydberg sounded thoughtful when he answered. "I think you'd better come back to town."

"What did she say?"

"Something you won't want to hear."

"I'll come to the hospital."

"It's better if you go to the station. She's dead, I told you."

Wallander hung up. "I've got to go," he said.

His father glared at him. "You don't like me," he said.

"I'll come back tomorrow," replied Wallander, wondering what to do about the squalor his father was living in. "I'll come tomorrow for sure. We can sit and talk. We can fix dinner. We can play poker if you want."

Even though Wallander was a miserable card player, he knew that a game would mollify his father. "I'll be here at seven," he said.

Then he drove back to Ystad.

At five minutes to eight he walked back in the same glass doors he had walked out of two hours earlier. Ebba nodded at him.

"Rydberg is waiting in the lunchroom," she said.

That's where he was, hunched over a cup of coffee. When Wallander saw the other man's face, he knew that something unpleasant was in store for him.

Chapter Four

Wallander and Rydberg were alone in the lunchroom. In the distance they could hear the ruckus a drunk was making, protesting loudly about being taken into custody. Otherwise it was quiet. Only the faint whine from the radiator could be heard.

Wallander sat down across from Rydberg.

"Take off your overcoat," said Rydberg. "Or else you'll freeze when you go back out in the wind again."

"First I want to hear what you have to say. Then I'll decide whether to take off my coat or not."

Rydberg shrugged. "She died," he said.

"So I understand."

"But she woke up for a while right before she died."

"And then she spoke?"

"That may be putting it too strongly. She whispered. Or wheezed."

"Did you get it on tape?"

Rydberg shook his head. "It wouldn't have worked anyway," he said. "It was almost impossible to hear what she was saying. Most of it was just raving. But I wrote down what I'm sure I understood."

Rydberg took a beat-up notebook out of his pocket. It was held together by a wide rubber band, and a pencil was stuck in between the pages.

"She said her husband's name," Rydberg began. "I think she was trying to find out how he was. Then she mumbled something I couldn't understand. That's when I tried to ask her, 'Who was it that came in the night? Did you know them? What did they look like?' Those were my questions. I repeated them for as long as she was conscious. And I actually think she understood what I was saying."

"So what did she answer?"

"I only managed to catch one word. 'Foreign.'"

"'Foreign'?"

"That's right. 'Foreign.'"

"Did she mean that whoever attacked both her and her husband were foreigners?"

Rydberg nodded.

"Are you sure?"

"Do I usually say I'm sure if I'm not?"

"No."

"Well then. So now we know that her last message to the world was the word 'foreign.' As a reply to who committed this insane crime."

Wallander took off his coat and got a cup of coffee.

"What the hell could she have meant?" he muttered.

"I've been sitting here thinking about that while I waited for you," replied Rydberg. "Maybe they looked un-Swedish. Maybe they spoke a foreign language. Maybe they spoke broken Swedish. There are lots of possibilities."

"What does an un-Swedish person look like?" asked Wallander.

"You know what I mean," said Rydberg. "Or rather, you can guess what she thought and what she meant."

"So it could have been her imagination?"

Rydberg nodded. "That's quite possible."

"But not particularly likely?"

"Why should she use the last minutes of her life to say something that wasn't true? Old people don't usually lie."

Wallander took a sip of his lukewarm coffee.

"This means we have to start looking for one or more foreigners," he said. "I wish she'd said something different."

"It's damn unpleasant, all right."

They sat in silence for a moment, each lost in his own thoughts. They could no longer hear the drunk out in the hall.

It was nineteen minutes to nine.

"You can just picture it," Wallander said after a while. "The only clue the police have to the double murder in Lenarp is that the perpetrators are probably foreigners."

"I can think of something much worse," replied Rydberg.

Wallander knew what he meant.

Twenty kilometers from Lenarp there was a big refugee camp that on several occasions had been the object of attacks against foreigners. Crosses had been burned at night in the courtyard, rocks had been thrown through windows, buildings had been spray-painted with slogans. The refugee camp in the old castle of Hageholm had been established despite vigorous protests from the surrounding communities. And the protests had continued.

Hostility to refugees was flaring up.

But Wallander and Rydberg knew something else that the general public did not know.

Some of the asylum seekers being housed at Hageholm had been caught red-handed breaking into a business that rented out farm machinery. Fortunately the owner was not among the fiercest opponents of taking in refugees, so it was possible to hush up the whole affair. The two men who had committed the break-in were no longer in Sweden either, since they had been denied asylum.

But Wallander and Rydberg had on several occasions discussed what might have happened if the incident had been made public.

"I have a hard time believing that any refugees seeking asylum could commit murder," said Wallander.

Rydberg gave Wallander a circumspect look. "You remember what I told you about the noose?"

"Something about the knot?"

"I didn't recognize it. And I know quite a bit about knots, since I spent my summers sailing when I was young."

Wallander looked at Rydberg attentively. "What are you getting at?" he mused.

"What I'm getting at is that this knot wasn't tied by anyone who was a member of the Swedish Boy Scouts."

"What the hell do you mean by that?"

"The knot was made by a foreigner."

Before Wallander could reply, Ebba came into the lunchroom to get some coffee.

"Go home and get some rest if you can," she said. "By the way, reporters keep calling and want you to make a statement."

"About what?" asked Wallander. "About the weather?"

"They seem to have found out that the woman died."

Wallander looked at Rydberg, who shook his head.

"We're not making a statement tonight," he said. "We're waiting till tomorrow."

Wallander got up and went over to the window. The wind had picked up, but the sky was still cloudless. It was going to be another cold night.

"We can hardly avoid mentioning what happened," he said. "The fact that she managed to say something before she died. And if we say that much, then we'll have to tell them what she said. And then all hell will break loose."

"We could try to keep it internal," said Rydberg, getting up and putting on his hat. "For investigative reasons."

Wallander looked at him in surprise.

"And risk having it come out later that we withheld important information from the press? That we were shielding foreign criminals?"

"It's going to affect so many innocent people," said Rydberg. "What do you think will happen at the refugee camp when it gets out that the police are looking for some foreigners?"

Wallander knew that Rydberg was right.

Suddenly he was full of doubt.

"Let's sleep on it till tomorrow," he said. "We'll have a meeting, just you and me, tomorrow morning at eight. Then we'll decide."

Rydberg nodded and limped toward the door. There he stopped and turned to Wallander again.

"There is one possibility we shouldn't overlook," he said. "That it really was refugees seeking asylum who did it."

Wallander rinsed out his coffee cup and put it in the dish rack.

Actually I hope it was, he thought. I really hope that the killers are at that refugee camp. Then maybe it'll put an end to this arbitrary, sloppy attitude that anyone at all, for any reason at all, can come across the Swedish border.

But of course he couldn't say that to Rydberg. It was an opinion he intended to keep to himself.

He fought his way through the heavy wind out to his car.

Even though he was tired, he had no desire to drive home.

Every evening the loneliness would set in.

He turned on the ignition and changed the cassette. The overture to *Fidelio* filled the darkness inside the car.

His wife's sudden departure had come as a complete surprise. But deep inside he realized, even though he still had a hard time accepting it, that he should have sensed the danger long before it happened. That he was living in a marriage that was slowly breaking apart because of its own dreariness. They had married when they were very young, and far too late they realized that they were growing apart. Of the three of them, maybe it was Linda who had reacted most openly to the emptiness surrounding them.

On that night in October when Mona had said that she wanted a divorce, he thought that he had actually been waiting for this to happen. But since the thought involved a threat, he had pushed it aside and blamed it on the fact that he was working so hard. Too late he realized that she had prepared her departure down to the smallest detail. One Friday evening she had talked about wanting a divorce, and by Sunday she had left him and moved into the apartment in Malmö, which she had rented in advance. The feeling of being abandoned had filled him with both shame and anger. In an impotent rage, all his feelings numbed, he had slapped her in the face.

Afterwards there was only silence. She had picked up some of her things during the daytime when he wasn't home. But she left most of her belongings behind, and he had been deeply hurt that she seemed prepared to trade in her entire past for a life that did not include him, even as a memory.

He had telephoned her. Late in the evenings their voices had met. Devastated by jealousy, he had tried to find out whether she had left him for another man.

"Another life," she had replied. "Another life, before it's too late." He had appealed to her. He had tried to give the impression that he was indifferent. He had begged her forgiveness for all the attention he had denied her. But nothing he said was able to alter her decision.

Two days before Christmas Eve the divorce papers had arrived in the mail.

When he opened the envelope and realized that it was all over, something had burst inside him. As if in an attempt to flee, he had called in sick over the Christmas holidays and had taken off on an aimless trip that had led him to Denmark. In northern Sjælland a sudden storm had left him snowbound, and he had spent Christmas in Gilleleje, in a freezing room at a pension near the beach. There he had written long letters to her, which he later tore to bits and strewed out over the sea in a symbolic gesture, signifying that in spite of everything he had begun to accept what had happened.

Two days before New Year's he had returned to Ystad and gone back to work. He spent New Year's Eve working on a serious case involving spousal abuse in Svarte, and he had a frightening revelation that he might just as well have been abusing Mona physically himself.

The music from *Fidelio* broke off with a screech.

The machine had eaten the tape.

The radio came on automatically, and he heard the play-by-play of a hockey game.

He pulled out of the parking lot and decided to head home to Mariagatan.

But he drove in the opposite direction instead, out along the coast road heading west to Trelleborg and Skanör. When he passed by the old prison he stepped on the gas. Driving had always distracted his thoughts...

Suddenly he realized that he had driven almost all the way to Trelleborg. A big ferry was just entering the harbor, and on a sudden impulse he decided to stay for a while.

He knew that some former police officers from Ystad had become immigration police at the ferry dock in Trelleborg. He thought some of them might be on duty tonight.

He walked across the harbor area, which was bathed in pale yellow light. A big truck came roaring toward him like a ghostly prehistoric beast.

But when he walked through the door with the sign "Authorized Personnel Only," he didn't know either of the officers.

Kurt Wallander nodded and introduced himself. The older of the two had a gray beard and a scar across his forehead.

"That's a nasty business you've got in Ystad," he said. "Did you catch them?"

"Not yet," replied Wallander.

The conversation was interrupted, since the passengers from the ferry were approaching passport control. The majority of them were Swedes returning from celebrating the New Year's holiday in Berlin. But there were also some East Germans trying out their newly won freedom by taking a trip to Sweden.

After twenty minutes there were only nine passengers left. All of them were trying in various ways to make it clear that they were seeking asylum in Sweden.

"It's pretty quiet tonight," said the younger of the two officers. "Sometimes up to a hundred asylum seekers arrive on one ferry. You can imagine."

Five of the asylum seekers belonged to the same Ethiopian family. Only one of them had a passport, and Wallander wondered how they had managed to make this long journey and cross all those borders with a single passport. Besides the Ethiopian family, two Lebanese and two Iranians were waiting at passport control.

Wallander had a hard time deciding whether the nine refugees looked expectant or whether they were just scared.

"What happens now?" he asked.

"Malmö will come and pick them up," replied the older officer. "It's their turn tonight. We get word over the radio when there are a lot of people without passports on the ferries. Sometimes we have to call for extra manpower."

"What happens in Malmö?" asked Wallander.

"They're put on one of the ships anchored out in the Oil Harbor. They have to stay there until they're shuttled on. If they're allowed to stay in Sweden, that is."

"What do you think about these people here?"

The policeman shrugged.

"They'll probably get in," he answered. "Do you want some coffee? It'll be a while before the next ferry."

Wallander shook his head.

"Some other time. I have to get going."

"Hope you catch them."

"Right," said Wallander. "So do I."

On the way back to Ystad he ran over a hare. When he saw the animal in the beam of his headlights he hit the brakes, but the hare struck the left front wheel with a soft thud. He didn't stop the car to get out and check whether the hare was still alive.

What's wrong with me? he thought.

That night Wallander slept uneasily. Just after five he awoke with a start. His mouth was dry, and he had dreamed that somebody was trying to strangle him. When he realized that he wouldn't be able to go back to sleep, he got up and made some coffee.

The thermometer outside the kitchen window showed -6° Celsius. The streetlight was swaying in the wind. He sat down at the kitchen table and thought about his conversation with Rydberg the night before. What he had feared had happened. The dead woman had revealed nothing that could give them a lead. Her words about something foreign were just too vague. He realized that they didn't have a single clue to go on.

At six thirty he got dressed and searched for a long time before finding the heavy sweater he was looking for.

He went outside, felt the wind tearing and biting at him, and then drove out Österleden and turned onto the main road toward Malmö. Before he met Rydberg at eight, he had to pay a return visit to the neighbors of the old couple that was killed. He couldn't shake the feeling that something didn't quite add up. Attacks on lonely old people were not often random. They were usually preceded by rumors of money stashed away. And even though the attacks could be brutal, they were hardly characterized by the methodical malice that he had witnessed at this murder scene.

People in the country get up early in the morning, he thought as he swung onto the narrow road that led to the Nyströms' house. Maybe they've had time to mull things over.

He stopped in front of the house and turned off the engine. At the same instant the light in the kitchen window went off.

They're scared, he thought. They probably think it's the killers coming back.

He left the lights on as he got out of the car and walked across the gravel to the steps.

He sensed rather than saw the muzzle flash coming from a bush beside the house. The ear-splitting noise made him dive for the ground. A pebble slashed his cheek, and for an instant he thought he had been hit.

"Police!" he yelled. "Don't shoot! Damn it, don't shoot!"

A flashlight shone on his face. The hand holding the flashlight was shaking, and the beam wobbled back and forth. Nyström was standing in front of him, an old shotgun in his hand.

"Is it you?" he said.

Wallander got up and brushed off the gravel.

"What were you aiming at?" he asked.

"I shot straight up in the air," said Nyström.

"Do you have a permit for that weapon?" Wallander queried. "Otherwise there could be trouble."

"I've been up all night, keeping watch," said Nyström. Wallander could hear how upset the man was.

"I have to turn off my lights," said Wallander. "Then we'll talk, you and I."

Two boxes of shotgun shells lay on the kitchen table. On the sofa lay a crowbar and a big sledgehammer. The black cat was in the window, staring menacingly at Wallander as he came in. The old woman stood at the stove stirring a pan of coffee.

"I had no idea it was the police coming," said Nyström, sounding apologetic. "And so early."

Wallander moved the sledgehammer and sat down.

"Mrs. Lövgren died last night," he said. "I thought I'd come out and tell you myself."

Every time Wallander was forced to notify someone of a death, he had the same feeling of unreality. To tell strangers that a child or a relative had suddenly died, and to do it with dignity, was impossible. The deaths that the police announced were always unexpected, and often violent and gruesome. Somebody drives off to buy something at the store and dies. A child on a bicycle is run over on the way home from the playground. Someone is abused or robbed, commits suicide or drowns. When the police are standing in the doorway, people refuse to accept the news.

The two old people in the kitchen were silent. The woman stirred the coffee with a spoon. The man fidgeted with his shotgun, and Wallander discreetly moved out of the line of fire.

"So, Maria is gone," the man said slowly.

"The doctors did everything they could."

"Maybe it was just as well," said the woman at the stove, unexpectedly forceful. "What did she have left to live for after he was dead?"

The man put the shotgun down on the kitchen table and stood up. Wallander noticed that he favored one knee.

"I'll go out and give the horse some hay," he said, putting on an old cap.

"Do you mind if I come with you?" asked Wallander.

"Why would I mind?" said the man, opening the door.

From her stall the mare whinnied as they entered the stable, which smelled like warm manure. With a practiced hand Nyström flung an armload of hay into the stall.

"I'll muck out later," he said, stroking the horse's mane.

"Why did they keep a horse?" Wallander wondered.

"To an old dairy farmer an empty stable is like a morgue," replied Nyström. "The horse was company."

Wallander thought that he might just as well start asking his questions here in the stable.

"You stayed up to keep watch last night," he said. "You're

scared, and I can understand that. You must have thought to yourself: Why were they the ones who were attacked? You must have
thought: Why them? Why not us?"

"They didn't have any money," said Nyström. "And nothing
else that was especially valuable. Anyway, nothing was stolen. I
told that to one of the policemen who were here yesterday. The
only thing that might have been stolen was an old wall clock."

"Might have been?"

"One of their daughters might have taken it. I can't remember everything."

"No money," said Wallander. "And no enemies."

A thought suddenly occurred to him.

"Do you keep any money in the house?" he asked. "Could it
be that whoever did this got the wrong house?"

"Everything we have is in the bank," replied Nyström. "And
we don't have any enemies either."

They went back to the house and drank coffee. Wallander saw
that the woman was red-eyed, as if she had been careful to cry
while they were out in the stable.

"Have you noticed anything unusual recently?" he asked.
"Anyone visiting the Lövgrens that you didn't recognize?"

The old folks looked at each other and then shook their heads.

"When was the last time you talked to them?"

"We were over there for coffee the day before yesterday," said
Hanna. "Just like always. We drank coffee together every day. For
over forty years."

"Did they seem afraid of anything?" asked Wallander.
"Worried?"

"Johannes had a cold," said Hanna. "But otherwise everything
was normal."

It seemed hopeless. Wallander didn't know what to ask them
about. Each reply he got was like a new door slamming shut.

"Did they have any acquaintances who were foreigners?" he
asked.

The man raised his eyebrows in surprise.

"Foreigners?"

"Anyone who wasn't Swedish," Wallander ventured.

"A few years ago there were some Danes camping on their field one midsummer."

Wallander looked at the clock. Almost seven thirty. At eight he was supposed to meet Rydberg, and he didn't want to be late.

"Try and think," he said. "Anything you can come up with might be of some help."

Nyström walked out to the car with him.

"I have a permit for the shotgun," he said. "And I didn't aim at you. I just wanted to scare you."

"You did a good job of it," replied Wallander. "But I think you ought to get some sleep tonight. Whoever did this isn't coming back."

"Would you be able to sleep?" asked Nyström. "Would you be able to sleep if your neighbors had been slaughtered like dumb animals?"

Since Wallander couldn't think of a good answer, he said nothing.

"Thanks for the coffee," he said, got in his car, and drove off.

This is all going to hell, he thought. Not a clue, nothing. Only Rydberg's strange knot, and the word "foreign." Two old people with no money under the bed, no antique furniture, are murdered in such a way that there seems to be something more than robbery behind it. A murder of hate or revenge.

There must be something, he thought. Something out of the ordinary about these two people.

If only the horse could talk!

There was something about that horse that made him uneasy. Something that was just a vague hunch. But he was too experienced a policeman to ignore his uneasiness. There was something about that horse.

At four minutes to eight he braked to a stop outside the police station in Ystad. The wind had died down to light gusts. Still, it felt a few degrees warmer today.

Just so we don't get snow, he thought. He nodded to Ebba at the switchboard. "Did Rydberg show up yet?"

"He's in his office," replied Ebba. "They've all started calling already. TV, radio, and the papers. And the county police commissioner."

"Stall them a while," said Wallander. "I have to talk with Rydberg first."

He hung up his jacket in his office before he went in to see Rydberg, whose office was a few doors down the hall. He knocked and heard a grunt in reply.

Rydberg was standing looking out the window when Wallander came in. It was obvious that he hadn't had enough sleep.

"Hi," said Wallander. "Shall I bring in some coffee?"

"Sure. But no sugar. I've cut it out."

Wallander left to get two plastic mugs of coffee and then went back to Rydberg's office.

Outside the door he suddenly stopped.

What's my plan, anyway? he thought. Should we keep her last words from the press for so-called investigative reasons? Or should we release them? What exactly is my plan?

I don't have any plan, he thought, annoyed, and pushed open the door with his foot.

Rydberg was sitting behind his desk combing his sparse hair. Wallander sank into a visitor's easy chair with worn-out springs.

"You ought to get a new chair," he said.

"There's no money for it," said Rydberg, putting away his comb in a desk drawer.

Wallander set his coffee cup on the floor beside his chair.

"I woke up so damned early this morning," he said. "I drove out and talked with the Nyströms again. The old man was waiting in a bush and took a shot at me with a shotgun."

Rydberg pointed at his cheek.

"Not from buckshot," said Wallander. "I hit the deck. He claimed he had a permit for the gun. Who the hell knows?"

"Did they have anything new to say?"

"Not a thing. Nothing unusual. No money, nothing. Provided they're not lying, of course."

"Why would they be lying?"

"No, why would they?"

Rydberg took a slurp of coffee and made a face.

"Did you know that cops are unusually susceptible to stomach cancer?" he asked.

"I didn't know that."

"If it's true, it's because of all the bad coffee we drink."

"But we solve our cases over our coffee mugs."

"Like now?"

Wallander shook his head. "What do we really have to go on? Nothing."

"You're too impatient, Kurt." Rydberg looked at him while he stroked his nose.

"You'll have to excuse me if I seem like an old schoolteacher," he went on. "But in this case I think we have to trust in patience."

They went over the progress of the investigation again. The police technicians had taken fingerprints and were checking them against the national centralized records. Hanson was busy investigating the location of all known criminals with records of assault on old people, to find out whether they were in prison or had alibis. Questioning of the residents of Lenarp would continue, and maybe the questionnaire they sent out would produce something. Both Rydberg and Wallander knew that the police in Ystad carried out their work precisely and methodically. Sooner or later something would turn up. A trace, a clue. It was just a matter of waiting. Of working methodically and waiting.

"The motive," Wallander persisted. "If the motive isn't money. Or the rumor of money hidden away. Then what is it? The noose? You must have thought the same thing I did. This double murder has revenge or hate in it. Or both."

"Let's imagine a couple of suitably desperate robbers," said Rydberg. "Let's assume that they were convinced that Lövgren had money squirreled away. Let's assume that they were sufficiently desperate and indifferent to human life. Then torture isn't out of the question."

"Who would be that desperate?"

"You know as well as I do that there are plenty of drugs that create such a dependency that people are ready to do anything at all."

Wallander knew that. He had seen the accelerating violence at first hand, and narcotics trafficking and drug dependency almost always lurked in the background. Even though Ystad's police district was seldom hit by visible manifestations of this increasing violence, he harbored no illusions that it was not steadily creeping closer and closer.

There were no protected zones anymore. A little insignificant town like Lenarp was confirmation of that fact.

He sat up straight in the uncomfortable chair.

"What are we going to do?" he said.

"You're the boss," replied Rydberg.

"I want to hear what you think."

Rydberg got up and went over to the window. With one finger he felt the dirt in a flowerpot. It was dry.

"If you want to know what I think, I'll tell you. But you should know that I'm by no means positive that I'm on the right track. I think that no matter what we decide to do, there's going to be a big fuss. But maybe it would be a good idea to keep at it for a few days anyway. There are plenty of things to investigate."

"Like what?"

"Did the Lövgrens have any foreign acquaintances?"

"I asked about that this morning. They may have known some Danes."

"There, you see."

"It couldn't be Danes camped out in tents, could it?"

"Why not? No matter what, we'll have to check it out. And there are more people than just the neighbors to question. If I understood you correctly yesterday, you said that the Lövgrens had a big family."

Wallander realized that Rydberg was right. There were investigative reasons to keep quiet about the fact that the police were searching for a person or persons with foreign connections.

"What do we actually know about foreigners who have committed crimes in Sweden?" he asked. "Do the National Police have special files on that?"

"There are files on everything," Rydberg replied. "Put some-one in front of a computer and hook into the central criminal data-base, and then maybe we'll find something."

Wallander stood up.

Rydberg gave him a quizzical look. "Aren't you going to ask about the noose?"

"I forgot."

"There's supposed to be an old sailmaker in Limhamn who knows all about knots. I read about him in a newspaper sometime last year. I thought I'd spend some time trying to track him down. Not because I'm sure anything will come of it. But just in case."

"I want you to come to the meeting first," said Wallander. "Then you can drive over to Limhamn."

At ten o'clock they were all gathered in Wallander's office.

The run-through was very brief. Wallander told them what the woman had said before she died. For the time being, this piece of information was not to be disclosed. No one seemed to have any objections.

Martinson was put on the computer to search for foreign crim-inals. The officers who were going to continue with the questioning in Lenarp went on their way. Wallander assigned Svedberg to con-centrate on the Polish family, who were presumably in the country illegally. He wanted to know why they were living in Lenarp. At quarter to eleven Rydberg left for Limhamn to look up the sailmaker.

When Wallander was alone in his office, he stood for a while looking at the map hanging on the wall. Where had the killers come from? Which way did they go afterwards?

Then he sat down at his desk and asked Ebba to start putting through calls. For over an hour he spoke with various reporters. But there was no word from the girl from the local radio station.

At quarter past twelve Norén knocked on the door.

"I thought you were going to Lenarp," Wallander said, surprised.

"I was," said Norén. "But I just thought of something."

Norén sat on the edge of a chair, since he was wet. It had started to rain. The temperature had now risen to +1° Celsius.

"This might not mean anything," said Norén. "It was just something that crossed my mind."

"Most things mean something," said Wallander.

"You remember that horse?" asked Norén.

"Sure, I remember the horse."

"You told me to give it some hay."

"And water."

"Hay and water. But I never did."

Wallander wrinkled his brow. "Why not?"

"It wasn't necessary. The horse already had hay. Water too."

Wallander sat in silence for a moment, looking at Norén.

"Go on," he said. "You're getting at something."

Norén shrugged his shoulders.

"We had a horse when I was growing up," he said. "When the horse was in its stall and was given hay, it would eat all of it. I just mean that someone must have given the horse some hay. Maybe just an hour or so before we got there."

Wallander reached for the phone.

"If you're thinking of calling Nyström, don't bother," said Norén.

Wallander let his hand drop.

"I talked to him before I came here. And he hadn't given the horse any hay."

"Dead men don't feed their horses," said Wallander. "Who did?"

Norén stood up. "It seems weird," he said. "First they kill a man. Then they put a noose on somebody else. And then they go out to the stable and give the horse some hay. Who the hell would do anything that weird?"

"You're right," said Wallander. "Who would do that?"

"It might not mean anything," said Norén.

"Or maybe it does," replied Wallander. "It was good of you to tell me."

Norén said goodbye and left.

Wallander sat and thought about what he had just heard.

The hunch he had been carrying around with him had proved to be right. There was something about that horse.

His thoughts were interrupted by the telephone.

Another reporter who wanted to talk with him.

At quarter to one he left the police station. He had to visit an old friend he hadn't seen in many, many years.

Chapter Five

Kurt Wallander turned off the E14 where a sign pointed toward the ruins of Stjärnsund Castle. He got out of the car and unzipped to take a leak. Through the noise of the wind he could hear the sound of accelerating jet engines at Sturup airport. Before he got back in the car, he scraped off the mud that had stuck to his shoes. The change in the weather had been abrupt. The thermometer in his car that showed the outside temperature indicated -5° Celsius. Ragged clouds were racing across the sky as he continued down the road.

Right outside the castle ruin the gravel road forked, and he kept to the left. He had never driven this route before, but he was positive it was the right way. Despite the fact that almost ten years had passed since the road had been described to him, he remembered the route in detail. He had a mind that seemed programmed for landscapes and roads.

After about a kilometer the road deteriorated. He crept forward, wondering how large vehicles ever managed to negotiate it.

The road suddenly sloped sharply downward, and a large farm with long wings of stables lay spread out before him. He drove into the large farmyard and stopped. A flock of crows was cawing overhead as he climbed out of the car.

The farm seemed strangely deserted. A stable door stood flapping in the wind. For a brief moment he wondered whether he had taken the wrong road after all.

What desolation, he thought.

The Scanian winter with its screeching flocks of black birds.

The clay that sticks to the soles of your shoes.

A teenage blonde girl suddenly emerged from one of the stable doors. For a moment he thought she looked like Linda. She had the same hair, the same thin body, the same ungainly movements as she walked. He watched her intently.

The girl started tugging at a ladder that led to the stable loft.

When she caught sight of him she let go of the ladder and wiped her hands on her gray riding pants.

"Hi," said Wallander. "I'm looking for Sten Widén. Is this the right place?"

"Are you a cop?" asked the girl.

"Yes," Wallander replied, surprised. "How did you know?"

"I could hear it in your voice," said the girl, once more pulling at the ladder, which seemed to be stuck.

"Is he home?" asked Wallander.

"Help me with the ladder," the girl said.

He saw that one of the rungs had caught on the wainscoting of the stable wall. He grabbed hold of the ladder and twisted it until the rung came free.

"Thanks," said the girl. "Sten is probably in his office."

She pointed to a red brick building a short distance from the stable.

"Do you work here?" asked Wallander.

"Yes," said the girl, climbing quickly up the ladder. "Now move!"

With surprisingly strong arms she began heaving bales of hay out through the loft doors. Wallander walked over toward the red building. Just as he was about to knock on the heavy door, a man came walking around the end of the building.

It was at least ten years since Wallander had seen Sten Widén, yet the man did not seem to have changed. The same tousled hair, the same thin face, the same red eczema near his lower lip.

"Well, this is a surprise," said the man with a nervous laugh. "I thought it was the blacksmith. And it's you instead. How long has it been, anyway?"

"Eleven years," said Wallander. "Summer of seventy-nine."

"The summer all our dreams fell apart," said Sten Widén. "Would you like some coffee?"

They went inside the red brick building. Wallander noticed a smell of oil coming from the walls. A rusty combine harvester stood inside in the darkness. Widén opened another door. A cat ran out as Wallander entered a room that seemed to be a combination of office and residence. An unmade bed stood along one wall. There were a TV and a VCR, and a microwave stood on a table. An old armchair was piled high with clothes. The rest of the room was taken up by a large desk. Sten Widén poured coffee from a thermos next to a fax machine in one of the wide window recesses.

Kurt Wallander was thinking about Widén's lost dreams of becoming an opera singer. About how in the late seventies the two of them had imagined a future for themselves that neither of them would be able to achieve. Wallander was supposed to become the impresario, and Sten Widén's tenor would resound from the opera stages of the world.

Wallander had been a cop back then. And he still was.

When Widén realized that his voice wasn't good enough, he had taken over his father's run-down stables for training race horses. Their earlier friendship had not been able to withstand the shared disappointment. At one time they had seen each other every day, but now eleven years had passed since their last meeting. Although they lived no more than fifty kilometers apart.

"You've put on weight," said Widén, moving a stack of newspapers from a spindle-backed chair.

"And you haven't," said Wallander, aware of his own annoyance.

"Race-horse trainers seldom get fat," said Widén, giving his nervous laugh once more. "Skinny legs and skinny wallets. Except for the big-time trainers, of course. Khan or Strasser. They can afford it."

"So how's it going?" asked Wallander, sitting down in the chair.

"So-so," said Widén. "I get by. I've always got some horse in training that does well. I get in a few new colts and manage to keep the whole place going. But actually —" He broke off without finishing his sentence.

Then he stretched, opened a desk drawer, and pulled out a half-empty bottle of whiskey.

"You want some?" he asked.

Wallander shook his head. "It wouldn't look good if a cop got caught for DWI," he replied. "Even though it does happen once in a while."

"Well, *skål,* anyway," said Widén, drinking from the bottle.

He took a cigarette from a crumpled pack and rummaged through the papers and racing forms before he found a lighter.

"How's Mona doing?" he asked. "And Linda? And your dad? And your sister, what's her name, Kerstin?"

"Kristina."

"That's it. Kristina. I've never had a very good memory, you know that."

"You never forgot the music."

"Didn't I?"

He drank from the bottle again, and Wallander noticed that something was eating him. Maybe he shouldn't have dropped by. Maybe Sten didn't want to be reminded of what once had been.

"Mona and I broke up," Wallander said, "and Linda's got her own place. Dad is the same as always. He keeps painting that picture of his. But I think he's becoming a little senile. I don't really know what to do with him."

"Did you know that I got married?" said Widén.

Wallander got the feeling he hadn't heard a word he'd said. "I didn't know that."

"I took over these goddamn stables, after all. When Dad finally realized that he was too old to take care of the horses, he started doing some serious drinking. Before, he always had control over how much he guzzled down. I realized that I couldn't handle him and his drinking buddies. I married one of the girls who worked here at the stables. Mostly because she was so good with Dad, I guess. She treated him like an old horse. Refused to go along with his habits, and set limits for him. Took the rubber hose and rinsed him off when he got too filthy. But when Dad died, it seemed as if she started to smell like him. So I got a divorce."

He took another slug from the bottle, and Wallander could see that he was beginning to get drunk.

"Every day I think about selling this place," he said. "I own the farm itself. I could probably get a million kronor for the whole thing. After the mortgage is paid off, I might have four hundred thousand left over. Then I'll buy an RV and hit the road."

"Where to?"

"That's just it. I don't know. There's nowhere I want to go."

Kurt Wallander felt uncomfortable listening to all this. Even though Widén was outwardly the same as ten years ago, inwardly he had gone through some big changes. It was the voice of a ghost talking to him, cracked and despairing. Ten years ago Sten Widén had been happy and high-spirited, the first one to invite you to a party. Now all his joy in life seemed to be gone.

The girl who had asked if Wallander was a cop rode past the window.

"Who's she?" he asked. "She could tell I was a cop."

"Her name is Louise," said Widén. "She could probably smell that you're a cop. She's been in and out of institutions since she was twelve years old. I'm her guardian. She's good with the horses. But she hates cops. She claims she was raped by a cop once."

He took another hit from the bottle and gestured toward the unmade bed.

"She sleeps with me sometimes," he said. "At least that's how it feels. That she's the one taking me to bed, and not the other way around. I suppose that's against the law, right?"

"Why should it be? She isn't a minor, is she?"

"She's nineteen. But do guardians have the right to sleep with their wards?"

Wallander thought he heard a hint of aggression in Widén's voice.

All of a sudden he was sorry he had come.

Even though he actually had a reason for the visit that was connected with the investigation, he now wondered whether it was merely an excuse. Had he come to visit Widén to talk about Mona? To seek some sort of consolation?

He no longer knew.

"I came here to ask you about horses," he said. "Maybe you saw in the paper that there was a double murder in Lenarp last night?"

"I don't read the papers," said Widén. "I read racing forms and starting lists. That's all. I don't give a damn about what's happening in the world."

"An old couple was killed," Wallander continued. "And they had a horse."

"Was it killed too?"

"No. But I think the killers gave it some hay before they left. And that's what I wanted to talk to you about. How fast does a horse eat an armload of hay?"

Widén emptied the bottle and lit another cigarette.

"Are you kidding?" he asked. "You came all the way out here to ask me how long it takes a horse to eat a load of hay?"

"Actually, I was thinking about asking you to come with me and take a look at the horse," said Wallander, making a quick decision. He could feel himself starting to get mad.

"I don't have time," said Widén. "The blacksmith is coming today. I've got sixteen horses that need vitamin shots."

"Tomorrow, then?"

Widén gave him a glazed look. "Is there money involved?"

"You'll be paid."

Widén wrote his telephone number on a dirty scrap of paper. "Maybe," he said. "Call me early in the morning."

When they stepped outside, Wallander noticed that the wind had picked up.

The girl came riding up on her horse.

"Nice horse," he said.

"Masquerade Queen," said Widén. "She'll never win a race in her life. The rich widow of a contractor in Trelleborg owns her. I was actually honest enough to suggest that she sell the horse to a riding school. But she thinks the horse can win. And I get my training fee. But there's no way in hell this horse will ever win a race."

They said goodbye at the car.

"You know how my dad died?" asked Widén suddenly.

"No."

"He wandered off to the castle ruin one autumn night. He used to sit up there and drink. Then he stumbled into the moat and drowned. The algae are so thick there that you can't see a thing. But his cap floated to the surface. 'Live Life,' it said on the cap. It was an ad for a travel bureau that sells sex trips to Bangkok."

"It was nice to see you," said Wallander. "I'll call you tomorrow."

"Whatever," said Widén and went off toward the stable.

Wallander drove away. In the rearview mirror he could see Sten Widén talking with the girl on the horse.

Why did I come here? he thought again.

Once a long time ago we were friends. We shared an impossible dream. When the dream burst like a phantom there was nothing left. It may be true that we both loved opera. But maybe that was just our imagination too.

He drove fast, as if he were letting his agitation control the pressure he put on the gas pedal.

Just as he braked for the stop sign at the main road, his car phone rang. The connection was so bad that he could hardly make out that it was Hanson on the line.

"You'd better come in," yelled Hanson. "Can you hear what I'm saying?"

"What happened?" Wallander yelled back.

"There's a farmer from Hagestad sitting here who says he knows who killed them," Hanson shouted.

Wallander could feel his heart beating faster.

"Who?" he shouted. "Who?"

The connection was abruptly cut off. The receiver hissed and squealed.

"Damn," he said out loud.

He drove back to Ystad. And much too fast, he thought. If Norén and Peters had been on traffic duty today, I would have kept to the speed limit.

On the way down the hill into the center of town, the engine suddenly started coughing.

He had run out of gas.

The dashboard light that was supposed to warn him was evidently on the blink.

He managed to make it to the gas station across from the hospital before the engine died completely. Getting out to put some money in the pump, he discovered that he didn't have any cash on him. He went next door to the locksmith shop in the same building and borrowed twenty kronor from the owner, who recognized him from an investigation of a break-in a few years back.

He pulled into his parking spot and hurried into the police station. Ebba tried to tell him something, but he dismissed her with a wave.

The door to Hanson's office was ajar, and Wallander went in without knocking.

It was empty.

In the hall he ran into Martinson, who was holding a stack of printouts.

"Just the man I'm looking for," said Martinson. "I dug up some stuff that might be interesting. I'll be damned if some Finns might not be behind this."

"When we don't have a lead, we usually say it's Finns," said Wallander. "I don't have time right now. You know where Hanson is?"

"He never leaves his office, you know that."

"Then we'll have to put out an APB on him. Anyway, he's not there now."

He poked his head in the lunchroom, but there was only an office clerk in there making an omelet.

Where the hell is that Hanson? he thought, flinging open the door to his own office.

Nobody there either. He called Ebba at the switchboard.

"Where's Hanson?" he asked.

"If you hadn't been in such a rush, I could have told you when you came in," said Ebba. "He told me he had to go down to the Union Bank."

"What was he going there for? Was anyone with him?"

"Yes. But I don't know who it was."

Wallander slammed down the phone.

What was Hanson up to?

He picked up the phone again.

"Can you page Hanson for me?" he asked Ebba.

"At the Union Bank?"

"If that's where he is."

He very seldom asked Ebba for help in tracking people down. He could never get used to the idea of having a secretary. If he needed something done, he was the one who had to do it. In the past he had thought it was a bad habit he carried with him from his upbringing. It was only rich, arrogant people who sent others out to do their footwork. Not being able to look up a number in the phone book and pick up the receiver was indefensible laziness.

The telephone rang, interrupting his thoughts. It was Hanson calling from the Union Bank.

"I thought I'd get back before you did," said Hanson. "You're probably wondering what I'm doing here."

"You can say that again."

"We were taking a look at Lövgren's bank account."

"Who's we?"

"His name is Herdin. But you'd better talk to him yourself. We'll be back in half an hour."

It was almost an hour and a quarter later before Wallander got to meet the man called Herdin. He was almost six foot six, thin and wiry, and when Wallander was introduced it was like shaking hands with a giant.

"It took a while," said Hanson. "But we got results. You've got to hear what Herdin has to say. And what we discovered at the bank."

Herdin was sitting erect and silent in a captain's chair.

Wallander had a feeling that the man had dressed up in his Sunday best before coming to the police station. Even if it was only a worn suit and a shirt with a frayed collar.

"It's probably best if we start at the beginning," said Wallander, grabbing a notebook.

Herdin gave Hanson a bewildered look.

"Should I start all over?" he asked.

"That would probably be best," said Hanson.

"It's a long story," Herdin began hesitantly.

"What's your name?" asked Wallander. "Let's start with that."

"Lars Herdin. I have a farm of forty acres near Hagestad. I'm trying to make ends meet by raising livestock. But things are a little slim."

"I've got all his personal data," Hanson interjected, and Wallander guessed that Hanson was in a hurry to get back to his racing forms.

"If I understand the matter correctly, you came here because you think you may have information relating to the murder of Mr. and Mrs. Lövgren," said Wallander, wishing he had expressed himself more simply.

"It's obvious it was the money," said Lars Herdin.

"What money?"

"All the money they had!"

"Could you clarify that a little?"

"The German money."

Wallander looked at Hanson, who shrugged discreetly. Wallander interpreted that as meaning he had to be patient.

"I think we're going to need a little more detail on this," he said. "Do you think you could be more specific?"

"Lövgren and his father made money during the war," said Herdin. "They secretly kept livestock on some forest pastures up in Småland. And they bought up worn-out old horses. Then they sold them on the black market to Germany. They made an obscene amount of money on the meat. And nobody ever caught them. Lövgren was both greedy and clever. He invested the money, and it's been growing over the years."

"You mean Lövgren's father?"

"He died right after the war. I mean Lövgren himself."

"So you're telling me that the Lövgrens were wealthy?"

"Not the family. Just Lövgren. She didn't know a thing about the money."

"Would he have kept his fortune a secret from his own wife?"

Lars Herdin nodded. "Nobody has ever been as badly deceived as my sister."

Wallander raised his eyebrows in surprise.

"Maria Lövgren was my sister. She was killed because he had stashed away a fortune."

Wallander heard the barely concealed bitterness. So maybe it *was* a hate murder, he thought.

"And this money was kept at home?"

"Only sometimes," replied Herdin.

"Sometimes?"

"When he made his large withdrawals."

"Could you try and give me a little more detail?"

Suddenly something seemed to spill over inside the man in the worn-out suit.

"Johannes Lövgren was a brute," he said. "It's better now that he's gone. But that Maria had to die, I can never forgive that."

Lars Herdin's outburst came so suddenly that neither Hanson nor Wallander had time to react. Herdin grabbed a thick glass ashtray that was on the table near him and flung it full force against the wall, right next to Wallander's head. Splinters of glass flew in every direction, and Wallander felt a shard strike his upper lip.

The silence after the outburst was deafening.

Hanson had sprung out of his chair and seemed ready to throw himself at the rangy Lars Herdin. But Wallander raised his hand to stop him, and Hanson sat back down.

"I beg your pardon," said Herdin. "If you have a broom and dustpan I'll clean up the glass. I'll pay for it."

"The cleaning women will take care of it," said Wallander. "I think we should continue talking."

Herdin now seemed totally calm.

"Johannes Lövgren was a beast," he repeated. "He pretended to be like everybody else. But the only thing he thought about was the money he and his father had made off the war. He complained that everything was so expensive and the farmers were so poor. But he had his money, which kept on growing and growing."

"And he kept this money in the bank?"

Herdin shrugged. "In the bank, in stocks and bonds, who knows what else."

"Why did he keep the money at home sometimes?"

"Johannes Lövgren had a mistress," said Herdin. "There was a woman in Kristianstad he had a child with in the fifties. Maria knew nothing about that either—the woman or the child. He probably spent more money on her every year than he gave Maria in her whole life."

"How much money are we talking about?"

"Twenty-five, thirty thousand. Two or three times a year. He withdrew the money in cash. Then he would think up some excuse and go to Kristianstad."

Wallander thought for a moment about what he had heard.

He tried to decide which questions were the most important. It would take hours to figure out all the details.

"What did they say at the bank?" he asked Hanson.

"If you don't have all the search warrants in order, the bank usually doesn't say anything," said Hanson. "They wouldn't let me look at his account balances. But I did get the answer to one question: Whether he had been to the bank recently."

"And he had?"

Hanson nodded. "Last Thursday. Three days before someone slaughtered him."

"Are you sure?"

"One of the tellers recognized him."

"And he withdrew a large sum of money?"

"They wouldn't say exactly. But the teller nodded when the bank director turned his back."

"We'll have to talk to the prosecutor after we write up this deposition," said Wallander. "Then we can look into his assets and get an idea of the situation."

"Blood money," said Lars Herdin.

Wallander wondered for a moment whether he was going to start throwing things again.

"There are plenty of questions left," he said. "But one is more

important than all the others right now. How come you know
about all this? You claim that Johannes Lövgren kept all this secret
from his wife. So how do you know about it?"

Herdin didn't answer the question. He stared mutely at the
floor.

Wallander looked at Hanson, who shook his head.

"You really have to answer the question," said Wallander.

"I don't have to answer at all," said Herdin. "I'm not the one
who killed them. Would I murder my own sister?"

Wallander tried to approach the question from another angle.
"How many people know about what you just told us?"

Herdin didn't answer.

"Whatever you say won't go beyond this room," Wallander
continued.

Herdin stared at the floor.

Wallander knew instinctively that he ought to wait.

"Would you get us some coffee?" he asked Hanson. "See if you
can find some pastries too."

Hanson vanished out the door.

Lars Herdin kept staring at the floor, and Wallander waited.

Hanson brought in the coffee, and Herdin ate a stale pastry.

Wallander thought it was time to ask the question again.
"Sooner or later you'll be forced to answer," he said.

Herdin raised his head and looked him straight in the eye.

"When they got married I already had a feeling that there
was somebody else behind Johannes Lövgren's friendly and taci-
turn front. I thought there was something fishy about him. Maria
was my little sister. I wanted the best for her. I was suspicious of
Johannes Lövgren from the first time he started coming around
and courting her at our parents' house. It took me thirty years to
figure out who he was. How I did it is my business."

"Did you tell your sister what you found out?"

"Never. Not a word."

"Did you tell anyone else? Your own wife?"

"I'm not married."

Wallander looked at the man sitting in front of him. There

was something hard and dogged about him. Like a man who had been brought up eating gravel.

"One last question for now," said Wallander. "Now we know that Johannes Lövgren had plenty of money. Maybe he also had a large sum of money at home the night he was murdered. We'll have to find that out. But who would have known about it? Besides you."

Lars Herdin looked at him. Wallander suddenly noticed a glint of fear in his eyes.

"I didn't know about it," said Herdin.

Wallander nodded.

"We'll stop here," he said, shoving aside the pad on which he had been taking notes the whole time. "But we're going to be needing your help again."

"Can I go now?" said Herdin, getting up.

"You can go," replied Wallander. "But don't leave the area without talking to us first. And if you think of anything else, let's hear from you."

At the door Herdin stopped as if there was something more he wanted to say.

Then he pushed open the door and was gone.

"Tell Martinson to run a check on him," said Wallander. "We probably won't find anything. But it's best to make sure."

"What do you think about what he said?" Hanson wondered.

Wallander thought about it before he answered.

"There was something convincing about him. I don't think he was lying or imagining things or making things up. I believe he did discover that Johannes Lövgren was living a double life. I think he was protecting his sister."

"Do you think he could have been involved?"

Wallander was certain when he replied. "Lars Herdin didn't kill them. I don't think he knows who did, either. I think he came to us for two reasons. He wanted to help us find one or more individuals so he can both thank them and spit in their face. As far as he's concerned, whoever murdered Johannes did him a favor. And whoever murdered Maria ought to be beheaded in the public square."

Hanson got up. "I'll tell Martinson. Anything else you need right now?"

Wallander looked at his watch.

"Let's have a meeting in my office in an hour. See if you can get hold of Rydberg. He was supposed to go into Malmö and find a guy who mends sails."

Hanson gave him a quizzical look.

"The noose," said Wallander. "The knot. You'll understand later."

Hanson left, and he was alone.

A breakthrough, he thought. All successful criminal investigations reach a point where we break through the wall. We don't know what we're actually going to find. But there's always a solution somewhere.

He went over to the window and looked out into the twilight. A cold draft was seeping through the window frame, and he could see from a swaying streetlight hanging on a wire over the street that the wind had picked up some more.

He thought about Nyström and his wife.

For a whole lifetime they had lived in close contact with a man who had not been the man he pretended to be at all.

How would they react when the truth was revealed?

With denial? Bitterness? Amazement?

He went back to the desk and sat down. The first feeling of relief that followed a breakthrough in a crime investigation often faded quite rapidly. Now there was a conceivable motive, the most common of all: money. But as yet there was no invisible finger pointing in a specific direction.

There was no murderer.

Wallander cast another glance at his watch. If he hurried, he could drive down to the hot-dog kiosk at the railway station and grab a bite to eat before the meeting. This day too was going to pass without a change in his eating habits.

He was just about to put on his jacket when the phone rang.

At the same time there was a knock on the door.

The jacket landed on the floor as he grabbed the phone and

shouted, "Come in."

Rydberg stood in the doorway. He was holding a large plastic bag.

He heard Ebba's voice on the phone.

"The TV people absolutely have to get hold of you," she said.

He quickly decided to talk to Rydberg first before he had to deal with the media again.

"Tell them I'm in a meeting and won't be available for half an hour," he said.

"Sure?"

"What?"

"That you'll talk to them in half an hour? Swedish TV doesn't like to be kept waiting. They presume that everyone's going to fall to their knees whenever they call."

"I'm not going to fall to my knees for their cameras. But I can talk to them in half an hour."

He hung up.

Rydberg had sat down in the chair by the window. He was busy drying off his hair with a paper napkin.

"I've got good news," said Wallander.

Rydberg kept on drying his hair.

"I think we've got a motive. Money. And I think we should look for the killers among people who were close to the Lövgrens."

Rydberg tossed the wet napkin into the wastebasket.

"I've had a miserable day," he said. "Good news is welcome."

Wallander spent five minutes recounting the meeting with Lars Herdin, the farmer. Rydberg stared gloomily at the glass shards on the floor.

"Strange story," said Rydberg when Wallander was finished. "It's strange enough to be completely true."

"I'll try to sum it all up," Wallander went on. "Someone knew that Johannes Lövgren occasionally kept large sums of money at home. This gives us robbery as a motive. And the robbery developed into a murder. If Lars Herdin's description of Johannes Lövgren is right, that he was an unusually stingy man, he would naturally have refused to reveal where he hid the money. Maria

Lövgren, who can't have understood much of what was happening on the last night of her life, was forced to accompany Johannes on his final journey. So the question is who, besides Lars Herdin, knew about these irregular but large cash withdrawals. If we can answer that, we can probably answer everything."

Rydberg sat there thinking after Wallander fell silent.

"Did I leave anything out?" asked Wallander.

"I'm thinking about what she said before she died," said Rydberg. "Foreign. And I'm thinking about what I've got in this plastic bag."

He got up and dumped the contents of the bag onto the desk.

It was a pile of pieces of rope. Each one with an artfully tied knot in it.

"I spent four hours with an old sailmaker in an apartment that smelled worse than anything you can imagine," said Rydberg with a grimace. "It turned out that this man was almost ninety years old and well on his way to senility. I wonder whether I shouldn't contact one of the social agencies. The old man was so confused that he thought I was his son. Later one of the neighbors told me that his son has been dead for thirty years. But he sure did know about knots. When I finally got out of there, it was four hours later. These pieces of rope were a present."

"Did you find out what you wanted to know?"

"The old man looked at the noose and said he thought the knot was ugly. Then it took me three hours to get him to tell me something about this ugly knot. In the meantime he managed to nod off for a while."

Rydberg gathered up the bits of rope in his plastic bag as he went on. "Suddenly he started talking about his days at sea. And then he said that he'd seen that knot in Argentina. Argentine sailors used to tie that knot as a leash for their dogs."

Wallander nodded.

"So you were right. The knot was foreign. The question now is how this all fits in with Lars Herdin's story."

They went out in the corridor. Rydberg went into his office, while Wallander went in to see Martinson and study the printouts.

It turned out that there were incredibly exhaustive statistics on foreign-born citizens who had either committed or been suspected of committing crimes in Sweden. Martinson had also managed to run a check of previous attacks on old people. At least four different individuals or gangs had committed assault on old isolated people in Skåne during the past year. But Martinson also found out that all of them were presently incarcerated in various penal institutions. He was still waiting for word on whether any of them had been granted leave on the day in question.

They held the meeting of the investigative team in Rydberg's office, since one of the office clerks had offered to vacuum the glass from Wallander's floor. The phone rang almost constantly, but she didn't feel like picking it up.

The investigative meeting was long. Everyone agreed that Lars Herdin's testimony was a breakthrough. Now they had a direction to go in. At the same time they went over everything that had been learned from the conversations with the residents of Lenarp, and the people who had telephoned the police or responded to the questionnaire they had sent out. A car that had driven through a town just a few kilometers from Lenarp at high speed late on Sunday night attracted special attention. A truck driver who had started a trip to Göteborg at three o'clock in the morning had encountered the car going around a tight curve and had almost been hit. When he heard about the double murder he started thinking, and then he called the police. He wasn't sure, but after going through pictures of various cars he decided it was probably a Nissan.

"Don't forget rental cars," said Wallander. "People on the move want to be comfortable these days. Robbers rent cars as often as they steal them."

It was already six o'clock by the time the meeting was over. Wallander realized that all his colleagues were now on the offensive. There was palpable optimism now, after Lars Herdin's visit.

He went to his office and typed up his notes from the conversation with Herdin. Hanson had turned in his already, so he could compare them. He realized at once that Lars Herdin had not been evasive. The information was the same in both.

Just after seven he put the paper aside. He had suddenly realized that the TV people had never called back. He asked the switchboard whether Ebba had left any message before she went home.

The girl who answered was a temp. "There's nothing here," she said.

He went out in the lunchroom and turned on the TV, on a hunch that he himself didn't understand. The local news had just started. He leaned on a table and distractedly watched a spot about some bad business deals made by the municipality of Malmö.

He thought about Sten Widén.

And Johannes Lövgren, who had sold meat to the Nazis during the war.

He thought about himself, and about his stomach, which was far too big.

He was just about to turn off the TV when the anchorwoman started talking about the double murder in Lenarp.

In astonishment he heard that the police in Ystad were concentrating their search on an as yet unidentified foreign citizen. But the police were convinced that the perpetrators were foreigners. It could not be ruled out that they might be refugees seeking asylum.

Finally the reporter talked about Wallander himself.

Despite repeated urging, it had been impossible to get any of the detectives in charge to comment on the information, which had been obtained from anonymous but reliable sources.

The reporter was speaking in front of a background shot of the Ystad police station.

Then she segued into the weather report.

A storm was approaching from the west. The wind would increase, but there was no risk of snow. The temperature would continue to stay above freezing.

Wallander switched off the TV.

He had a hard time deciding whether he was upset or merely tired. Or maybe he was just hungry.

But someone at the police station had leaked the information.

Perhaps nowadays people got paid for passing on confidential information.

Did the state-run television monopoly have slush funds too?

Who? he thought.

It could have been anyone except me.

And why?

Was there some other explanation besides money?

Racial hatred? Fear of refugees?

As he walked back to his room, he could hear the phone ringing all the way out in the hall.

It had been a long day. Most of all he would have liked to drive home and fix some dinner. With a sigh he sat down in his chair and pulled over the phone.

I guess I'll have to get started, he thought. Start denying the information on the TV.

And hope that nobody burns another wooden cross in the days to come.

Chapter Six

Overnight a storm moved in over Skåne. Kurt Wallander was sitting in his untidy apartment while the winter wind tore at the roof tiles. He was drinking whiskey and listening to a German recording of *Aida* when everything suddenly went dark and silent around him. He went over to the window and looked out into the darkness. The wind was howling, and somewhere an advertising sign was banging against the wall of a building.

The glow-in-the-dark hands on his wristwatch were pointing at ten minutes to three. Oddly enough, he did not feel in the least tired. It had been almost twelve thirty by the time he got away from the police station that night. The last person to call him had been a man who refused to give his name. He had proposed that the police join forces with the domestic nationalist movements and chase all the foreigners out of the country once and for all. For a moment Wallander had tried to listen to what the anonymous man was saying. Then he had slammed down the receiver, called the switchboard, and had all incoming calls held. He turned off the lights in his office, walked down the silent corridor, and drove straight home. When he unlocked his front door, he had decided to find out who on the police force had leaked the confidential information. It wasn't really his business at all. If conflicts arose within the police force, it was the duty of the chief of police to intervene. In a few days Björk would be back from his winter vacation. Then he could take over. The truth would have to come out.

But by the time Wallander had drunk his first glass of whiskey, he realized that Björk wouldn't do a thing. Even though each individual police officer was bound by an oath of silence, it could hardly be considered a criminal offense if an officer called up a contact at Swedish Television and told him what was discussed at an internal meeting in the investigative group. It would hardly be possible to prove any irregularities, either, if Swedish Television had paid its secret informant. Wallander wondered for an instant how Swedish Television entered such an expense in their books.

Then he thought that Björk wouldn't be inclined to question internal loyalty while they were in the middle of a murder case.

By the second glass of whiskey he was again worrying about who could have been the source of the leak. Apart from himself he felt he could safely eliminate Rydberg. But why was he so sure of Rydberg? Could he see more deeply into him than into any of the others?

Now the storm had knocked out the power and he was sitting alone in the dark.

His thoughts about the murdered couple, about Lars Herdin, and about the strange knot on the noose were mixed with thoughts of Sten Widén and Mona, of Linda and his old father. Somewhere in the dark a vast meaninglessness was beckoning to him. A grinning face that laughed scornfully at all his vain attempts to manage his life.

He woke up when the power came back on. From his watch he could see that he had slept for over an hour. The record was still spinning on the phonograph. He emptied his glass and went to lie down on his bed.

I've got to talk to Mona, he thought. I've got to talk to her after all that's happened. And I've got to talk to my daughter. I have to visit my father and see what I can do for him. On top of all that I really ought to catch a murderer too.

He must have dozed off again. He thought he was in his office when the telephone rang. Drowsily he stumbled into the kitchen and grabbed the phone. Who could be calling him at a quarter past four in the morning?

Before he answered, the thought crossed his mind that he hoped it was Mona.

At first he thought that the man on the line sounded like Sten Widén.

"Now you've got three days to make good," said the man.

"Who is this?" said Wallander.

"It doesn't matter who I am," replied the man. "I'm one of the Ten Thousand Redeemers."

"I refuse to talk to anyone when I don't know who it is," said Wallander, now wide awake.

"Don't hang up," said the man. "You now have three days to make up for shielding foreign criminals. Three days, no more."

"I don't understand what you're talking about," said Wallander, feeling ill at ease at the unknown voice.

"Three days to catch the killers and put them on display," said the man. "Or else we'll take over."

"Take over what? Who's 'we'?"

"Three days. No more. Then something's going to burn."

The connection was broken off.

Wallander turned on the kitchen light and sat down at the table. He wrote down the conversation in an old notebook that Mona used to use for her shopping lists. At the top of the pad it said "bread." He couldn't read what she had written below that.

It wasn't the first time that Wallander had received an anonymous threat during his years as a cop. A man who considered himself unjustly convicted of assault and battery had harassed him with insinuating letters and nighttime phone calls several years earlier. That time it was Mona who finally got fed up and demanded that he do something about it. Wallander had sent Svedberg to the man with a warning that he was risking a long jail sentence if he didn't stop harassing him. Another time someone had slashed his tires.

But this man's message was different.

Something's going to burn, he had said. Wallander realized that it could be anything from refugee camps to restaurants to houses owned by foreigners.

Three days. Seventy-two hours. That meant Friday, or Saturday the thirteenth at the latest.

He went and lay down on top of the bed again and tried to sleep.

The wind tore and ripped at the walls of the houses.

How could he sleep when he kept waiting for the man to call again?

At six thirty he was back at the police station. He exchanged a few words with the duty officer and learned that the stormy night had been peaceful at least. A tractor-trailer rig had tipped over outside Ystad, and a building under construction had blown down in Skårby. That was all.

He got some coffee and went into his office. With an old electric shaver that he kept in a desk drawer he got rid of the stubble on his cheeks. Then he went out for the morning papers. The more he looked through them, the more displeased he became. Despite the fact that he had been on the telephone talking to a number of reporters until late the night before, they printed only vague and incomplete denials that the police were concentrating their investigation on some foreign citizens. It was as though the papers had only reluctantly accepted the truth.

He decided to call another press conference for that afternoon and to present an account of the status of the investigation. He would also report on the anonymous threat he had received during the night.

He took down a folder from a shelf behind his desk. There he kept information on the various refugee conduits in the vicinity. Besides the big refugee camp in Ystad, several smaller units were scattered throughout the district.

But what was there to prove that the threat actually had to do with a refugee camp in Ystad's police district? Nothing. Besides, the threat might just as well be directed at a restaurant or a residence. For instance, how many pizzerias were there in the Ystad area? Fifteen? More?

There was one thing he was quite sure of. The threat in the night had to be taken seriously. In the past year there had been too many incidents confirming the fact that there were organized forces in Sweden that would not hesitate to resort to open violence against foreign citizens or refugees seeking asylum.

He looked at his watch. Quarter to eight. He picked up the phone and dialed the number of Rydberg's house. After ten rings he hung up. Rydberg was on his way.

Martinson stuck his head in the door.

"Hi," he said. "What time is the meeting today?"

"Ten o'clock," said Wallander.

"How about this weather?"

"As long as we don't get snow, I don't care if it's windy."

While he waited for Rydberg, he looked for the piece of paper he had received from Sten Widén. After Lars Herdin's visit he realized that perhaps it wasn't so unusual that someone had given the horse some hay during the night. If the killers were among Johannes and Maria Lövgren's acquaintances, or even members of their family, then they would naturally know about the horse. Maybe they also knew that Johannes Lövgren made a habit of going out to the stable at night.

Wallander had only a vague idea of what Sten Widén would be able to add. Maybe the real reason he had called him was to avoid losing touch with him again.

No one answered, even though he let the phone ring for over a minute. He hung up and decided to try again a little later.

He also had another phone call he hoped to finish before Rydberg arrived. He dialed the number and waited.

"District attorney's office," a cheerful female voice said.

"This is Kurt Wallander. Is Åkeson there?"

"He's on leave of absence this spring. Did you forget?"

He had forgotten. It had completely slipped his mind that District Attorney Per Åkeson was taking some university courses. And they had had dinner together as recently as the end of November.

"I can connect you with his deputy, if you like," said the receptionist.

"Do that," said Wallander.

To his surprise a woman answered. "Anette Brolin."

"I'd like to talk with the prosecutor," said Wallander.

"Speaking," said the woman. "What is this regarding?"

Wallander realized that he had not introduced himself. He gave her his name and went on, "It's about this double murder. I think it's time we presented a report to the DA's office. I had forgotten that Per was on leave."

"If you hadn't called this morning, I would have called you," said the woman.

Wallander thought he detected a reproachful tone in her voice. Bitch, he thought. Are you going to teach me how the police are supposed to cooperate with the DA's office?

"We actually don't have much to tell you," he said, noticing that his voice sounded a little hostile.

"Is an arrest imminent?"

"No. I was thinking more of a short briefing."

"All right," said the woman. "Shall we say eleven o'clock at my office? I've got a detention hearing at ten fifteen. I'll be back by eleven."

"I might be a little late. We have a meeting of the investigative team at ten. It might run long."

"Try to make it by eleven."

She hung up, and he sat there holding the receiver.

Cooperation between the police and the district attorney's office wasn't always easy. But Wallander had established an unbureaucratic relationship of trust with Per Åkeson. They often called each other up to ask advice. They seldom disagreed on when detention or release was justified.

"Damn," he said out loud. Anette Brolin, who the hell is she?

Just then he heard the unmistakable sound of Rydberg limping out in the hall. He stuck his head out the door and asked him to come in. Rydberg was dressed in an outmoded fur jacket and beret. When he sat down he grimaced.

"Bothering you again?" asked Wallander, pointing at his leg.

"Rain is okay," said Rydberg. "Or snow. Or cold. But this damned leg can't stand the wind. What do you want?"

Wallander told him about the anonymous threat he had received during the night.

"What do you think?" he asked when he was done. "Serious or not?"

"Serious. At least we have to act as if it is."

"I'm thinking about a press conference this afternoon. We'll present the status of the investigation and zero in on Lars Herdin's story. Without mentioning his name, of course. Then I'll tell about the threat. And say that all rumors about foreigners are groundless."

"But that's actually not true," Rydberg mused.

"What do you mean?"

"The woman said what she said. And the knot may be Argentine."

"How did you intend to make that fit in with a robbery that was presumably committed by someone who knew Johannes Lövgren very well?"

"I don't know yet. I think it's too soon to draw conclusions. Don't you?"

"Provisional conclusions," said Wallander. "All police work deals with drawing conclusions. Which you later discard or keep building on."

Rydberg shifted his sore leg.

"What are you thinking of doing about the leak?" he asked.

"I'm thinking of giving them hell at the meeting," said Wallander. "Then Björk can take care of it when he gets back."

"What do you think he'll do?"

"Nothing."

"Exactly."

Wallander threw his arms wide.

"We might as well admit it right now. Whoever leaked it to the TV people isn't going to get his nose twisted off. By the way, how much do you think Swedish Television pays to snitching cops?"

"Probably way too much," said Rydberg. "That's why they don't have money for any good programs."

He got up from his chair.

"Don't forget one thing," he said as he stood with his hand on the door frame. "A cop who snitches can snitch again."

"What do you mean?"

"He can insist that one of our leads does point toward foreigners. It's true, after all."

"It's not even a lead," said Wallander. "It's the last confused word of a groggy old woman who was dying."

Rydberg shrugged.

"Do as you like," he said. "See you in a while."

The meeting went as badly as an investigative meeting can go. Wallander had decided to start with the leak and its possible consequences. He would describe the anonymous phone call he had received and then entertain suggestions on what should be done before the deadline ran out. But when he angrily complained that someone among those present was apparently so disloyal that he spread confidential information and possibly also took money for it, he was met by equally angry protests. Several of the police officers thought that the rumor might well have been leaked from the hospital. Hadn't both doctors and nurses been present when the old woman uttered her last words?

Wallander tried to refute their objections, but they kept protesting. By the time he finally managed to steer the discussion to the investigation itself, a sullen mood had settled over the room. Yesterday's optimism had been replaced by a slack, uninspired atmosphere. Wallander realized that he had gotten off on the wrong foot.

The attempt to identify the car with which the truck driver had almost collided had yielded no results. To increase efficiency, an additional man was assigned to concentrate on the car.

The investigation of Lars Herdin's past was ongoing. On the first check nothing remarkable had come to light. Lars Herdin had no record and no conspicuous debts.

"We're going to run a vacuum over this guy," said Wallander. "We have to know everything there is to know. I'm going to be meeting with the prosecutor in a few minutes. I'll request authorization to go into the bank."

Peters was the one who brought the biggest news of the day.

"Johannes Lövgren had two safe-deposit boxes," he said. "One at the Union Bank and one at the Merchants' Bank. I went through the keys on his key ring."

"Good," said Wallander. "We'll go check them out later today."

The charting of Lövgrens' family, friends, and relatives would continue.

It was decided that Rydberg should take care of the daughter who lived in Canada, who would be arriving at the hovercraft terminal in Malmö just after three in the afternoon.

"Where's the other daughter?" asked Wallander. "The handball player?"

"She's already arrived," said Svedberg. "She's staying with relatives."

"You go talk to her," said Wallander. "Do we have any other tips that might produce something? Ask the daughters if either of them received a wall clock, by the way."

Martinson had sifted through the tips. Everything that the police learned was fed into a computer. Then Martinson did a rough sort. The most ridiculous tips never got beyond the printouts.

"Hulda Yngveson phoned from Vallby and said that it was the disapproving hand of God that dealt the blow," said Martinson.

"She always calls," sighed Rydberg. "If a calf runs off, it's because God is displeased."

"I put her on the CF list," said Martinson.

The sullen atmosphere was broken by a little amusement when Martinson explained that CF stood for "crazy fools."

They hadn't received any tips of immediate interest. But everything would be checked out in time.

Finally the question remained of Johannes Lövgren's secret relationship in Kristianstad and the child they had together.

Wallander looked around the room. Thomas Näslund, a thirty-year veteran who seldom called attention to himself but who did solid, thorough work, was sitting in a corner, pulling on his lower lip as he listened.

"You can come with me," said Wallander. "See if you can do a little footwork first. Call up Herdin and pump him for everything you can about this woman in Kristianstad. And the child too, of course."

The press conference was set for four o'clock. By then Kurt Wallander and Thomas Näslund hoped to be back from Kristianstad. If they were late, Rydberg promised to preside.

"I'll write the press release," said Wallander. "If no one has anything more, we'll adjourn."

It was eleven twenty-five when he knocked on Per Åkeson's door in another part of the police building.

The woman who opened the door was very striking and very young. Wallander stared at her.

"Seen enough yet?" she said. "You're half an hour late, by the way."

"I told you the meeting might run over," he countered.

When he entered her office, he hardly recognized it. Per Åkeson's spartan, colorless space had been transformed into a room with colorful curtains and big flowerpots along the walls.

He followed her with his eyes as she sat down behind her desk. He thought she couldn't be more than thirty years old. She was dressed in a rust-brown suit that he was sure was of good quality and no doubt quite expensive.

"Have a seat," she said. "Maybe we ought to shake hands, by the way. I'll be filling in for Åkeson the entire time he's away. So we'll be working together for quite a while."

He put out his hand and noticed at the same time that she was wearing a wedding ring. To his surprise he realized that he felt disappointed.

She had dark brown hair, cut short and framing her face. A bleached lock of hair curled down beside one ear.

"I'd like to say welcome to Ystad," he said. "I have to admit that I totally forgot that Per was on leave."

"I assume we'll be using our first names. Mine is Anette."

"Kurt. How do you like Ystad?"

She shook off the question with a curt reply. "I don't really know yet. Stockholmers no doubt have a hard time getting used to the leisurely pace of Skåne."

"Leisurely?"

"You're half an hour late."

Wallander could feel himself getting angry. Was she provoking him? Didn't she understand that a meeting of an investigative team could run over? Did she view all Scanians as leisurely?

"I don't think Scanians are any lazier than anyone else," he said. "All Stockholmers aren't stuck-up, are they?"

"Pardon?"

"Forget it."

She leaned back in her chair. He noticed that he was having a hard time looking her in the eye.

"Perhaps you could give me a rundown," she said.

Wallander tried to make his report as concise as possible. He could tell that, without really intending it, he had wound up in a defensive position.

He avoided mentioning the leak in the police department.

She interjected a few brief questions, which he answered. He could see that despite her youth she did have professional experience.

"We have to go take a look at Lövgren's bank balances," he said. "He also has two safe-deposit boxes we want to open."

She wrote up the documents he needed.

"Does a judge have to look at this?" asked Wallander as she shoved the documents over to him.

"We'll do that later," she said. "Then I'd appreciate receiving ongoing copies of all the investigative material."

He nodded and got ready to leave.

"This article in the papers," she inquired "About foreigners who may have been involved?"

"A rumor," replied Wallander. "You know how it is."

"Do I?" she asked.

When he left her office he noticed that he was sweating.

What a babe, he thought. How the hell can someone like that become a prosecutor? Devote her life to catching small-time crooks and keeping the streets clean?

He stopped in the big reception area of the police station, unable to decide what to do next.

Eat, he decided. If I don't get some food now, I never will. I can write the press release while I eat.

When he walked out of the police station he was almost blown over.

The storm had not died down.

He thought he ought to drive home and make himself a simple salad. Despite the fact that he had hardly eaten a thing all day, his stomach felt heavy and bloated. But then he allowed himself to be tempted to eat at the Lurhorn Blower down by the square instead. He wasn't going to tackle his eating habits seriously today either.

At quarter to one he was back at the station. Since he had once again eaten too fast, he had an attack of diarrhea and ran to the toilet. When his stomach had settled somewhat, he turned in the press release to one of the office clerks and then headed for Näslund's room.

"I can't get hold of Herdin," said Näslund. "He's out on some kind of winter hike with a conservation group in Fyle Valley."

"Then I guess we'll have to drive out there and look for him," said Wallander.

"I thought I might as well do that, then you can go check the safe-deposit boxes. If everything was so hush-hush with this woman and their kid, maybe there's something locked up in there. We'll save time that way, I mean."

Wallander nodded. Näslund was right. He barged forward like an impatient locomotive.

"Okay, that's what we'll do," he said. "If we don't make it today we'll go up to Kristianstad tomorrow morning."

Before he got into his car to drive down to the bank, he tried once more to get hold of Sten Widén. There was no answer this time either.

He dropped off the slip with Ebba at the reception desk.

"See if you can get an answer," he said. "Check whether this number is right. It's supposed to be in the name of Sten Widén. Or a racehorse stable that might have a name I don't know."

"Hanson probably knows," said Ebba.

"I said racehorses, not trotters."

"He plays anything that moves," said Ebba with a laugh.

"I'll be at the Union Bank if there's anything urgent," said Wallander.

He parked the car across from the bookstore on the square. The powerful wind almost blew the parking stub out of his hand after he put the money in the automat. The town seemed abandoned. The strong winds were keeping people indoors.

He stopped at the radio store by the square. In an attempt to combat the sadness in the evenings, he was considering buying a VCR. He looked at the prices and tried to figure out whether he could afford the purchase this month. Or should he invest in a new stereo instead? After all, it was music he turned to when he lay tossing and turning and couldn't sleep.

He tore himself away from the display window and turned down the pedestrian street by the Chinese restaurant. The Union Bank was right next door. When he walked in through the glass doors, he found only one customer inside the small bank lobby. A farmer with a hearing aid, complaining about the high interest rate in a high, shrill voice. To the left a door stood open to an office where a man sat studying a computer screen. He assumed that's where he was supposed to go. When he stood in the doorway the man looked up quickly, as if Wallander were a possible bank robber.

He walked into the room and introduced himself.

"We're not happy about this at all," said the man behind the desk. "In all the years I've been at this bank we've never had any trouble with the police."

Wallander was instantly annoyed by the man's uncooperative attitude. Sweden had turned into a country where people more than anything else seemed to be afraid of being bothered. Nothing was holier than ingrained routine.

"It can't be helped," said Wallander, taking out the documents that Anette Brolin had drawn up.

The man read them carefully.

"Is this really necessary?" he asked. "The whole point of a safe-deposit box is that it's protected from inspection by outsiders."

"It's necessary," said Wallander. "And I haven't got all day."

With a sigh the man got up from his desk. Wallander realized that he had prepared himself for a visit from the police. They passed through a barred doorway and entered the safe-deposit vault. Johannes Lövgren's box was at the bottom in one corner. Wallander unlocked it, pulled out the drawer, and set it on the table.

Then he raised the lid and started going through the contents. There were some papers for burial arrangements and some title deeds to the farm in Lenarp. Some old photographs and a pale envelope with old stamps on it. That was all.

Nothing, he thought. Nothing of what I had hoped for.

The bank man stood to the side watching him. Wallander wrote down the number of the title deed and the names on the burial documents. Then he closed the box.

"Will that be all?" asked the bank official.

"For the time being," said Wallander. "Now I'd like to take a look at the accounts he had here at the bank."

On the way out of the vault something occurred to him. "Did anyone else besides Johannes Lövgren have access to his safe-deposit box?" he asked.

"No," replied the bank official.

"Do you know whether he opened the box recently?"

"I looked at the visitor register," the official replied. "It has to be many years since he last opened the box."

The farmer was still complaining when they returned to the bank lobby. Now he had started in on a tirade about the declining price of grain.

"I have all the information in my office," said the man.

Wallander sat down by his desk and went through two full sheets of printouts. Johannes Lövgren had four different accounts. Maria Lövgren was a joint signatory on two of them. The total amount in these two accounts was 90,000 kronor. Neither of the accounts had been touched in a long time. In the past few days interest had been posted. The third account was left over from Lövgren's days as an active farmer. The balance in that one was 132 kronor and 97 öre.

There was one more account. Its balance was almost a million kronor. Maria Lövgren was not a signatory to it. On January 1, interest of more than 90,000 kronor had been posted to the account. On January 4, Johannes Lövgren had withdrawn 27,000 kronor.

Wallander looked up at the man sitting on the other side of the desk.

"How far back can you trace this account?" he asked.

"In principle, for ten years. But it'll take some time, of course. We'll have to run a computer search."

"Start with last year. I want to see all activity in this account during 1989."

The bank official rose and left the room. Wallander started studying the other document. It showed that Johannes Lövgren had almost 700,000 kronor in various mutual funds that the bank administered.

So far Lars Herdin's story seems to check out, he thought.

He recalled the conversation with Nyström, who had sworn that his neighbor didn't have any money.

That's how much you know about your neighbors, he thought.

After about five minutes the man came back from the lobby. He handed Wallander another printout.

On three occasions in 1989 Johannes Lövgren had withdrawn a total of 78,000 kronor. The withdrawals were made in January, July, and September.

"May I keep these papers?" he asked.

The man nodded.

"I'd very much like to speak with the teller who paid out the money to Johannes Lövgren the last time," he said.

"Britta-Lena Bodén," said the man.

The woman who entered the office was quite young. Wallander thought she was hardly more than twenty years old.

"She knows what it's all about," said the man.

Wallander nodded and introduced himself. "Tell me what you know."

"It was quite a lot of money," said the young woman. "Otherwise I wouldn't have remembered it."

"Did he seem uneasy? Nervous?"

"Not that I recall."

"How did he want the money?"

"In thousand-krona bills."

"Just thousands?"

"He took a few five hundreds too."

"What did he put the money in?"

The young woman had a good memory.

"A brown briefcase. One of those old-fashioned ones with a strap around it."

"Would you recognize it if you saw it again?"

"Maybe. The handle was ragged."

"What do you mean by ragged?"

"The leather was cracked."

Wallander nodded. The woman's memory was excellent. "Do you remember anything else?"

"After he got the money, he left."

"And he was alone?"

"Yes."

"You didn't see whether anyone was waiting for him outside?"

"I wouldn't be able to see that from the teller's window."

"Do you remember what time it was?"

The woman thought before she replied. "I went to lunch right afterwards. It was around noon."

"You've been a great help. If you remember anything else, please let me know."

Wallander got up and went out to the bank lobby. He stopped for a moment and looked around. The young woman was right. From the tellers' windows it was impossible to see whether anyone was waiting on the street outside.

The hard-of-hearing farmer was gone, and new customers had arrived. Someone speaking a foreign language was changing money at one of the tellers' windows.

Wallander went outside. The Merchants' Bank was on Hamngatan close by.

A considerably friendlier bank officer accompanied him down

to the vault. When Wallander opened the steel drawer, he was disappointed at once. The box was completely empty.

No one but Johannes Lövgren had access to this safe-deposit box either. He had rented it in 1962.

"When was he here last?" asked Wallander.

The answer gave him a start.

"On January fourth," the official replied after studying the register of visitors. "At one fifteen in the afternoon, to be precise. He stayed for twenty minutes."

But even when Wallander asked all the employees, no one remembered whether Lövgren had anything with him when he left the bank. No one remembered his briefcase either.

The young woman from the Union Bank, he thought. Every bank ought to have someone like her.

Wallander struggled down windblown back streets to Fridolf's Bakery, where he drank some coffee and ate a cinnamon roll.

I would like to know what Johannes Lövgren did between noon and one fifteen, he thought. What did he do between his first and second bank visits? And how did he arrive in Ystad? How did he get back? He didn't own a car.

He took out his notebook and brushed some crumbs off the table. After half an hour he had drawn up a summary of the questions that had to be answered as soon as possible.

On the way back to the car he went into a menswear shop and bought a pair of socks. He was shocked at the price but paid without protesting. Before, it had always been Mona who bought his clothes. He tried to remember the last time he had bought a pair of socks.

When he got back to his car, a parking ticket had been stuck under one windshield wiper.

If I don't pay it, they'll eventually start legal proceedings against me, he thought. Then acting district attorney Anette Brolin will be forced to stand up in court and take me to task.

He tossed the parking ticket into the glove compartment and thought once again about how good-looking she was. Good-looking and charming. Then he thought about the roll he'd just eaten.

It was three o'clock before Thomas Näslund called in. By that time Wallander had already decided to postpone the trip to Kristianstad to the next day.

"I'm soaked," said Näslund on the phone. "I've tramped around in the mud after Herdin all over Fyle Valley."

"Pump him good," said Wallander. "Put a little pressure on him. We want to know everything he knows."

"Should I bring him in?" asked Näslund.

"Go home with him. Maybe he'll talk more freely at home at his own kitchen table."

The press conference started at four. Wallander looked for Rydberg, but nobody knew where he was.

The room was full of reporters. Wallander saw that the female reporter from the local radio was there, and he quickly decided to find out what she really knew about Linda.

He could feel his stomach churning.

I'm repressing things, he thought. Along with everything else I don't have time for. I'm searching for the slayers of the dead and can't even manage to pay attention to the living.

For a dizzying instant his entire consciousness was filled with only one urge.

To take off. Flee. Disappear. Start a new life.

Then he climbed up on the little dais and welcomed his audience to the press conference.

After fifty-seven minutes it was over. Wallander thought that he probably came off pretty well by denying all rumors that the police were searching for some foreign citizens in connection with the double murder. He hadn't been asked any questions that gave him trouble. When he stepped down from the podium, he felt satisfied.

The young woman from the local radio waited while he was interviewed for television. As always when a TV camera was pointed at his face, he got nervous and stumbled over his words. But the reporter was satisfied and didn't ask for another take.

"You'll have to get yourself some better informants," said Wallander when it was all over.

"I might have to at that," replied the reporter and laughed.

When the TV crew had left, Wallander suggested that the young woman from the local radio station accompany him to his office.

He was less nervous in front of a radio microphone than in front of the camera.

When she was finished, she turned off the tape recorder. Wallander was just about to bring up Linda when Rydberg knocked on the door and came in.

"We're almost done," said Wallander.

"We're done now," said the young woman, getting up.

Crestfallen, Wallander watched her go. He hadn't managed to get in one word about Linda.

"More trouble," said Rydberg. "They just called from the refugee receiving unit here in Ystad. A car drove into the courtyard and threw a bag of rotten turnips at an old man from Lebanon and hit him in the head."

"Damn," said Wallander. "What happened?"

"He's at the hospital getting bandaged up. But the director is nervous."

"Did they get the license number?"

"It all happened too fast."

Wallander thought for a moment.

"Let's not do anything conspicuous right now," he said. "In the morning there will be strong denials about the foreigners in all the papers. It'll be on TV tonight. Then we just have to hope that things calm down. We could ask the night patrols to check out the camp."

"I'll tell them," said Rydberg.

"Come back afterwards and we'll do an update," said Wallander.

It was half past eight when Wallander and Rydberg finished.

"What do you think?" asked Wallander as they gathered up their papers.

Rydberg scratched his forehead. "It's obvious that this Herdin lead is a good one. As long as we can get hold of that mystery woman and the boy. There's a lot to indicate that the solution might be close at hand. So close that it's hard to see. But at the same time..." Rydberg broke off his sentence.

"At the same time?"

"I don't know," Rydberg went on. "There's something funny about all this. Especially that noose. I don't know what it is."

He shrugged and stood up.

"We'll have to continue tomorrow," he said.

"Do you remember seeing a brown briefcase at Lövgren's house?" Wallander asked.

Rydberg shook his head.

"Not that I can recall," he said. "But a whole bunch of old junk fell out of the wardrobes. I wonder why old people turn into such pack rats?"

"Send someone out there tomorrow morning to look for an old brown briefcase," said Wallander. "With a cracked handle."

Rydberg left. Wallander could see that his lame leg was bothering him a lot. He thought he'd better find out whether Ebba had gotten hold of Sten Widén. But he didn't bother. Instead he looked up Anette Brolin's home address in a department directory. To his surprise he discovered that she was almost his neighbor.

I could ask her to dinner, he thought.

Then he remembered that she wore a wedding ring.

He drove home through the storm and took a bath. Then he lay down on his bed and leafed through a book about the life of Giuseppe Verdi.

He woke up with a start a few hours later because he was cold.

His watch showed a few minutes to midnight.

He felt dejected about waking up. Now he'd have another sleepless night.

Driven by his despondency, he got dressed. He thought he might as well spend a few nighttime hours at his office.

Outside he noticed that the wind had died down. It had started to get cold again.

Snow, he thought. It'll be here soon.

He turned onto Österleden. A lone taxi was headed in the opposite direction. He drove slowly through the empty town.

Suddenly he decided to drive past the refugee camp on the west side of town.

The camp consisted of a number of barracks in long rows in an open field. Bright floodlights lit up the green-painted buildings.

He stopped at a parking lot and got out of the car. The waves breaking on the beach were not far away.

He looked at the refugee camp.

Put a fence around it and it'd be a concentration camp, he thought.

He was just about to get back in his car when he heard a faint crash of glass breaking.

In the next instant there was a dull boom.

Then tall flames were shooting out of one of the barracks.

Chapter Seven

He had no idea how long he stood there, stunned by the flames blazing in the winter night. Maybe it was several minutes, maybe only a few seconds. But when he managed to break through his paralysis, he had enough presence of mind to grab the car phone and call in the alarm.

The static on the phone made it difficult to hear the man who answered.

"The refugee camp in Ystad is on fire!" shouted Wallander. "Get the fire department out here! The wind is blowing hard."

"Who am I speaking with?" asked the man at the emergency switchboard.

"This is Wallander of the Ystad police. I just happened to be driving past when the fire started."

"Can you identify yourself?" continued the voice on the phone, unmoved.

"Damn it! Four-seven-one-one-two-one! Move your butt!"

He hung up the phone to avoid answering any more questions. Besides, he knew that the emergency switchboard could identify all the police officers on duty in the district.

Then he ran across the road toward the burning barracks. The fire was sizzling in the wind. He wondered fleetingly what would have happened if the fire had started the night before, during the heavy storm. But right now the flames were already getting a firm grip on the barracks next door.

Why didn't someone sound the alarm? he thought. But he didn't know whether there were refugees living in all the barracks.

The heat of the fire hit him in the face as he pounded on the door of the barracks that had so far only been licked by the flames.

The barracks where the fire had started was now completely engulfed. Wallander tried to approach the door, but the fire drove him back. He ran around to the other side of the building. There was only one window. He banged on the glass and tried to look inside, but the smoke was so thick that he found himself staring straight into a white haze. He looked around for something to break the glass with but found nothing. Then he tore off his jacket, wrapped it around his arm, and smashed his fist through the windowpane. He held his breath to keep from inhaling the smoke and groped for the window latch. Twice he had to leap back to catch his breath before he managed to open the window.

"Get out!" he shouted into the fire. "Get out! Get out!"

Inside the barracks were two bunk beds. He hauled himself up onto the window ledge and felt the splinters of glass cutting into his thigh. The upper bunks were empty. But someone was lying on one of the lower bunks.

Wallander yelled again but got no response. Then he heaved himself through the window, hitting his head on the edge of a table as he landed on the floor. He was almost suffocating from the smoke as he fumbled his way toward the bed. At first he thought he was touching a lifeless body. Then he realized that what he had taken for a person was merely a rolled-up mattress. At the same moment his jacket caught fire and he threw himself headfirst out the window. From far off he could hear sirens, and as he stumbled away from the fire he saw crowds of half-dressed people milling around outside the barracks. The fire had now ignited two more of the low buildings. Wallander threw open doors and saw that people were living in these barracks. But those who had been asleep inside were already out. His head was pounding and his thigh hurt, and he felt sick from the smoke he had inhaled into his lungs. At that moment the first fire truck arrived, followed closely by an ambulance. He saw that the fire captain on duty was Peter Edler, a thirty-five-year-old man who flew kites in his spare time. Wallander had heard only favorable things about him. He was a man who was never bothered by uncertainty. Wallander staggered over to Edler, noting at the same time that he had burns on one arm.

"The barracks that are burning are empty," he said. "I don't know about the other ones."

"You look like shit," said Edler. "I think we can handle the other barracks."

The firefighters were already hosing down the closest barracks. Wallander heard Edler order a tractor to tow away the barracks that were already on fire in order to isolate the hot spots.

The first police car came to a skidding stop, its blue light flashing and siren wailing. Wallander saw that it was Peters and Norén. He hobbled over to their car.

"How's it going?" asked Norén.

"It'll be okay," said Wallander. "Start cordoning off the area and ask Edler if he needs any help."

Peters stared at him. "You sure look like shit. How'd you happen to be here?"

"I was out driving around," replied Wallander. "Now get moving."

For the next hour a peculiar mixture of chaos and efficient firefighting prevailed. The dazed director of the refugee camp was wandering around aimlessly, and Wallander had to take him to task to find out how many refugees were at the camp and then do a count. To his great surprise, it turned out that the Immigration Service's record of the refugees in residence at Ystad was completely and hopelessly confused. And he got no help from the dazed director either. In the meantime a tractor towed away the smoldering barracks, and the firefighters soon had the blaze under control. The medics had to take only a few of the refugees to the hospital. Most of them were suffering from shock. But there was a little Lebanese boy who had fallen and hit his head on a rock.

Edler pulled Wallander aside. "Go get yourself patched up."

Wallander nodded. His arm was stinging and burning, and he could feel that one leg was sticky with blood.

"I don't dare think about what might have happened if you hadn't called in the alarm the instant the fire broke out," said Edler.

"Why the hell do they put the barracks so close together?" asked Wallander.

Edler shook his head. "The old boss here is starting to get tired. Of course you're right; the buildings are too damn close to each other."

Wallander went over to Norén, who had just finished the job of cordoning off the area.

"I want that director in my office first thing tomorrow morning," he said.

Norén nodded.

"Did you see anything?" he asked.

"I heard a crash. Then the barracks exploded. But no cars. No people. If it was set, then it was done with a delayed-action detonator."

"Shall I drive you home or to the hospital?"

"I can drive myself. But I'm leaving now."

At the hospital emergency room Wallander realized that he was more battered than he had thought. On one forearm he had a large burn, his groin area and one thigh had been lacerated by the glass, and above his right eye he had a big lump and several nasty abrasions. He had also evidently bitten his tongue without being aware of it.

It was almost four o'clock by the time Wallander could leave the hospital. His bandages were too tight, and he still felt sick from the smoke he had inhaled.

As he left the hospital, a camera flashed in his face. He recognized the photographer from the biggest morning newspaper in Skåne. He waved his hand to dismiss a reporter who popped up out of the shadows, wanting an interview. Then he drove home.

To his own great amazement he was actually feeling sleepy. He undressed and crawled under the covers. His body ached, and flames were dancing in his head. And yet he fell asleep at once.

At eight o'clock Wallander woke up because somebody was pounding a sledgehammer inside his head. When he opened his eyes, he became aware of the throbbing in his temples. He had once again dreamed of the unknown black woman who had visited him before in his dreams. But when he stretched out his hand for her, Sten Widén was suddenly standing there with the whiskey bottle in his hand, and the woman had turned her back on Wallander and gone off with Sten instead.

He lay completely still, taking stock of how he felt. His neck and arm were stinging. His head was pounding. For a moment he was tempted to turn to the wall and go back to sleep. Forget all about the murder investigation and the conflagration that had blazed in the night.

He didn't get a chance to decide. His thoughts were interrupted by the ringing of the telephone.

I don't feel like answering it, he thought.

Then he quickly slipped out of bed and stumbled out to the kitchen.

It was Mona on the phone.

"Kurt," she said. "It's Mona."

He was filled with an overwhelming sense of joy.

Mona, he thought. Dear God! Mona! How I've missed you!

"I saw your picture in the paper," she said. "How are you doing?"

He remembered the photographer outside the hospital during the night. The camera that had flashed.

"Fine," he said. "Just a little sore."

"Are you sure?"

Suddenly his joy was gone. Now the bad feelings came back, the sharp pain in his stomach.

"Do you really care how I am?"

"Why shouldn't I care?"

"Why should you?"

He heard her breathing in his ear.

"I think you're so brave," she said. "I'm proud of you. In the paper it said that you risked your life to save people."

"I didn't save anybody! What kind of crap is that?"

"I just wanted to make sure you weren't hurt."

"What would you have done if I was?"

"What would I have done?"

"If I was hurt. If I was dying. What would you have done then?"

"Why do you sound so angry?"

"I'm not angry. I'm just asking you. I want you to come back home. Back here. To me."

"You know I can't do that. I just wish we could talk to each other."

"I never hear from you! So how are we supposed to talk to each other?"

He heard her sigh. That made him furious. Or maybe scared.

"Of course we can meet," she said. "But not at my place. Or at yours."

Suddenly he made up his mind. What he had said was not entirely true. But it wasn't really a lie either.

"There are a lot of things we need to talk about," he told her. "Practical matters. I can drive over to Malmö if you like."

There was a pause before she answered.

"Not tonight," she said. "But I can do it tomorrow."

"Where? Shall we have dinner? The only places I know are the Savoy and the Central."

"The Savoy is expensive."

"Then how about the Central? What time?"

"Eight o'clock?"

"I'll be there."

The conversation was over. He looked at his pummeled face in the hall mirror.

Was he looking forward to the meeting? Or was he feeling uneasy?

He couldn't make up his mind. All his thoughts were confused. Instead of picturing his meeting with Mona, he saw himself with Anette Brolin at the Savoy. And even though she was still the acting district attorney in Ystad, she was suddenly transformed into a black woman.

Wallander got dressed, skipped his morning coffee, and went out to his car. There was no wind at all. It had turned warmer again. The remnants of a damp fog were drifting in over the town from the sea.

He was greeted with friendly nods and pats on the back when he entered the police station. Ebba gave him a hug and a jar of pear preserves. He felt both embarrassed and a little proud of himself.

If only Björk had been here, he thought.

In Ystad instead of in Spain.

This was the kind of thing he dreamed of. Heroes on the police force...

By nine thirty everything had returned to normal. By then he had already managed to give the director of the refugee camp a fierce lecture about the sloppy supervision of the refugees who occupied the barracks. The director, who was short and plump and radiated a large measure of apathetic laziness, had vigorously defended himself by insisting that he had followed the rules and regulations of the Immigration Service to the letter.

"It's the responsibility of the police to guarantee our safety," he said, trying to twist the entire discussion around 180 degrees.

"How are we supposed to guarantee anything at all when you have no idea how many people are living in those damned barracks or who they are?"

The director was red-faced with fury when he left Kurt Wallander's office.

"I'm going to file a complaint," he said. "It's the responsibility of the police to guarantee the safety of the refugees."

"Complain to the king," replied Wallander. "Complain to the prime minister. Complain to the European Court. Complain to whoever the hell you like. But from now on you're going to have precise lists of how many people there are at your camp, what their names are, and which barracks they live in."

Right before the meeting with the investigative team was due to start, Peter Edler called.

"How are you doing?" he asked. "The hero of the day."

"Kiss my ass," replied Wallander. "Have you found anything?"

"It wasn't hard," replied Edler. "A handy little detonator that ignited some rags soaked in gasoline."

"Are you sure?"

"You're damn right I'm sure! You'll have the report in a few hours."

"We'll have to try and run the arson investigation parallel with the double homicide. But if anything else happens, I'm going to need reinforcements from Simrishamn or Malmö."

"Are there any police in Simrishamn? I thought the station there was closed down."

"It was the volunteer firefighters who were disbanded. In fact, I've heard rumors that we're going to have some new positions opening up down here."

Wallander started the investigative meeting by reporting what Peter Edler had told him. A brief discussion followed concerning possible reasons for the attack. Everyone agreed that it was most likely a rather well-organized boyish prank. But no one denied the seriousness of what had occurred.

"It's important for us to get them," said Hanson. "Just as important as catching the killers at Lenarp."

"Maybe it was the same people who threw the turnips at the old man," said Svedberg.

Wallander noticed an unmistakable hint of contempt in his voice.

"Talk to him. Maybe he can give you a description."

"I don't speak Arabic," said Svedberg.

"We have interpreters, for God's sake! I want to know what he has to say no later than this afternoon." Wallander could feel that he was angry.

The meeting was extremely brief. This was one of those days when the police officers were in the midst of an intense investigative phase. Conclusions and results were sparse.

"We'll skip the afternoon meeting," Wallander decided. "Provided nothing out of the ordinary happens. Martinson will go out to the camp. Svedberg, maybe you could take over whatever Martinson was doing that can't wait."

"I'm searching for the car that the truck driver saw," said Martinson. "I'll give you my paperwork."

When the meeting was over, Näslund and Rydberg stayed behind in Wallander's office.

"We're starting to go into overtime," said Wallander. "When is Björk coming back from Spain?"

Nobody knew.

"Does he have any idea about what's happened?" Rydberg wondered.

"Does he care?" Wallander countered.

He called Ebba and got an immediate reply. She even knew which airline he would be coming in on.

"Saturday night," he told the others. "But since I'm the acting chief, I'm going to authorize all the overtime we need."

Rydberg changed the subject to his visit to the farm where the murder was committed.

"I've been snooping around," he said. "I've turned the whole place upside down. I've even dug around in the hay bales out in the stable. But there was no brown briefcase."

Wallander knew this had to be true. Rydberg never gave up until he was one hundred percent sure.

"So now we know this much," he said. "One brown briefcase containing twenty-seven thousand kronor is missing."

"People have been killed for much less," said Rydberg.

They sat in silence for a moment, pondering Rydberg's words.

"I can't understand why it should be so hard to locate that car," said Wallander, touching the tender lump on his forehead. "I gave the description of the car at the press conference and asked the driver to contact us."

"Patience," said Rydberg.

"What came out of the conversations with the daughters? If there are any reports, I can read them in the car on the way to Kristianstad. By the way, do either of you think that the attack last night had anything to do with the threat I received?"

Both Rydberg and Näslund shook their heads.

"I don't either," said Wallander. "That means that we need to be prepared for something to happen on Friday or Saturday. I thought that you, Rydberg, could think through this matter and come up with some suggestions for action by this afternoon."

Rydberg made a face.

"I'm not good at things like that."

"You're a good cop. You'll do just fine."

Rydberg gave him a skeptical look.

Then he stood up to go. He stopped at the door.

"The daughter that I talked to, the one from Canada, had her husband with her. The one who's the Mountie. He wondered why we don't carry side arms."

"In a few years we probably will," said Wallander.

He was just about to start talking to Näslund about his conversation with Lars Herdin when the phone rang. Ebba told him that the head of the Immigration Service was on the line.

Wallander was surprised when he realized that he was speaking to a woman. In his mind, high government officials were still elderly gentlemen with an air of guarded dignity and arrogant self-esteem.

The woman had a pleasant voice. But what she said annoyed him instantly. It occurred to him that it might be a breach of conduct for an acting police chief in a small town to contradict what the high priest of a government civil service agency had to say.

"We are most displeased," said the woman. "The police have to guarantee the safety of our refugees."

She sounds just like that damned director, thought Wallander.

"We do what we can," he said, trying not to reveal that he was angry.

"Clearly that is not sufficient."

"It would have been considerably easier if we had received updated information about how many refugees were assigned to the various camps."

"The service has complete data on the refugees."

"That's not my impression at all."

"The Minister of Immigration is quite concerned."

Wallander visualized a red-haired woman who was regularly interviewed on TV.

"She's welcome to contact us," said Wallander, making a face at Näslund, who was leafing through some papers.

"It's clear that the police are not allocating enough resources to protecting the refugees."

"Or maybe there are just too many coming in. And you have

no idea where they're living."

"What do you mean by that?"

The polite voice was suddenly cool. Wallander felt his anger grow.

"Last night's fire revealed an enormous disarray at the camp. That's what I mean. In general, it's difficult to get any clear directives from the Immigration Service. You often tell the police to instigate deportations. But we have no idea where to find the deportees. Sometimes we have to search for several weeks before we find the people we are supposed to expel."

What he said was true. He had heard about his colleagues in Malmö who were driven to despair by the inability of the Immigration Service to handle its job.

"That's a lie," said the woman. "I'm not going to waste my valuable time arguing with you."

The conversation was over.

"Bitch," said Wallander, slamming down the phone.

"Who was that?" asked Näslund.

"A director general," replied Wallander, "who doesn't know a thing about reality. Feel like getting some coffee?"

Rydberg turned in transcripts of the interviews that he and Svedberg had held with Lövgren's two daughters. Wallander quickly recounted his phone conversation.

"The Minister of Immigration will be calling soon, and she'll be concerned," said Rydberg, laughing wickedly.

"You can talk to her," said Wallander. "I'll try to be back from Kristianstad by four."

When Näslund came back with the two mugs of coffee, Wallander no longer wanted any. He felt a need to get out of the building. His bandages were too tight, and his head ached. A drive might do him good.

"You can tell me about it in the car," he said, pushing the coffee away.

Näslund looked doubtful.

"I don't really know where we should go. Lars Herdin knew virtually nothing about this mystery woman's identity, even though he was well informed about Lövgren's financial assets."

"He must have known something."

"I interrogated him up and down," said Näslund. "I actually think he was telling the truth. The only thing he knew for sure was that she existed."

"How did he know that?"

"By coincidence he was once in Kristianstad and saw Lövgren and the woman on the street."

"When was that?"

Näslund flipped through his notes.

"Eleven years ago."

Wallander sipped his coffee.

"It doesn't fit," he said. "He has to know more, much more. How can he be so sure that there's a child? How does he know about the payments? Didn't you try to squeeze it out of him?"

"He claimed that somebody had written to him and told him about the situation."

"Who?"

"He wouldn't say."

Wallander thought about this for a moment.

"We'll go to Kristianstad anyway," he said. "Our colleagues up there will have to help us. Then I'm going to take on Lars Herdin myself."

They took one of the squad cars. Wallander crawled into the back seat and let Näslund drive. When they were outside of town, Wallander noticed that Näslund was driving much too fast.

"This isn't an emergency," said Wallander. "Drive slower. I have to read these papers and think."

Näslund slowed down.

The landscape was gray and foggy. Wallander stared out at the dreary desolation. Although he felt at home in the Scanian spring and summer, he felt alienated by the barren silence of fall and winter.

He leaned back and closed his eyes. His body ached and his arm burned. He also noticed that he was having palpitations.

Divorced men have heart attacks, he thought. We put on weight eating too much and feel tormented about being abandoned. Or else we throw ourselves into new relationships, and finally our hearts just give out.

The thought of Mona made him both furious and sad.

He opened his eyes and looked out at the landscape of Skåne again.

Then he read through the transcripts of the interviews the police had conducted with Lövgren's two daughters.

There was nothing to give them a lead. No enemies no pent-up hostilities.

And no money either.

Johannes Lövgren had kept even his own daughters in the dark about his vast financial assets.

Wallander tried to imagine this man. How had he operated? What had driven him? What did he think would happen to all the money after he was gone?

He was startled by his own thought.

Somewhere there ought to be a will.

But if it wasn't in one of the safe-deposit boxes, then where was it? Did the murdered man have another safe-deposit box somewhere else?

"How many banks are there in Ystad?" he asked Näslund.

Näslund knew everything about the town. "Around ten."

"Tomorrow I want you to investigate the ones we haven't visited so far. Did Johannes Lövgren have more safe-deposit boxes? I also want to know how he got back and forth from Lenarp. Taxi, bus, whatever."

Näslund nodded. "He might have taken the school bus."

"Someone must have seen him."

They took the route past Tomelilla. They crossed the main road to Malmö and continued north.

"What did the inside of Lars Herdin's house look like?" Wallander asked.

"Old-fashioned. But clean and tidy. Strangely enough, he uses a microwave oven to do his cooking. He offered me homemade rolls. He has a big parrot in a cage. The farm is well cared for.

The whole place looks neat. No tumbledown fences."
"What kind of car does he have?"
"A red Mercedes."
"A Mercedes?"
"Yes, a Mercedes."
"I thought he told us it was hard making ends meet."
"That Mercedes of his cost over three hundred thousand."
Wallander thought for a moment. "We need to know more about Lars Herdin. Even if he has no idea who killed them, he might actually know something without realizing it himself."
"What's that got to do with the Mercedes?"
"Nothing. I've just got a hunch that Lars Herdin is more important to us than he realizes. Then we might wonder how a farmer today can afford to buy a car for three hundred thousand kronor. Maybe he has a receipt that says he bought a tractor."
They drove into Kristianstad and parked outside the police station just as rain mixed with snow started to fall. Wallander noticed the first vague prickles in his throat, warning him that a cold was coming on.
Damn, he thought. I can't get sick now. I don't want to meet Mona with a fever and sniffles.
The Ystad police and the Kristianstad police had no special relationship with each other other than cooperating whenever the situation called for it. But Wallander knew several of the officers rather well from various conferences on the county level. He was hoping, above all, that Göran Boman would be on duty. He was the same age as Wallander, and they had met while sitting over a whiskey at Tylösand. They had both endured a tedious study day organized by the educational delegation of the National Police. The purpose was to inspire them to improve and make more effective the staff policies at their respective workplaces. In the evening they sat and shared half a bottle of whiskey and soon discovered that they had a lot in common. In particular, both their fathers had been extremely resistant when the sons had decided to go into police work.
Wallander and Näslund stepped into the lobby. The young woman at the switchboard, who oddly enough spoke with a lilting

Norrland accent, told them that Göran Boman was on duty.

"He's in an interrogation," said the woman. "But it probably won't last long."

Wallander went out to use the toilet. He gave a start when he caught sight of himself in the mirror. The bruises and abrasions were bright red. He splashed his face with cold water. At that moment he heard Boman's voice out in the hall.

The reunion was a hearty one. Wallander realized that he was overjoyed to see Boman again. They got some coffee and took it to his office. Wallander discovered that both of them had exactly the same kind of desk. But otherwise Boman's office was better furnished. It made his office look better, the same way that Anette Brolin had transformed the sterile office she had taken over.

Göran Boman knew, of course, about the double homicide in Lenarp, as well as the attack on the refugee camp and Kurt Wallander's rescue attempt that had been so exaggerated in the papers. They talked for a while about refugees. Boman had the same impression as Wallander that people seeking asylum were dealt with in a chaotic and disorganized fashion. The police in Kristianstad also had numerous examples of deportation orders that could be carried out only with great difficulty. As recently as a few weeks before Christmas they had been advised that several Bulgarian citizens were supposed to be expelled. According to the Immigration Service, they were living at a camp in Kristianstad. Only after several days' work did the police manage to find out that the Bulgarians were living at a camp in Arjeplog, over a thousand kilometers to the north.

Then they switched to the real reason for their visit. Wallander gave Boman a detailed rundown.

"And you want us to find her for you," said Boman when he was done.

"That wouldn't be a bad idea."

Up until then Näslund had been sitting in silence.

"I've got an idea," he said. "If Johannes Lövgren had a child by this woman, and we assume that the child was born in this town, we should be able to look it up in the vital statistics records. Lövgren must have been listed as the child's father, don't you think?"

Wallander nodded. "Besides, we know approximately when the child was born. We can concentrate on a ten-year period, from about 1947 to 1957, if Lars Herdin's story is correct. And I think it is."

"How many children are born over a ten-year period in Kristianstad?" asked Boman. "It would have taken an awfully long time to check it out before we had computers."

"Of course it's possible that Johannes Lövgren was listed as 'father unknown,'" said Wallander. "But then we just have to go through all of those cases with extra care."

"Why don't you go ahead and put out a public appeal for the woman?" asked Boman. "Ask her to contact you."

"Because I'm quite sure that she wouldn't do that," said Wallander. "It's just a feeling I have. It may not be particularly professional. But I think I'd rather try this route instead."

"We'll find her," said Boman. "We live in a society and an age when it's almost impossible to disappear. Unless you commit suicide in such an ingenious fashion that your body is completely obliterated. We had a case like that last summer. At least that's what I assume happened. A man who was sick of it all. He was reported missing by his wife. His boat was gone. We never found him. And I don't think we're ever going to, either. I think he put out to sea, scuttled the boat, and drowned himself. But if this woman and her child exist, we'll find them. I'll put a man on it right away."

Wallander's throat hurt.

He noticed that he had started to sweat.

Most of all he would have liked to stay sitting there, discussing the double homicide with Göran Boman in peace and quiet. He had the feeling that Boman was a talented cop. His opinion would be valuable. But Wallander suddenly felt too tired.

They concluded their conversation. Boman followed them out to the car.

"We'll find her," he repeated.

"Let's get together some evening," said Wallander. "In peace and quiet. And have some whiskey."

Boman nodded.

"Maybe on another meaningless study day," he said.

The wet snow was still coming down. Wallander felt the dampness seeping into his shoes. He crawled into the back seat and huddled up in the corner. Soon he fell asleep.

He didn't wake up until Näslund pulled up in front of the police station in Ystad. He was feeling feverish and miserable. The wet snow was still coming down, and he asked Ebba for a couple of aspirin. Even though he realized that he ought to go home to bed, he couldn't resist getting an update on what had happened during the day. Besides, he wanted to hear what Rydberg had come up with regarding protection for the refugees.

His desk was covered with phone messages. Anette Brolin was among the many people who had called. And his father. But not Linda. Or Sten Widén. He shuffled through the messages and then put them aside except for the ones from Anette Brolin and his father. Then he called Martinson on the phone.

"Bingo," said Martinson. "I think we've found the car. A vehicle that fits the description was rented last week by an Avis office in Göteborg. It hasn't been returned. There's just one thing that's strange."

"What's that?"

"The car was rented by a woman."

"What's so strange about that?"

"I have a little trouble picturing a woman committing the double murder."

"Now you're on the wrong track. We have to get hold of that car. And the driver. Even if it *is* a woman. Then we'll see if they had anything to do with it. Eliminating someone from an investigation is just as important as getting a positive lead. But give the license number to the truck driver and see whether he recognizes it after all."

He hung up and went into Rydberg's office.

"How's it going?" he asked.

"This is certainly not much fun," replied Rydberg gloomily.

"Who ever said police work was supposed to be fun?"

But Rydberg had made a thorough job of it, exactly as Wallander had known he would. The various camps were cordoned off, and

Rydberg had drawn up a brief memo about each one. For the time being he suggested that as a precaution the night patrols should make regular rounds of the camps according to a cleverly devised timetable.

"Good," said Wallander. "Just make sure the patrols understand that it's a serious matter."

He gave Rydberg a report of the results from his visit to Kristianstad. Then he stood up.

"I'm going home now," he said.

"You're looking a little bedraggled."

"I'm coming down with a cold. But everything seems to be moving along by itself right now."

He drove straight home, made some tea, and crawled into bed. When he woke up several hours later, the teacup was standing next to his bed untouched. It was quarter to seven. He was feeling a little better after getting some sleep. He threw out the cold tea and made coffee instead. Then he called his father.

Wallander realized at once that his father had heard nothing about the fire in the night.

"Weren't we going to play cards?" snapped his father.

"I'm sick," said Wallander.

"But you're never sick."

"I've got a cold."

"I don't call that being sick."

"Not everybody is as healthy as you are."

"What do you mean by that?"

Kurt Wallander sighed.

If he didn't come up with something, this conversation with his father was going to be unbearable.

"I'll come out to see you early in the morning," he said. "Around eight o'clock. If you're up by then."

"I never sleep past four thirty."

"But I do."

He ended the conversation and hung up the phone.

At the same instant he regretted having made this appointment with his father. Starting off the day by driving out to visit him was equivalent to accepting a whole day filled with depression and guilt feelings.

He looked around his apartment. There were thick layers of dust everywhere. Even though he frequently aired out the place, it still smelled musty. Lonely and musty.

All of a sudden he started thinking about the black woman he had been dreaming about lately. The woman who willingly came to him, night after night. Where did she come from? Where had he seen her? Was it a picture in the newspaper, or did he catch a glimpse of her on TV?

He wondered why it was that in his dreams he had an erotic obsession that differed completely from his experiences with Mona.

The thought got him excited. Again he wondered whether he should call up Anette Brolin. But he couldn't talk himself into it. Angrily he sat down on the floral-patterned sofa and switched on the TV. It was one minute to seven. He rolled through to one of the Danish channels, where the news broadcast was just about to start.

The anchorman reviewed the top stories. Another catastrophic famine. Terror was on the rise in Romania. A huge quantity of drugs had been confiscated in Odense.

Wallander grabbed the remote control and turned off the TV. Suddenly he couldn't take any more news.

He thought about Mona. But his thoughts took an unexpected turn. All of a sudden he was no longer sure that he really wanted her back. What guarantee was there that anything would be better?

None. He was just fooling himself.

Feeling restless, he went out to the kitchen and drank a glass of juice. Then he sat down and wrote a detailed status report of the investigation. When he was done, he spread out all his notes on the table and looked at them as if they were pieces of a puzzle. He suddenly had a strong feeling that they might not be too far from finding a solution. Even though there were still a lot of loose ends, a number of details did fit together.

It wasn't possible to point to a particular person. There weren't even any possible suspects. But he still had the feeling that the police were close. This made him feel both gratified and uneasy. Too many times he had headed up complicated criminal investigations that seemed promising at first but later petered out in dead ends which they never managed to get out of, and in the worst instances they had to drop these cases altogether.

Patience, he thought. Patience.

It was almost nine o'clock. Again he was tempted to call Anette Brolin. But he resisted. He had no idea what he would say to her. And maybe her husband would answer the phone.

He sat down on the couch and switched on the TV again.

To his immense surprise he found himself staring at his own face. In the background he heard the droning voice of a woman reporter. The story was about the fact that Wallander and the police in Ystad seemed to be showing a deplorable lack of interest in guaranteeing the safety of the various refugee camps.

Wallander's face disappeared and was replaced by a woman who was being interviewed outside a large office complex. When her name appeared on the screen, he realized that he should have recognized her. It was the head of the Immigration Service, whom he had talked to on the phone that very day.

"It cannot be ruled out that there may be an element of racism behind the lack of interest shown by the police," she stated.

Bitter anger welled up inside him.

That bitch, he thought. What you're saying is a total lie. And why didn't those damned reporters contact me? I could have showed them Rydberg's protection plan.

Racists? What was she talking about? His fury was mixed with shame at being unjustly accused.

Then the phone rang. He considered not answering it. But then he went out to the hallway and grabbed the receiver.

The voice was the same as last time. A little hoarse, muffled. Wallander guessed that the man was holding a handkerchief over the mouthpiece.

"We're waiting for results," said the man.

"Go to hell!" roared Wallander.

"By Saturday at the latest," continued the man.

"Were you the bastards who set the fire last night?" he shouted into the phone.

"By Saturday at the latest," repeated the man, unmoved. "Saturday at the latest."

The line went dead.

Wallander suddenly felt sick. He couldn't rid himself of a sense of foreboding. It was like an ache in his body that was slowly spreading.

Now you're scared, he thought. Now Kurt Wallander is scared.

He went back to the kitchen and stood at the window and looked out into the street.

All of a sudden he realized that there was no wind. The street light was hanging motionless.

Something was going to happen. He was positive of that.

But what? And where?

Chapter Eight

In the morning he took out his best suit.

Despondently he stared at a spot on one lapel.

Ebba, he thought. This is a good project for her. When she hears that I'm going to meet Mona, she'll put her heart into getting rid of this spot. Ebba is a woman who thinks that the number of divorces is a considerably greater threat to the future of our society than the increase in crime and violence.

At quarter past seven he laid the suit on the back seat and drove off. A thick cloud cover hung over the town.

Is it snow? he wondered. The snow that I really don't want.

He drove slowly eastward, through Sandskogen, past the abandoned golf course, and turned off toward Kåseberga.

For the first time in days he felt that he had had enough sleep. He had slept nine hours straight. The swelling on his forehead had started to go down, and his burned arm didn't sting anymore.

Methodically he went through the summary he had written up the night before. The main thing now was to find Johannes Lövgren's mystery woman. And the son. Somewhere, in the circles surrounding these people, the perpetrators would be found. It was quite obvious that the double murder was connected to the missing 27,000 kronor, and maybe even to Lövgren's other assets.

Someone who knew about the money, and who had taken time to give the horse some hay before he disappeared. One or more persons who knew Johannes Lövgren's habits.

The rental car from Göteborg didn't fit into the picture. Maybe it had nothing to do with the case at all.

He looked at his watch. Twenty to eight. Thursday, January eleventh.

Instead of driving straight to his father's house, he went a few kilometers past it and turned off on the little gravel road that wound through rolling sand dunes up toward Bäckakra, Dag Hammarskjöld's estate, which the statesman had bequeathed to the Swedish public. Wallander left the car in the empty parking lot and walked up the hill; from there he could see the sea stretched out below.

There was a stone circle there. A stone circle of contemplation, built some years earlier. It was an invitation to solitude and peace of mind.

He sat down on a stone and looked out over the sea.

He had never been particularly inclined to philosophical meditation. He had never felt a need to delve into himself. Life was a continual interplay among various practical questions awaiting a solution. Whatever was out there was something inescapable which he could not affect no matter how much he worried about some meaning that probably didn't even exist.

Having a few minutes of solitude was another thing altogether. It was the vast peace that lay hidden in not having to think at all. Just listen, observe, sit motionless.

There was a boat on its way somewhere. A large sea bird glided soundlessly on the updrafts. Everything was very quiet.

After ten minutes he stood up and went back to the car.

His father was in his studio painting when Wallander walked in. This time it was going to be a canvas with a wood grouse.

His father looked at him crossly.

Wallander could see that the old man was filthy. And he smelled bad too.

"Why are you here?" his father said.

"We made a date yesterday."

"Eight o'clock, you said."

"Good grief, I'm only eleven minutes late."

"How the hell can you be a cop if you can't keep track of time?"

Wallander didn't answer. Instead he thought about his sister

Kristina. Today he would have to make time to call her. Ask her whether she was aware of their father's rapid decline. He had always imagined that senility was a slow process. That wasn't the case at all, he realized now.

His father was searching for a color with his brush on the palette. His hands were still steady. Then he confidently daubed a nuance of pale red on the grouse's plumage.

Wallander had sat down on the old sled to watch.

The stench of his father's body was acrid. Wallander was reminded of a foul-smelling man lying on a bench in the Paris Metro when he and Mona were on their honeymoon.

I have to say something, he thought. Even if my father is on his way back to his childhood, I still have to speak to him like a grownup.

His father kept on painting with great concentration.

How many times has he painted that same motif? thought Wallander.

A quick and incomplete reckoning in his head came up with the figure of seven thousand.

Seven thousand sunsets.

He poured coffee out of the kettle that stood steaming on the kerosene stove.

"How are you feeling?" he asked.

"When you're as old as I am, how you're feeling is how you're feeling," his father replied dismissively.

"Have you thought about moving?"

"Where would I move to? And why should I move anyway?"

The questions he countered with came like the cracks of a whip.

"To a retirement home."

His father pointed his brush at him ferociously, as if it were a weapon.

"Do you want me to die?"

"Of course not! I'm thinking of your own good "

"How do you think I'd survive with a bunch of old fogies? And they certainly wouldn't let me paint in my room."

"Nowadays you can have your own apartment."

"I've already got my own house. Maybe you didn't notice that. Or maybe you're too sick to notice?"

"I just have a little cold."

At that moment he realized that the cold had never broken out. It had vanished as quickly as it came. He had been through this a few times before. When he had a lot to do, he refused to permit himself to get sick. But once the investigation was over, an illness could often break out instantly.

"I'm going to see Mona tonight," he said.

Continuing to talk about an old folks' home or an apartment in a building for senior citizens was pointless, he realized. First he had to talk with his sister about it.

"If she left you, she left you. Forget her."

"I have absolutely no wish to forget her."

His father kept on painting. Now he was working on the pink clouds. The conversation had stopped.

"Is there anything you need?" asked Wallander.

His father replied without looking at him. "Are you leaving already?"

The reproach in the words was evident. Wallander knew it was impossible to try and stifle the guilt that instantly flared up.

"I've got a job to do," he said. "I'm the acting chief of police. We're trying to solve a double murder. And track down some pyromaniacs."

His father snorted and scratched his crotch. "Chief of police. Is that supposed to impress me?"

Wallander got up.

"I'll be back, Dad," he said. "I'm going to help you clean up this mess."

His father's outburst took him completely by surprise.

The old man flung his brush to the floor and stood in front of his son shaking his fist.

"You think you can come here and tell me this place is a mess?" he shouted. "You think you can come here and meddle in my life? Let me tell you this, I have both a cleaning woman and a housekeeper here. By the way, I'm taking a trip to Rimini for winter vacation. I'm going to have a show there. I'm demanding twenty-five thousand kronor per canvas. And you come here talking about old folks' homes. But you're not going to kill *me* off, I can tell you that."

He left the studio, slamming the door behind him.

He's nuts, thought Wallander. I've got to put a stop to this. Maybe he really imagines he has a cleaning woman and a housekeeper. That he's going to Italy to open a show.

He wasn't sure if he should go inside after his father, who was banging around in the kitchen. It sounded as if he was throwing pots and pans around.

Then Wallander went out to his car. The best thing would be to call his sister. Now, right away. Together maybe they could get their father to admit that he couldn't go on like this.

At nine o'clock he went through the door of the police station and left his suit with Ebba, who promised to have it cleaned and pressed by that afternoon.

At ten o'clock he called a meeting for all the team members who weren't out. The ones who had seen the spot on the news the night before shared his indignation. After a brief discussion they agreed that Wallander should write a sharp rebuttal and distribute it on the wire service.

"Why doesn't the chief of the National Police respond?" Martinson wondered.

His question was met with disdainful laughter.

"That guy?" said Rydberg. "He only responds if he has something to gain from it. He doesn't give a damn about how the police in the provinces are doing."

After this comment their focus shifted to the double homicide.

Nothing remarkable had happened that demanded the attention of the investigators. They were still laying the groundwork.

Material was collected and gone over, various tips were checked out and entered in the daily log.

The whole team agreed that the mystery woman and her son in Kristianstad were the hottest lead. No one had any doubt either that the murder they were trying to solve had robbery as a motive.

Wallander asked whether things had been quiet at the various refugee camps.

"I checked the nightly report," said Rydberg. "It was calm. The most dramatic thing last night was a moose running around on E14."

"Tomorrow is Friday," said Wallander. "Yesterday I got another anonymous phone call. The same individual. He repeated the threat that something was going to happen tomorrow, Friday."

Rydberg suggested that they contact the National Police. Let them decide whether additional manpower should be committed.

"Let's do that," said Wallander. "We might as well be on the safe side. In our own district we'll send out an extra night patrol to concentrate on the refugee camps."

"Then you'll have to authorize overtime," said Hanson.

"I know," said Wallander. "I want Peters and Norén on this special night detail. Then I want someone to call and talk with the directors at all the camps. Don't scare them. Just ask them to be a little more vigilant."

After about an hour the meeting was over.

Wallander was alone in his office, getting ready to write the response to Swedish Television.

Then the telephone rang.

It was Göran Boman in Kristianstad.

"I saw you on the news last night," he said, laughing.

"Wasn't that a bitch?"

"Yeah, you ought to protest."

"I'm writing a letter right now."

"What the hell are those reporters thinking of?"

"Not about what's true, that's for sure. But about what big headlines they can get."

"I've got good news for you."

Wallander felt himself tense up.

"Did you find her?"

"Maybe. I'm faxing you some papers. We think we've found nine possibles. The register of citizens isn't such a stupid thing to have. I thought you ought to take a look at what we came up with. Then you can call me and tell me which ones you want us to check out first."

"Great, Göran," said Wallander. "I'll call you back."

The fax machine was out in the lobby. A young female temp he had never seen before was just taking a piece of paper out of the tray.

"Which one is Kurt Wallander?" she asked.

"That's me," he said. "Where's Ebba?"

"She had to go to the dry cleaners," said the woman.

Wallander felt ashamed. He was making Ebba run his private errands.

Boman had sent a total of four pages. Wallander returned to his room and spread them out on the desk. He went through one name after another, their birthdates, and when their babies with unknown fathers had been born. It didn't take long for him to eliminate four of the candidates. That left five women who had borne sons during the fifties.

Two of them were still living in Kristianstad. One was listed at an address in Gladsax outside Simrishamn. Of the two others, one lived in Strömsund and the other had emigrated to Australia.

He smiled at the thought that the investigation might require sending someone to the other side of the world.

Then he called up Göran Boman.

"Great," he said again. "This looks promising. If we're on the right track, we've got five to choose from."

"Should I start bringing them in for a talk?"

"No, I'll take care of it myself. Or rather, I thought we could do it together. If you have time, I mean."

"I'll make time. Are we starting today?"

Wallander looked at his watch.

"Let's wait till tomorrow," he said. "I'll try to get up there by nine. If there's no trouble tonight, that is."

He quickly told Göran about the anonymous threats.

"Did you catch whoever set the fire the other night?"

"Not yet."

"I'll set things up for tomorrow. Make sure none of them has moved."

"Maybe I should meet you in Gladsax," Wallander suggested. "It's about halfway."

"Nine o'clock at the Hotel Svea in Simrishamn," said Boman. "A cup of coffee to start the day with."

"Sounds good. See you there. And thanks for your help."

Now, you bastards, thought Wallander after he hung up the phone. Now I'm going to let you have it.

He wrote the letter to Swedish Television. He did not mince words, and he decided to send copies to the Immigration Service, the Immigration Ministry, the County Chief of Police, and the Chief of the National Police.

Standing in the corridor, Rydberg read through what he had written.

"Good," he said. "But don't think they'll do anything about it. Reporters in this country, especially on television, can do no wrong."

He dropped the letter off to be typed and went into the lunch-room for coffee. He hadn't had time to think about food yet. It was almost one o'clock, and he decided to go through all his phone messages before he went out to eat.

The night before, he had felt sick to his stomach when he took the anonymous phone call. Now he had cast off all sense of foreboding. If anything happened, the police were ready.

He punched in the number for Sten Widén. But before the phone started to ring on the other end, he abruptly hung up. Widén could wait. There would be plenty of time later to amuse themselves by timing how long it took for a horse to finish off a ration of hay.

Instead he tried the number of the DA's office.

The woman at the switchboard told him that Anette Brolin was in.

He got up and walked down to the other wing of the police building. Just as he raised his hand to knock, the door opened.

She had her coat on. "I'm just on my way to lunch."

"May I join you?"

She seemed to think about it for a moment. Then she gave him a quick smile. "Why not?"

Wallander suggested the Continental. They got a window table facing the station, and they both ordered salted salmon.

"I saw you on the news yesterday," said Anette Brolin. "How can they broadcast such incomplete and insinuating reports?"

Wallander, who had instantly braced himself for criticism, relaxed.

"Reporters view the police as fair game," he said. "Whether we do too much or too little, we get criticized for it. And they don't understand that sometimes we have to hold back certain information for investigative purposes."

Without hesitating, he told her about the leak. How furious he had been when information from the investigative meeting had gone straight to a TV broadcast.

He noticed that she was listening. Suddenly he thought he had discovered someone else behind the prosecutor role and the tasteful clothes.

After lunch they ordered coffee.

"Did your family move here too?" he asked.

"My husband is still in Stockholm," she said. "And the kids won't have to change schools for a year."

Wallander could feel his disappointment.

Somehow he had hoped that the wedding ring meant nothing after all.

The waiter came with the check, and Wallander reached out to pay.

"We'll split it," she said.

They got refills on the coffee.

"Tell me about this town," she said. "I've looked through a number of criminal cases for the last few years. It's a lot different from Stockholm."

"That's changing fast," he said. "Soon the entire Swedish countryside will be nothing but one solid suburb of the big cities. Twenty years ago, for example, there were no narcotics here. Ten years ago drugs had come to towns like Ystad and Simrishamn, but we still had some control over what was happening. Today drugs are everywhere. When I drive by some beautiful old Scanian farm I sometimes think: there might be a huge amphetamine factory hidden in there."

"There are fewer violent crimes," she said. "And they're not quite as brutal."

"It's coming," he said. "Unfortunately, I guess I'm supposed to say. But the differences between the big cities and the countryside have been almost totally wiped out. Organized crime is widespread in Malmö. The open borders and all the ferries coming in are like candy for the underworld. We have one detective who moved down here from Stockholm a few years ago. Svedberg is his name. He moved here because he couldn't stand Stockholm anymore. A few days ago he said he was thinking about moving back."

"Still, there's a sense of calm here," she said pensively. "Something that's been totally lost in Stockholm."

They left the Continental. Wallander had parked his car on Stickgatan nearby.

"Are you really allowed to park here?" she asked.

"No," he replied. "But when I get a ticket I usually pay it. Otherwise it might be an interesting experience to say the hell with it and get taken to court."

They drove back to the police station.

"I was thinking of asking you to dinner some evening," he said. "I could show you around the area."

"I'd like that," she said.

"How often do you go home?" he asked.

"Every other week."

"And your husband? The kids?"

"He comes down when he can. And the kids when they feel like it."

I love you, thought Kurt Wallander.

I'm going to see Mona tonight and I'm going to tell her that I love another woman.

They said goodbye in the lobby of the police station.

"You'll get a briefing on Monday," said Wallander. "We're starting to get a few leads to go on."

"Is an arrest imminent?"

"No. Not yet. But the investigations at the banks produced some good results."

She nodded.

"Preferably before ten on Monday," she said. "The rest of the day I have detention hearings and negotiations in district court."

They settled on nine o'clock.

Wallander watched her as she disappeared down the corridor.

He felt strangely exhilarated when he returned to his office.

Anette Brolin, he thought. In a world where everything is said to be possible, anything could happen.

He devoted the rest of the day to reading the notes from various interrogations that he had only skimmed before. The definitive autopsy report had also arrived. Once more he was shocked at the senseless violence to which the old couple had been subjected. He read the reports of the interviews with the two daughters and the accounts of what had been learned from the door-to-door canvassing in Lenarp.

All the information matched and added up

No one had any idea that Johannes Lövgren was a significantly more complex person than he outwardly seemed. The simple farmer had been a split personality in disguise.

Once during the war, in the fall of 1943, he had been taken to district court in a case of assault and battery. But he had been acquitted. Someone had dug up a copy of the report, and Wallander read through it carefully. But he could see no reasonable motive for revenge. It seemed to have been an ordinary quarrel that led to blows at Erikslund community center.

At half past three Ebba brought in his dry-cleaned suit.

"You're an angel," he said.

"Hope you have a wonderful time tonight," she said with a smile.

Wallander got a lump in his throat. She had really meant what she said.

He spent the time until five o'clock filling in a soccer lottery coupon, making an appointment to have his car serviced, and thinking through the important interviews for him the following day. Then he wrote a reminder to himself that he had to prepare a memo for Björk when he came back from vacation.

At three minutes after five Thomas Näslund stuck his head in the door.

"Are you still here?" he said. "I thought you'd gone home."

"Why would I have done that?"

"That's what Ebba said."

Ebba keeps watch over me, he thought with a smile. Tomorrow I'll bring her some flowers before I leave for Simrishamn.

Näslund came into the room.

"Do you have time right now?" he asked.

"Not much."

"I'll make it quick. It's this Klas Månson."

Wallander had to think for a moment before he remembered who that was.

"The one who robbed that minimart?"

"That's the guy. We have witnesses who can identify him, even though he had some crappy stocking over his head. A tattoo on his wrist. There's no doubt that he's the one. But this new prosecutor doesn't agree with us."

Wallander raised his eyebrows. "What do you mean?"

"She thinks the investigation was sloppy."

"Was it?"

Näslund looked at him in amazement.

"It was no sloppier than any other investigation. It's a clear-cut case."

"So what did she say?"

"If we can't come up with more convincing proof she's considering opposing the detention order. It's bullshit that a Stockholm bitch like that can come here and pretend she's somebody!"

Wallander could feel himself getting mad, but he was careful to keep his feelings to himself.

"Pelle wouldn't have given us any problems," Näslund went on. "It's obvious that this punk is the one who robbed the store."

"Have you got the report?" asked Wallander.

"I asked Svedberg to read through it."

"Leave it here for me so I can look at it tomorrow."

Näslund got ready to leave.

"Somebody ought to tell that bitch," he said

Wallander nodded and smiled. "I'll do it. It's obvious we can't have a prosecutor from Stockholm who doesn't do things the way we're used to."

"I thought you'd say that," said Näslund and left.

An excellent excuse to have dinner, thought Wallander. He put on his jacket, hung the dry-cleaned suit over his arm, and switched off the ceiling light.

After a quick shower he made it to Malmö just before seven. He found a parking space near Stortorget and went down the steps to Kock's Tavern. He would toss back a couple of drinks before he met Mona at the restaurant of the Central Hotel.

Even though the price was outrageous, he ordered a double whiskey. He preferred to drink malt whiskey, but an ordinary blend would have to do.

At the first gulp he spilled some on himself.

Now he'd have a new spot on his lapel. Almost in the same place as the old one.

I'm going home, he thought, full of self-reproach. I'll go home and go to bed. I can't even hold a glass without spilling it on me. At the same time he knew this feeling was pure vanity. Vanity and incurable nervousness about this meeting with Mona. It might be their most important meeting since the time he proposed to her.

Now he had taken on the task of stopping a divorce that was already set in motion.

But what did he really want?

He wiped off his lapel with a paper napkin, drained the glass, and ordered another whiskey.

In ten minutes he would have to go.

By then he would need to make up his mind What was he going to say to Mona?

And what would her answer be?

His new drink came and he tossed it off. The liquor burned in his temples, and he could feel himself starting to sweat.

He didn't come up with any solution.

Deep inside he hoped that Mona would say the words he was waiting to hear.

She was the one who had wanted the divorce.

So she was also the one who should take the initiative and cancel it.

He paid the bill and left. He walked slowly so that he would not arrive too early.

He decided two things while he waited for the light to turn green at the corner of Vallgatan.

He was going to have a serious talk with Mona about Linda. And he would ask her advice with regard to his father. Mona knew him well. Even though they had never really gotten along, she knew from experience about his changeable moods.

I should have called Kristina, he thought as he crossed the street.

I probably forgot about it on purpose.

He walked across the canal bridge and was passed by a carload of punks. A drunken youth was hanging halfway out the open window and bellowing something.

Wallander remembered how he used to walk across this bridge more than twenty years before. In these neighborhoods the city had looked exactly the same. He had walked the beat here as a young policeman, usually with an older partner, and they would go into the train station to check up on things. Sometimes they had to throw out someone who was drunk and didn't have a ticket. There was seldom any violence.

That world doesn't exist anymore, he thought.

It's gone, lost forever.

He went into the train station. A lot had changed since the last time he had walked the beat here. But the stone floor was the same. And the sound of the screeching train cars and the braking locomotives.

Suddenly he caught sight of his daughter.

At first he thought he was seeing things. It could just as well have been the girl tossing hay bales at Sten Widén's farm. But then he was sure. It was Linda.

She was standing with a coal-black man and trying to get a ticket out of the automat. The African was almost a foot and a half taller than she was. He had thick curly hair and was dressed in purple overalls.

As if he were on a stakeout, Wallander swiftly drew back behind a pillar.

The African said something and Linda laughed.

He realized it must have been years since he had seen his daughter laugh.

What he saw depressed him. He sensed that he couldn't reach her. She was gone from him, despite the fact that she was standing so near.

My family, he thought. I'm in a railroad station spying on my daughter. At the same time that her mother, my wife, has probably already arrived at the restaurant so that we can meet and eat dinner and maybe manage to talk with each other without starting to yell and scream.

Suddenly he noticed that he was having a hard time seeing. His eyes were misted over with tears.

He hadn't had tears in his eyes for a long time. It was as distant a memory as the last time he had seen Linda laugh.

The African and Linda were walking toward the exit to the platform. He wanted to rush after her, pull her to him.

Then they were gone from his field of vision, and he continued his hastily instigated surveillance. He slunk along in the shadows of the platform where the icy wind from the sound was blowing through. He watched them walk hand in hand, laughing. The last thing he saw was the blue doors hissing shut and the train leaving toward Landskrona or Lund.

He tried to focus on the fact that she had looked happy. Just as carefree as when she was a young girl. But all he seemed to feel was his own misery.

Kurt Wallander. The pathetic cop with his pitiful family life.

And now he was late. Maybe Mona had already turned on her heel and left. She was always punctual and hated having to wait.

Especially for him.

He started running along the platform. A fire-engine red locomotive screeched alongside him like an angry wild beast.

He was in such a hurry that he stumbled on the stairs leading to the restaurant. The crew-cut doorman gave him a dirty look.

"Where do you think you're going?" asked the doorman.

Wallander was completely paralyzed by the question. Its implication was suddenly clear to him.

The doorman thought he was drunk. He wasn't going to let him in.

"I'm going to have dinner with my wife," he said.

"No, I don't think you are," said the doorman. "I think you'd better go on home."

Kurt Wallander felt his blood boil.

"I'm a police officer!" he shouted. "And I'm not drunk, if that's what you think. Now let me in before I really get mad."

"Kiss my ass!" said the doorman. "Now go home before I call the cops."

For a moment he felt like punching the doorman in the nose. Then he regained his composure and calmed down. He pulled his ID out of his inside pocket.

"I really am a police officer," he said. "And I'm not drunk. I stumbled. And it is actually true that my wife is waiting for me."

The doorman gave the ID card a suspicious look.

Then his face suddenly lit up.

"Hey, I recognize you," he said. "You were on TV the other night."

Finally I'm getting some benefit from the TV, he thought.

"I'm with you," said the doorman. "All the way."

"With me about what?"

"Keeping those damn niggers on a short leash. What kind of shit are we letting into this country, going around killing old folks? I'm with you, we should kick 'em all out. Chase 'em out with a stick."

Wallander could tell it was pointless to get into a discussion with the doorman. Instead he attempted a smile.

"Well, I guess I'll go eat, I'm starving," he said.

The doorman held the door open for him.

"You understand we've got to be careful, right?"

"No problem," replied Wallander and went into the warmth of the restaurant.

He hung up his coat and looked around.

Mona was sitting at a window table with a view over the canal. He wondered whether she had been watching him arrive.

He sucked in his stomach as best he could, ran his hand over his hair, and walked over to her.

Everything went wrong right from the start.

He saw that she had noticed the spot on his lapel, and it made him furious.

And he didn't know if he totally succeeded in concealing his fury.

"Hi," he said, sitting down across from her.

"Late as usual," she said. "You've really put on weight!"

She had to start off with an insult. No friendliness, no affection.

"But you look just the same. You've really got a tan."

"We spent a week on Madeira."

Madeira. First Paris, then Madeira. The honeymoon. The hotel perched way out on the cliffs, the little fish restaurant down by the beach. And now she had been there again. With someone else.

"I see," he said. "I thought Madeira was our island."

"Don't be childish!"

"I mean it."

"Then you *are* being childish."

"Of course I'm childish! What's wrong with that?"

The conversation was spinning out of control. When a friendly waitress came to their table it was like being rescued from a frigid hole in the ice.

When the wine arrived the mood improved.

Kurt Wallander sat looking at the woman who had been his wife and thought that she was extremely beautiful. At least in his eyes. He tried to avoid thoughts that gave him a sharp stab of jealousy.

He tried to give the impression of being very calm, which he definitely was not, but it was something he strived for.

They said *skål* and raised their glasses.

"Come back," he begged. "Let's start over."

"No," she said. "You've got to understand that it's finished. It's all over."

"I went into the station while I was waiting for you," he said. "I saw our daughter there."

"Linda?"

"You seem surprised."

"I thought she was in Stockholm."

"What would she be doing in Stockholm?"

"She was supposed to visit a college to see if it might be the right place for her."

"I'm not blind. It was her."

"Did you talk to her?"

Wallander shook his head. "She was just getting on the train. I didn't have time."

"Which train?"

"Lund or Landskrona. She was with an African."

"That's good, at least."

"What do you mean by that?"

"I mean that Herman is the best thing that's happened to Linda in a long time."

"Herman?"

"Herman Mboya. He's from Kenya."

"He was wearing purple overalls!"

"He does have an amusing way of dressing sometimes."

"What's he doing in Sweden?"

"He's in medical school. He'll be a physician soon."

Wallander listened in amazement. Was she pulling his leg?

"A physician?"

"Yes! A physician! A doctor, or whatever you call it. He's friendly, thoughtful, and has a good sense of humor."

"Do they live together?"

"He has a student apartment in Lund."

"I asked you if they were living together!"

"I think Linda has finally decided."

"Decided what?"

"To move in with him."

"Then how can she go to the college in Stockholm?"

"It was Herman who suggested that."

The waitress refilled their wine glasses. Wallander could feel himself starting to get a buzz.

"She called me one day," he said. "She was in Ystad. But she never came by to say hello. If you see her, you can tell her that I miss her."

"She does what she wants."

"All I'm asking is for you to tell her!"

"I will! Don't yell!"

"I'm not yelling!"

Just then the roast beef arrived. They ate in silence. Wallander couldn't taste a thing. He ordered another bottle of wine and wondered how he was going to get home.

"You seem to be doing well," he said.

She nodded, firmly and maybe spitefully too.

"And you?"

"I'm having a hell of a time. Otherwise, everything's fine."

"What was it you wanted to talk to me about?"

He had forgotten that he was supposed to think of some excuse for their meeting. Now he had no idea what to say.

The truth, he thought ironically. Why not try the truth?

"I just wanted to see you," he said. "The other stuff I said was all lies."

She smiled.

"I'm glad that we could see each other," she said.

Suddenly he burst into tears.

"I miss you terribly," he mumbled.

She reached out her hand and put it on his. But she didn't say anything.

And it was in that instant that Kurt Wallander knew that it was over. The divorce wouldn't change anything. Maybe they'd have dinner once in a while. But their lives were irrevocably going in different directions. Her silence did not lie.

He started thinking about Anette Brolin. And the black woman who visited him in his dreams.

He had been unprepared for loneliness. Now he would be forced to accept it and maybe gradually find the new life that no one but himself could create.

"Tell me one thing," he said. "Why did you leave me?"

"If I hadn't left you, I would have died," she said. "I wish you could understand that it wasn't your fault. I was the one who felt the breakup was necessary, I was the one who decided. One day you'll understand what I mean."

"I want to understand now."

When they were about to leave she wanted to pay her share. But he insisted and she gave in.

"How are you getting home?" she asked.

"There's a night bus," he replied. "How are you getting home?"

"I'm walking," she said.

"I'll walk with you partway."

She shook her head.

"We'll say goodbye here," she said. "That would be best. But call me again sometime. I want to stay in touch."

She kissed him quickly on the cheek. He watched her walk across the canal bridge with a vigorous stride. When she disappeared between the Savoy and the tourist bureau, he followed her. Earlier that evening he had shadowed his daughter. Now he was tailing his wife.

Near the radio store at the corner of Stortorget a car was waiting. She got into the front seat. Wallander ducked into a stairwell as the car drove past. He got a quick glimpse of the man behind the wheel.

He walked to his own car. There was no night bus to Ystad. He went into a phone booth and called Anette Brolin at home. When she answered he hung up at once.

He got into his car and pushed in the cassette of Maria Callas and closed his eyes.

He woke up with a start because he was cold. He had slept for almost two hours. Even though he wasn't sober, he decided to drive home. He would take the back roads through Svedala and Svaneholm. That way he wouldn't risk running into any police patrols.

But he did anyway. He had completely forgotten that the night patrols from Ystad were watching the refugee camps. And he was the one who had given the order.

Peters and Norén came upon an erratic driver between Svaneholm and Slimminge, after they had checked that everything was quiet at Hageholm. Normally both of them would have recognized Wallander's car, but it never occurred to them that he might be out driving around at night. Besides, the license plate was so covered with mud that it was unreadable. Not until they had stopped the car and knocked on the windshield, and Kurt Wallander had rolled down the window did they recognize their acting chief.

None of them said a word. Norén's flashlight shone on Wallander's bloodshot eyes.

"Everything quiet?" asked Wallander.

Norén and Peters looked at each other.

"Yes," said Peters. "Everything seems quiet."

"That's good," said Wallander, about to roll up the window. Then Norén stepped forward.

"You'd better get out of the car," he said. "Now, right away."

Wallander looked inquiringly at the face he could hardly recognize in the sharp glare from the flashlight.

Then he obeyed and did as he was told.

He got out of the car.

The night was cold. He could feel that he was freezing.

Something had come to an end.

Chapter Nine

The last thing Kurt Wallander felt like was a laughing policeman as he stepped into the Svea Hotel in Simrishamn at seven o'clock on Friday morning. An almost impenetrable mixture of snow and rain was falling over Skåne, and water had seeped through his shoes on his way from the car to the hotel.

He also had a headache.

He asked the waitress for a couple of headache tablets. She came back with a glass of water fizzing with white powder.

As he drank his coffee, he noticed that his hand was shaking. He figured it was just as much from fear as from relief.

A few hours earlier, when Norén had ordered him to get out of his car on the two-lane road between Svaneholm and Slimminge, he had thought that it was all over. Now he wouldn't be a cop anymore. The serious charge of driving under the influence would mean immediate suspension. And even if someday he were allowed to return to active duty on the police force, after having served a jail sentence, he would never be able to look his former colleagues in the eye.

He quickly imagined the possibility that he might become head of security for some company. Or he might slip through the background check of some less choosy guard service. But his twenty-year career with the police would be over. And he was a cop to the core.

He didn't even consider trying to bribe Peters and Norén. He knew that was impossible. The only thing he could do was plead. Appeal to their team spirit, to their camaraderie, to their friendship, which didn't really exist.

But he didn't have to do that.

"Ride with Peters, and I'll drive your car home," Norén had said.

Kurt Wallander recalled his feeling of relief, but also the unmistakable hint of contempt in Norén's voice.

Without a word he got into the back seat of the patrol car. Peters was silent and uncommunicative during the whole drive to Mariagatan in Ystad.

Norén had followed close behind; he parked the car and handed the keys to Wallander.

"Did anyone see you?" asked Norén.

"Nobody but you."

"You were damn lucky."

Peters nodded. And then Wallander realized that nothing was going to happen. Norén and Peters were committing a serious breach of duty for his sake. He had no idea why.

"Thank you," he said.

"That's all right," Norén replied.

And then they had driven off.

Wallander went into his apartment and polished off the last of an almost empty bottle of whiskey. Then he fell asleep for several hours, lying on top of his bed. Without thinking, without dreaming. At six fifteen he got into his car again, after giving himself a cursory shave.

He knew, of course, that he was still intoxicated. But now there was no danger of running into Peters and Norén. They went off duty at six.

He tried to concentrate on what was in store for him. He was going to meet Göran Boman, and together they would go in search of a missing link in the investigation of the double murder at Lenarp.

Wallander pushed all other thoughts aside. He would let them come back when he had the energy to deal with them. When he no longer had a hangover, when he had managed to put everything in perspective.

He was the only person in the hotel dining room. He gazed out at the gray sea, barely visible through the wet snowfall. A fishing boat was on its way out of the harbor, and he tried to make out the number painted in black on the hull.

A beer, he thought. A good old pilsner is what I need right now.

It was a strong temptation. He also thought that he ought to try to drop in at the state liquor store, so he would have something to drink in the evening.

He realized that he wasn't ready to sober up too quickly.

A rotten policeman, that's what I am, he thought.

A dubious cop.

The waitress refilled his coffee cup. He imagined himself going into the hotel and she would come with him. Behind drawn curtains he would forget that he existed, forget everything around him, and sink into a world that had nothing to do with reality.

He drank the coffee and picked up his briefcase. He still had a little time to read through the investigation reports.

Filled with a sudden restlessness, he went out to the lobby and called the police station in Ystad. Ebba answered.

"Did you have a nice evening?" she asked.

"Couldn't have been better," he replied. "And thanks again for your help with my suit."

"Any time.'

"I'm calling from the Svea Hotel in Simrishamn. If you need to get hold of me. Later I'm going to drive around with Boman from the Kristianstad police. But I'll call in."

"Everything's quiet. Nothing has happened at the refugee camps."

He hung up and went into the men's room to wash his face. He avoided looking at himself in the mirror. With his fingertips he gingerly touched the bump on his forehead. It hurt. But the stinging in his arm was almost gone.

Only when he stretched did he notice a twinge shoot through his thigh.

When he returned to the dining room, he ordered breakfast. As he ate, he leafed through all his papers.

Göran Boman was punctual. At the stroke of nine he entered the dining room.

"What awful weather!" he said.

"At least it's better than a snowstorm," said Wallander.

While Boman drank his coffee they figured out what had to be done during the course of the day.

"It seems we're in luck," said Boman. "It's going to be possible to get hold of the woman in Gladsax and the two in Kristianstad without much trouble."

They started with the woman in Gladsax.

"Her name is Anita Hessler," said Boman. "Fifty-eight years old. She married a couple of years ago; her husband is a real estate agent."

"Is Hessler her maiden name?" wondered Wallander.

"Her name is Johanson now. Her husband is Klas Johanson. They live in a residential area not far outside the town. We've done a little snooping. As far as we know, she's a housewife."

He checked his papers.

"On March 9, 1951, she gave birth to a son at Kristianstad's maternity ward. At four thirteen in the morning, to be exact. As far as we know, he's her only child. But Klas Johanson has four children from a previous marriage. He's also six years younger than she is."

"So her son is thirty-nine," said Wallander.

"He was christened Stefan," said Boman. "He lives in Åhus and works as a tax-assessment supervisor in Kristianstad. His finances are in order. He has a row house, a wife, and two kids."

"Do tax-assessment supervisors usually commit murder?" asked Wallander.

"Not very often," replied Boman.

They drove out to Gladsax. The wet snow had now changed to a steady rain. Just before entering the town, Göran Boman turned left.

The two-story houses in the residential neighborhood were in sharp contrast to the low white buildings of the town itself. Wallander thought that it could just as well have been a well-to-do suburb outside any large city.

The house was at the end of a row. A huge satellite dish stood on a slab of cement next to the house. The yard was well kept.

They sat in the car for a few minutes and stared at the red-brick building. A white Nissan was parked in the driveway in front of the garage.

"The husband probably isn't home," said Boman. "His office is in Simrishamn. He apparently specializes in selling property to well-heeled Germans."

"Is that legal?" asked Wallander, in surprise.

Göran Boman shrugged.

"They use dummy owners," he said. "The Germans pay well and the deeds are placed in Swedish hands. There are people in Skåne who make a good living by assuming the illegal ownership of real estate."

All of a sudden they caught a glimpse of movement behind the curtains. It happened so fast that only the trained eyes of the police would have noticed.

"Somebody's home," said Wallander. "Shall we go and say hello?"

The woman who opened the door was astoundingly attractive. Her radiance was unmistakable, even though she was wearing a baggy jogging suit. The fleeting thought occurred to Wallander that she didn't look Swedish.

He also thought that their initial introductions might be just as important as all their questions put together.

How would she react when they told her that they were cops?

The only thing he noticed was that she raised one eyebrow slightly. Then she smiled, revealing even rows of white teeth. Wallander wondered whether Boman was right. Was she really fifty-eight years old? If he hadn't known better, he would have guessed forty-five.

"This is unexpected," she said. "Come in."

They stepped into a tastefully furnished living room. The walls were covered with crowded bookshelves. A top-of-the-line Bang & Olufsen TV stood in the corner. Tiger-striped fish swam in an aquarium. Wallander had trouble connecting this living room with Johannes Lövgren. There was nothing to indicate a connection.

"Can I offer you gentlemen anything?" asked the woman.

They declined and sat down.

"We've come to ask you some routine questions," said Wallander. "My name is Kurt Wallander, and this is Göran Boman from the Kristianstad police."

"How exciting to have a visit from the police," said the woman, still smiling. "Nothing unusual ever happens here in Gladsax."

"We just wanted to ask you whether you know a man named Johannes Lövgren," said Wallander.

She gave him a look of surprise.

"Johannes Lövgren? No. Who's he?"

"Are you sure?"

"Of course I'm sure!"

"He was murdered along with his wife in a town called Lenarp a few days ago. Maybe you read about it in the newspapers."

Her surprise seemed quite genuine.

"I don't understand," she said. "I remember seeing something about it in the paper. But what does this have to do with me?"

Nothing, thought Wallander and glanced at Boman, who seemed to share his opinion. What did this woman have to do with Johannes Lövgren?

"In 1951 you gave birth to a son in Kristianstad," said Boman. "On all the documents in various records you listed the father as unknown. Is it possible that a man by the name of Johannes Lövgren might be this unknown father?"

She gazed at them for a long time before she answered.

"I don't understand why you're asking these questions," she said. "And I understand even less what this has to do with that murdered farmer. But if it's any help, I can tell you that Stefan's father was named Rune Stierna. He was married to someone else. I knew what I was getting into, and I chose to thank him for the child by keeping his identity secret. He died twelve years ago. And Stefan got along well with his father during his whole childhood."

"I know that these questions must seem strange," said Wallander. "But sometimes we have to ask odd questions."

They asked a few more questions and took some notes. Then it was over.

"I hope you will forgive us for disturbing you," said Wallander as he got to his feet.

"Do you think I'm telling the truth?" she asked all of a sudden.

"Yes," said Wallander. "We think you're telling the truth. But if you're not, we'll find out. Sooner or later."

She burst out laughing. "I'm telling the truth," she said. "I'm not a very good liar. But feel free to come back if you have more strange questions."

They left the house and went back to the car.

"Well, that's that," said Boman.

"She's not the one," said Wallander.

"Do we need to talk to the son in Åhus?"

"I think we can skip him. For the time being, at any rate."

They got into Wallander's car and drove straight back toward Kristianstad.

When they reached the hills around Brösarp the rain stopped and the clouds began to dissipate.

Outside the police station in Kristianstad they switched cars and continued on in one of the police vehicles.

"Margareta Velander," said Boman. "Forty-nine years old, owns a beauty shop called 'The Wave' on Krokarpsgatan. Three children, divorced, remarried, divorced again. Lives in a row house out toward Blekinge. Gave birth to a son in December 1958. The son's name is Nils. Evidently quite an entrepreneur. Used to go around the marketplaces selling imported knickknacks. Also listed as the owner of a company dealing in women's specialty underwear. Lives in Sölvesborg, of all places. Who the hell would buy women's specialty underwear sold by a mail-order company from a town like that?"

"Plenty of people," said Wallander.

"Once did time for assault and battery," Boman continued. "I haven't seen the report. But he got one year. That means the assault must have been pretty bad."

"I want to see that report," said Wallander. "Where did it happen?"

"He was sentenced by the Kalmar district court. They're looking for the paperwork on the case."

"When did it happen?"

"In 1981, I think."

Wallander sat and thought while Boman drove through the town.

"So she was only seventeen when the boy was born. And if we're picturing Johannes Lövgren as the father, there was a big age difference."

"I've thought of that. But that could mean a lot of things."

The beauty shop was in an ordinary apartment building on the outskirts of Kristianstad. It was located on the basement level.

"Maybe I should get a haircut more often," said Boman. "Who cuts your hair, by the way?"

Wallander was just about to say that his wife Mona took care of that.

"It varies," he replied evasively.

There were three chairs in the beauty shop. All of them were occupied as they came in.

Two women were sitting under hair dryers while a third woman was having her hair washed.

The woman who was washing the customer's hair looked up at them in surprise.

"I only work by appointment," she said. "I'm booked up today. And tomorrow too. If you want to make an appointment for your wives."

"Margareta Velander?" asked Göran Boman.

He showed her his ID.

"We'd like to talk to you," he said.

Wallander could see that she was scared.

"I can't leave right now," she said.

"We'd be happy to wait," said Boman.

"You can wait in the back room," said Margareta Velander. "I won't be long."

It was a very small room. A table covered with oilcloth and a couple of chairs took up practically all the space. A shelf held a number of tabloids between some coffee cups and a grimy coffee maker. Wallander studied a black-and-white photograph pinned up on the wall. It was blurry and faded, showing a young man in

a sailor's uniform. Wallander could read the word "Halland" on band around the cap.

"'Halland,'" he said. "Was that a cruiser or a destroyer?"

"A destroyer. Scrapped long ago."

Margareta Velander came into the room. She was drying her hands on a towel.

"I've got a few minutes now," she said. "What's it about?"

"We wonder whether you know a man named Johannes Lövgren," began Wallander.

"Is that so," she said. "Would you like some coffee?"

They both declined, and Wallander was annoyed that she had turned her back to him when he asked the question.

"Johannes Lövgren," he repeated. "A farmer from a little town outside of Ystad. Did you know him?"

"The man who was murdered?" she asked, looking him straight in the eye.

"Yes," he said. "The man who was murdered. That's the one."

"No," she replied, pouring coffee into a plastic cup. "Why should I know him?"

The police officers exchanged glances. There was something about her voice that indicated she was feeling pressured.

"In December 1958 you gave birth to a son who was christened Nils," said Wallander. "You listed the father as unknown."

The instant he mentioned the name of her son, she started to cry. The coffee cup tipped over and fell to the floor.

"What has he done?" she asked. "What has he done now?"

They waited until she calmed down before they continued their questioning.

"We're not here to bring you bad news," Wallander assured her. "But we'd like to know whether Johannes Lövgren is the name of Nils's father."

"No."

Her answer was not exactly convincing.

"Then we'd like you to tell us the name of his father."

"Why do you want to know?"

"It's important for our investigation."

"I've already told you that I don't know anybody named Johannes Lövgren."

"What's the name of Nils's father?"

"I can't tell you."

"It won't go any further than this room."

She paused a little too long before she answered. "I don't know who Nils's father was."

"Women usually know things like that."

"I was sleeping with more than one man at the time. I don't know who it was. That's why I listed the father as unknown."

She stood up quickly.

"I've got to get back to work," she said. "The old ladies are going to be boiled alive under those dryers."

"We can wait."

"But I don't have anything else to tell you!"

She seemed more and more upset.

"We have some more questions."

Ten minutes later she was back. She was holding some bills that she stuffed into her purse, which was hanging on the back of a chair. She now seemed composed and ready for an argument.

"I don't know anyone named Lövgren," she said.

"And you insist that you don't know who the father was of your son who was born in 1958?"

"That's right."

"Do you realize that you may have to answer these questions under oath?"

"I'm not lying."

"Where can we find your son Nils?"

"He travels a lot."

"According to our records, his place of residence is in Sölvesborg."

"So go out there then!"

"That's what we plan to do."

"I have nothing more to say."

Wallander hesitated for a moment. Then he pointed at the blurry, faded photograph pinned up on the wall.

"Is that Nils's father?" he asked.

She had just lit a cigarette. When she exhaled, it sounded like a hiss.

"I don't know any Lövgren. I don't know what you're talking about."

"All right then," said Göran Boman, bringing the conversation to a close. "We'll be going now. But you may be hearing from us again."

"I have nothing more to say. Why can't you leave me alone?"

"Nobody gets left alone when the police are looking for a double murderer," said Boman. "That's the way it goes."

When they came outdoors, the sun was shining. They stood next to the car for a moment.

"What do you think?" asked Boman.

"I don't know. But there's something there."

"Shall we try to locate the son before we move on to the third woman?"

"I think so."

They drove over to Sölvesborg and with great difficulty located what was supposedly the right address. A dilapidated wooden house outside the center of town, surrounded by junked cars and pieces of machinery. A furious German shepherd was yanking and pulling on its iron chain. The house looked deserted. Boman leaned forward and looked at a nameplate with sloppy lettering that was nailed to the door.

"Nils Velander," he said. "This is the place."

He knocked several times. But no one answered. They walked all the way around the house.

"What a damn rat hole," said Boman.

When they got back to their starting point, Wallander tried the door handle.

The house wasn't locked.

Wallander looked at Boman, who shrugged.

"If it's open, it's open," he said. "Let's go in."

They stepped into a musty entryway and listened. There wasn't a sound, until they both jumped when a hissing cat leaped out of a dark corner and vanished up the stairs to the second floor. The room on the left seemed to be some sort of office. There were two battered file cabinets and an exceedingly messy desk with a phone and an answering machine. Wallander lifted the top of a box sitting on the desk. Inside was a set of black leather underwear and a mailing label.

"Fredrik Åberg of Dragongatan in Alingsås ordered this stuff," he said with a grimace. "Plain brown wrapper, no doubt."

They moved on to the next room, which was a storeroom for Nils Velander's specialty underwear. There were also a number of whips and dog collars.

Everything was jumbled up in the storeroom, with no sign of organization.

The next room was the kitchen, with dirty dishes on the counter. A half-eaten chicken lay on the floor. The whole room smelled of cat piss.

Wallander threw open the door to the pantry.

There was a home distillery and two large carboys.

Boman snickered and shook his head.

They went upstairs and peeked into the bedroom. The sheets were dirty and clothing was heaped on the floor. The curtains were drawn, and together they counted seven cats scurrying off as they approached.

"What a pigsty," repeated Boman. "How can anybody live like this?"

The house looked as if it had been vacated in a hurry.

"Maybe we'd better go," said Wallander. "We'll need a search warrant before we can give the place a thorough going-over."

They went back downstairs. Boman stepped into the office and punched the button on the answering machine.

Nils Velander, assuming it was him, stated that no one was in the Raff-Sets office at the moment, but you were welcome to leave your order on the answering machine.

The German shepherd jerked on its chain as they came out into the yard.

Right at the corner, on the left-hand side of the house,

Wallander discovered a basement door almost hidden behind the remains of an old mangle.

He opened the unlocked door and stepped into the darkness. He fumbled his way over to a fuse box. An old oil furnace stood in the corner. The rest of the basement room was filled with empty birdcages. He called to Boman, who joined him down in the basement.

"Leather underpants and empty birdcages," said Wallander. "What exactly is this guy up to?"

"I think we'd better find out," replied Boman.

As they were about to leave, Wallander noticed a small steel cabinet behind the furnace. He bent down and pressed on the handle. It was unlocked, like everything else in the house. He put his hand in and grabbed hold of a plastic bag. He pulled it out and opened it.

"Look at this," he said to Boman.

The plastic bag held a stack of thousand-krona bills.

Wallander counted twenty-three.

"I think we're going to have to have a talk with this guy," said Boman.

They stuffed the money back and went outside. The German shepherd was barking.

"We'll have to talk to our colleagues here in Sölvesborg," said Boman. "They can check this guy out for us."

At the Sölvesborg police station they met an officer who was quite familiar with Nils Velander.

"He's probably mixed up in all kinds of illegal activities," said the policeman. "But the only thing we have on him is suspicion of illegally importing caged birds from Thailand. And operating a home still."

"He was once sentenced for assault and battery," said Boman.

"He doesn't usually get into fights," replied the police officer. "But I'll try to check him out for you. Do you really think he's turned to murdering people?"

"We don't know," said Wallander. "But we want to get hold of him."

They returned to Kristianstad. It had started raining again. They both had a good impression of the police officer in Sölvesborg and were counting on him to find Nils Velander for them.

But Wallander was having doubts.

"We don't know anything," he said. "Thousand-krona bills in a plastic bag aren't proof of anything."

"But something is going on there," said Boman.

Wallander agreed. There was something about the beauty-shop owner and her son.

They stopped for lunch at a motel restaurant just outside Kristianstad.

Wallander thought he ought to check in with the police station in Ystad.

The pay phone that he tried was broken.

It was one thirty by the time they got back to Kristianstad. Before they continued on to the third woman, Boman wanted to check in at his office.

The young woman at the reception desk flagged them down.

"There was a call from Ystad," she said. "They want Kurt Wallander to call back."

"Let's go to my office," said Boman.

Full of foreboding, Wallander punched in the number while Boman went to get some coffee.

Without a word Ebba connected him to Rydberg.

"You'd better come back," said Rydberg. "Some idiot has shot a Somali refugee at Hageholm."

"What the hell do you mean by that?"

"Exactly what I said. This Somali was out taking a little walk. Someone blasted him with a shotgun. I've had a hell of a time tracking you down. Where have you been?"

"Is he dead?"

"His head was blown off."

Wallander felt sick to his stomach. "I'm on my way," he said.

He hung up the phone just as Boman came in, balancing two mugs of coffee. Wallander gave him a brief rundown on what had happened.

"I'll get you emergency transport," said Boman. "I'll send your car over later with one of the boys."

Everything happened fast.

In a few minutes Wallander was on his way to Ystad in a car with wailing sirens. Rydberg met him at the police station and they drove at once to Hageholm.

"Do we have any leads?" asked Wallander.

"None. But the newsroom at *Sydsvensan* got a call only a few minutes after the murder. A man said that it was revenge for the murder of Johannes Lövgren. Next time they struck, they would take a woman for Maria Lövgren."

"This is insane," said Wallander. "We don't suspect foreigners anymore, do we?"

"Somebody seems to have a different opinion. Thinks that we're shielding some foreigners."

"But I've already denied that."

"Whoever did this doesn't give a shit about your denials. They see a perfect opportunity to pull out a gun and start shooting foreigners."

"This is crazy!"

"You're damn right it's crazy. But it's true!"

"Did the newspaper tape the phone conversation?"

"Yes."

"I want to hear it. To see if it's the same person who's been calling me."

The car raced through the landscape of Skåne.

"What are we going to do now?" asked Wallander.

"We've got to catch the Lenarp killers," said Rydberg. "And damned fast."

At Hageholm everything was in chaos. Distressed and weeping refugees had gathered in the dining hall, reporters were conducting interviews, and phones were ringing. Wallander stepped out of the car onto a muddy dirt road several hundred meters from the residential buildings. The wind had started blowing again, and he turned up the collar of his jacket. An area near the road had been cordoned off. The dead man was lying face down in the mud.

Wallander cautiously lifted the sheet covering the body.

Rydberg hadn't been exaggerating. There was almost nothing left of the head.

"Shot at close range," said Hanson who was standing nearby. "Whoever did this must have jumped out of hiding and fired the shots from a few meters away."

"The shots?" said Wallander.

"The camp director says that she heard two shots, close together."

Wallander looked around.

"Car tracks?" he asked. "Where does this road go?"

"Two kilometers farther along you come out on E14."

"And no one saw anything?"

"It's hard to question refugees who speak fifteen different languages. But we're working on it."

"Do we know who the dead man is?"

"He had a wife and nine children."

Wallander stared at Hanson in disbelief. "Nine children?"

"Just imagine the headlines tomorrow morning," said Hanson. "Innocent refugee murdered taking a walk. Nine children left without a father."

Svedberg came running from one of the police cars.

"The police chief is on the phone," he said.

Wallander looked surprised.

"I thought he wasn't due back from Spain until tomorrow."

"Not him. The chief of the *National* Police."

Wallander got into the car and picked up the phone. The chief's voice was emphatic, and Wallander was immediately annoyed by what he said.

"This looks very bad," said the chief. "We don't need racist murders in this country."

"No," said Wallander.

"This investigation must be given top priority."

"Yes. But we already have the double homicide in Lenarp on our hands."

"Are you making any progress?"

"I think so. But it takes time."

"I want you to report to me personally. I'm going to take part in a discussion program on TV tonight, and I need all the information I can get."

"I ll see to it."

He hung up the phone.

Wallander remained sitting in the car.

Näslund will have to handle this, he thought He'll have to feed the paperwork to Stockholm.

Wallander felt depressed. His hangover was gone, and he thought about what had happened the night before. He was also reminded of it because he saw Peters approaching from a police car that had just arrived.

Then he thought about Mona and the man who had picked her up.

And Linda laughing. The black man at her side.

His father, painting his eternal landscape.

He thought about himself too.

A time to live, and a time to die.

Then Wallander forced himself to get out of the car to take charge of the criminal investigation.

Nothing else had better happen, he thought.

We can't handle anything else.

It was three fifteen. Once again it had started to rain.

Chapter Ten

Kurt Wallander stood freezing in the pouring rain. It was almost five o'clock, and the police had rigged floodlights around the murder scene. He watched two ambulance attendants who came squishing through the mud with a stretcher. They were taking away the dead Somali. When he looked at the sea of mud he wondered whether even as skillful a detective as Rydberg would be able to find any tracks.

Still, at the moment he felt slightly relieved. Until ten minutes ago the officers had been surrounded by a hysterical wife and nine howling children. The wife of the dead man had thrown herself into the mud, and her wails were so piercing that several of the policemen couldn't stand the sound and had moved away. To his surprise, Wallander had realized that the only one who was able to handle the grieving woman and the dismayed children was Martinson. The youngest cop on the force, who so far in his career had never even been forced to notify someone of a relative's death. He had held the woman, kneeling in the mud, and in some way the two were able to understand each other across the language barrier. A minister who had been hurriedly called was unable to do anything, of course. Gradually Martinson succeeded in getting the woman and the children back to the main building, where a doctor was ready to take care of them.

Rydberg came tramping through the mud. His pants were splotched all the way up his thighs.

"What a hell of a mess," he said. "But Hanson and Svedberg have done a fantastic job. They managed to find two refugees and an interpreter who actually think they saw something."

"What?"

"How should I know? I don't speak either Arabic or Swahili. But they're on their way to Ystad right now. The Immigration Service has promised us some interpreters. I thought it would be best if you handled the interrogations."

Wallander nodded. "Have we got anything to go on?"

Rydberg took out his grimy notebook.

"He was killed at precisely one o'clock," he said. "The director was listening to the wire-service news on the radio when she heard the noise. There were two shots. But you know that already. He was dead before he hit the ground. It seems to have been regular buckshot. Gyttorp brand, I think. Nytrox 36, probably. That's about all."

"That's not much."

"I think it's absolutely nothing. But maybe the eyewitnesses will have something to tell us."

"I've authorized overtime for everyone," said Wallander. "Now we'll have to bust our butts night and day if necessary."

Back at the station, the first interrogation almost drove him to despair. The interpreter, who was supposed to know Swahili, couldn't understand the dialect spoken by the witness, a young man from Malawi. It took Wallander almost half an hour before he realized that the interpreter wasn't translating what the witness said at all. Then it took almost twenty more minutes before he learned that the man from Malawi, for some strange reason, knew Luvale, a language that was spoken in parts of Zaire and Zambia. But then they had a stroke of luck. One of the Immigration Service representatives knew an old missionary who spoke fluent Luvale. She was close to ninety years old and lived in a retirement apartment in Trelleborg. After calling his colleagues there, he received a promise that the missionary would be given police transport to Ystad. Wallander suspected that a ninety-year-old missionary might not be very sharp. But he was wrong. A little white-haired lady with lively eyes suddenly stood on the threshold of his office, and before he knew it she was involved in an intense conversation with the young man.

Unfortunately, it turned out that the man hadn't seen a thing.
"Ask him why he volunteered as a witness," Wallander said wearily.

The missionary and the young man went off into a lengthy exchange.

"He probably just thought it was rather exciting," she said at last. "And that's understandable."

"Is it?" Wallander wondered.

"You were probably young once yourself," said the old woman.

The young man from Malawi was sent back to Hageholm, and the missionary returned to Trelleborg.

The next witness actually had something to tell them. He was an Iranian interpreter who spoke good Swedish. Just like the dead Somali, he had been out for a walk in the area around Hageholm when the shots were fired.

Wallander picked out a section of the topographic map that showed the area around Hageholm. He put an X at the murder scene, and the interpreter was able to point out at once where he had been when he heard the two shots. Wallander calculated the distance as about three hundred meters.

"After the shots I heard a car," said the interpreter.

"But you didn't see it?"

"No. I was in the woods. I couldn't see the road."

The interpreter pointed again. To the south.

Then he gave Wallander a real surprise.

"It was a Citroën," he said.

"A Citroën?"

"The one you call a turtle here in Sweden."

"How can you be sure of that?"

"I grew up in Teheran. When we were kids we learned to recognize the makes of cars by the sound of the engine. Citroëns are easy. Especially the turtle."

Wallander had a hard time believing what he heard. Then he made a quick decision.

"Come out in the courtyard with me," he said. "And when you get outside, turn your back and shut your eyes."

Outside in the rain he started his Peugeot and drove around the parking lot. He watched the interpreter carefully the whole time.

"All right," he said when he returned. "What was that?"

"A Peugeot," replied the interpreter with the utmost confidence.

"Good," said Wallander. "Damned amazing."

He sent the witness home and gave the order to put out an APB on a Citroën that might have been seen between Hageholm and E4 to the west. The wire service was also informed that the police were now searching for a Citroën that was assumed to be involved in the murder.

The third witness was a young woman from Romania. She sat in Wallander's office nursing her baby during the interrogation. The interpreter spoke poor Swedish, but Wallander still thought he got a good idea of what the woman was saying.

She had walked the same way as the murdered Somali, and she had met him on the way back to the camp.

"How long?" asked Wallander. "How long was it from when you met him and when you heard the shots?"

"Maybe three minutes."

"Did you see anyone else?"

The woman nodded, and Wallander leaned over the desk in suspense.

"Where?" he asked. "Show me on the map!"

The interpreter held the infant while the woman searched on the map.

"There," she said, pressing the pen to the map.

Wallander saw that the spot was right near the murder scene.

"Tell me about it," he said. "Take your time. Think carefully."

The interpreter translated and the woman took her time.

"A man in blue overalls," she said. "He was standing out in the field."

"What did he look like?"

"He didn't have much hair."

"How tall was he?"

"Normal height."

"Am I a man of normal height?"

Wallander stood up straight.

"He was taller."

"How old was he?"

"He wasn't young. Not old either. Maybe forty-five."

"Did he see you?"

"I don't think so."

"What was he doing out in the field?"

"He was eating."

"Eating?"

"He was eating an apple."

Wallander thought for a moment. "A man in blue overalls standing in a field near the road and eating an apple. Did I understand you correctly?"

"Yes."

"Was he alone?"

"I didn't see anyone else. But I don't think he was alone."

"Why not?"

"He seemed to be waiting for someone."

"Did this man have a weapon of any kind?"

The woman thought again. "There might have been a brown package at his feet. Maybe it was just mud."

"What happened after you saw the man?"

"I hurried home as fast as I could."

"Why were you in a hurry?"

"It's not a good idea to run into strange men in the woods."

Wallander nodded. "Did you see a car?" he asked.

"No. No car."

"Can you describe the man in more detail?"

She thought for a long time before she replied. The baby was asleep in the interpreter's arms.

"He looked strong," she said. "I think he had big hands."

"What color was his hair? What little he had."

"Swedish color."

"Blond hair?"

"Yes. And he was bald like this."

She drew a half moon in the air.

Then she was allowed to go back to the camp. Wallander went to get a cup of coffee. Svedberg asked if he wanted pizza. He nodded.

At nine o'clock that night the team met in the lunchroom. Wallander thought that everyone except Näslund still looked surprisingly alert. Näslund had a cold and a fever but stubbornly refused to go home.

As they divided up the pizzas and sandwiches, Wallander tried to sum up. At one end of the room he had taken down a picture and projected a slide that showed a map of the murder scene. He had put an *X* at the site of the crime and drawn in the location and movements of both witnesses.

"So we aren't totally out in the cold here," he began his presentation. "We've got the time, and we have two reliable witnesses. A few minutes before the first shot, the female witness sees a man in blue overalls standing in a field right next to the road. This fits exactly with the time it should have taken the deceased to reach that point. Then we know that the killer took off in a Citroën and headed southwest."

The presentation was interrupted when Rydberg came into the lunchroom. All the team members broke out laughing. Rydberg was covered in mud all the way up to his chin. He kicked off his filthy wet shoes and took a sandwich that someone handed him.

"You're just in time," said Wallander. "What have you found?"

"I've been slogging around in that field for two hours," replied Rydberg. "The Romanian woman pointed out pretty well where the man was probably standing. We took casts of some footprints there. From rubber boots. And she said that's what the man was wearing. Ordinary green rubber boots. Then I found an apple core."

Rydberg took a plastic bag out of his pocket.

"With a little luck we might get some prints off it," he said.

"Can you take fingerprints from an apple core?" Wallander wondered.

"You can take prints from anything," said Rydberg. "There might be a strand of hair, a little saliva, skin fragments."

He set the plastic bag on the table carefully, as if it were made of porcelain.

"Then I followed the footprints," he went on. "And if this Apple Man is the killer, then this is how I think it happened."

Rydberg took his pen out of the notebook and went over to the map projected on the wall.

"He saw the Somali coming up the road. Then he threw away the apple core and walked straight onto the road in front of him. It looked as if his boots had dragged some mud onto the road. There he fired off his two shots at a distance of about four meters. Then he turned around and ran about fifty meters down the road from the murder scene. The path turns there, and the road widens a little, making it possible for a car to turn around. Sure enough, there were tire tracks. And I also found two cigarette butts."

He took the next plastic bag from his pocket.

"Then the man hopped in the car and drove south. That's how I think it happened. By the way, I think I'll send my dry-cleaning bill to the police department."

"I'll sign for it," promised Wallander. "But now we have to think."

Rydberg raised his hand, as if he were in school.

"I've got a couple of ideas," he said. "First of all, I'm sure there were two of them. One waiting by the car and one shooter."

"Why do you think that?" asked Wallander.

"People who choose to eat an apple in a tense situation are probably not smokers. I think there was one person waiting by the car. A smoker. And a killer who ate an apple."

"That sounds reasonable."

"Also, I've got a feeling that the whole thing was carefully planned. It doesn't take much to figure out that the refugees at Hageholm use this road to take walks. Most often they probably go in groups. But now and then someone will be walking alone. If you then dress like a farmer, no one would think it looked suspicious. And the spot was well chosen, because the car could wait on the road right nearby without being seen. So I think that this senseless act was a cold-blooded execution. The only thing the killers didn't know was who would come walking up that road alone. And they didn't care."

Silence fell over the lunchroom. Rydberg's analysis had been so clear that no one had anything to say. The ruthlessness of the murder was now blatantly apparent.

It was Svedberg who finally broke the silence. "A messenger brought over a cassette tape from *Sydsvensan*," he said.

Someone got a tape recorder.

Wallander recognized the voice. It was the same man who had called him twice and threatened him.

"We'll send this tape up to Stockholm," said Wallander. "Maybe they can figure out something by analyzing it."

"I also think we should find out what kind of apple he was eating," said Rydberg. "With a little luck we might track down the store where he bought it."

Then they started talking about the motive.

"Racial hatred," said Wallander. "That can be so many things. But I assume we have to start poking around in these Neo-Swedish groups. Obviously we've entered a new and more serious phase. Now they're not just painting slogans anymore. Now they're throwing fire bombs and killing people. But I don't think the same people did this as set fire to the barracks in Ystad. I still think that was more of a prank or the act of some drunk who got worked up about refugees in general. This murder is different. It's individuals either acting on their own or somehow involved in one of these movements. And we'll have to give them a good shakeup. We also need to go out and appeal to the public for tips. I'm thinking of asking Stockholm for help in charting these Neo-Swedish movements. This murder has the status of a national alarm. That means we can have all the resources we need. Besides, someone must have seen that Citroën."

"There's a club for Citroën owners," said Näslund in a hoarse voice. "We could match their list against the list of registered vehicles. The people in the club probably know about every Citroën on the road in the whole country."

The assignments were given out. It was almost ten thirty before the meeting was over. No one even thought of going home.

Wallander arranged an improvised press conference in the lobby of the police station. Again he urged anyone who had seen a Citroën on E14 to get in touch with the police. He also gave the preliminary description of the murderer.

When he was finished, the questions rained down on him.

"Not now," he said. "I've said all I'm going to say."

When Wallander was on the way back to his office, Hanson came and asked if he wanted to see a videotape of the discussion program on which the chief of the National Police had been a guest.

"I'd rather not," he replied. "Not right now, at least."

He cleaned off his desk. He stuck the note reminding him to call his sister on the receiver of the telephone. Then he called Göran Boman at home.

Boman himself answered. "How's it going?" he asked.

"We've got a good deal to go on," said Wallander. "We'll have to work on it."

"I've got good news for you too."

"I was hoping you would."

"Our colleagues in Sölvesborg found Nils Velander. Apparently he has a boat at some shipyard that he goes out and works on once in a while. The transcript of the interrogation is coming tomorrow, but they told me the most important things. He claims that he earned the money in the plastic bag in his underwear business. And he agreed to exchange the bills for new ones, so we can check for fingerprints."

"The Union Bank here in Ystad," said Wallander. "We have to find out whether the serial numbers can be traced."

"The money is arriving tomorrow. But honestly, I don't think he's the one."

"Why not?"

"I don't know."

"I thought you said you had good news?"

"I do. Now I'm getting to the third woman. I didn't think you'd mind if I looked her up by myself."

"Of course not."

"As you recall, her name is Ellen Magnusson. She's sixty years old and works at one of the pharmacies here in Kristianstad. I actually met her once before. Several years ago she ran over a highway worker in a traffic accident and killed him. That was outside the airport at Everöd. She claimed that she had been blinded by the sun. Which was no doubt true. In 1955 she gave birth to a son and listed the father as unknown. The son's name is Erik, and he lives in Malmö. He's a civil service employee at the county council. I drove out to her house. She seemed frightened and upset, as if she'd been waiting for the police to show up. She denied that Johannes Lövgren was the father of her boy. But I had a strong feeling that she was lying. If you trust my judgment, I'd like to focus on her. But of course I won't forget about that bird dealer and his mother."

"For the next twenty-four hours I probably won't be able to do much beyond what I'm working on right now," said Wallander. "I'm grateful for all the time you're devoting to this."

"I'll send over the papers," said Boman. "And the banknotes. I assume you'll have to give us a receipt for them."

"When all this is over we'll sit down and have a whiskey," said Wallander.

"There's going to be a conference at Snogeholm Castle in March on the new narcotics routes in Eastern Europe," said Boman. "How would that be?"

"I think that sounds fine," said Wallander.

They hung up, and he went over to Martinson's room to hear whether any tips had come in on the Citroën they were looking for.

Martinson shook his head. Still nothing.

Wallander went back to his office and put his feet up on his desk. It was eleven thirty. Slowly he let his thoughts fall into place. First he methodically replayed in his mind the murder outside the refugee camp. Had he forgotten anything? Was there any hole in Rydberg's account of the events, or something else that they ought to be working on right away?

In his opinion, the investigation was rolling along as efficiently as could be expected. All they had to do now was wait for the various technical analyses and hope that the vehicle could be traced.

He shifted in his chair, loosened his tie, and thought about what Göran Boman had told him. He had full confidence in his judgment.

If Boman felt the woman was lying, then that was undoubtedly the case.

But why was he going so easy on Nils Velander?

He took his feet down from the desk and pulled over a blank sheet of paper. Then he made a list of everything he had to do in the next few days. He also decided to try to get the Union Bank to open its doors for him tomorrow, even though it was Saturday.

When he finished his list, he stood up and stretched. It was just after midnight. Out in the corridor he could hear Hanson talking with Martinson, but he couldn't hear what they were saying.

Outside the window a streetlight was swaying in the wind. He felt sweaty and dirty and considered taking a shower downstairs in the police locker room. He opened the window and breathed in the cold air. It had stopped raining.

He could feel that he was restless. How would they be able to stop the murderer from striking again?

The next one would be a woman, in retribution for Maria Lövgren's death.

He sat down at his desk and pulled over the folder with the data on the refugee camps in Skåne.

It was unlikely that the murderer would return to Hageholm. But there were countless conceivable alternatives. And if the murderer selected his victim as randomly as he had at Hageholm, they had even less to go on.

Besides, it was impossible to require the refugees to stay indoors.

He shoved the folder aside and rolled a sheet of paper into his typewriter.

It was almost half past twelve. He thought he might as well write his memo to Björk.

Just then the door opened and Svedberg came in.

"News?" asked Wallander.

"You might call it that," said Svedberg, looking unhappy.

"What is it?"

"I don't quite know how to tell you. But we just got a call from a farmer out by Löderup."

"Did he see the Citroën?"

"No. But he claimed that your father was walking around out in a field in his pajamas. With a suitcase in his hand."

Wallander was completely stunned. "What the hell are you talking about?"

"The guy who called seemed lucid enough. It was you he actually wanted to talk to. But the switchboard put it through to me by mistake. I thought you ought to decide what to do."

Wallander sat quite still, his expression blank.

Then he stood up. "What field?" he asked.

"It sounded like your father was walking down by the main highway."

"I'll handle this myself. I'll be back as soon as I can. Tell them to give me a car with a radio, so you can call me if anything happens."

"Do you want me or somebody else to go along?"

Wallander shook his head.

"My father is senile," he said. "I have to see about getting him into a home somewhere."

Svedberg saw to it that Wallander was given the keys to a squad car with a radio.

Just as Wallander was going out the main doors, he noticed a man standing in the shadows outside. He recognized him as a reporter on one of the afternoon papers.

"I don't want him following me," he told Svedberg.

Svedberg nodded. "Wait till you see me back out and stall my engine in front of his car. Then you can leave."

Wallander got into his car and waited.

He saw the reporter quickly run over to his own car. Thirty seconds later, Svedberg drove up. He switched off the ignition.

The car was blocking the reporter from backing out. Wallander drove away.

He drove fast. Much too fast. He ignored the speed limit

through Sandskogen. Besides, he was almost alone on the road.
Terrified hares fled across the rain-slick asphalt.

When he reached the town where his father lived, he didn't
even have to look for him. His headlights caught the old man, in
his blue-trimmed pajamas, squishing barefoot through a field.
He was wearing his old hat and carrying a big suitcase. When
the headlights blinded him, his father held his hand in front of
his eyes in annoyance. Then he kept on walking. Energetically,
as if he were on his way to some specific destination.

Kurt Wallander turned off his engine but left the headlights on.
Then he walked out into the field.

"Dad!" he yelled. "What the hell are you doing?"

His father didn't answer but kept going. Wallander followed
him. He tripped and fell and got wet up to his belt.

"Dad!" he shouted again. "Stop! Where are you going?"

No response. His father seemed to pick up speed. Soon they
would be down by the main highway. Wallander ran and stumbled to catch up to him, grabbing him by the arm. But his father
pulled away and kept going.

Then Kurt Wallander got mad. "Police," he yelled. "If you
don't stop, we'll fire a warning shot."

His father stopped short and turned around. Wallander saw
him blinking in the glare of the headlights.

"What did I tell you?" the old man screamed. "You want to
kill me!"

Then he flung his suitcase at Wallander. The lid flew open and
revealed the contents: dirty underwear, tubes of paint, and brushes.

Wallander felt a huge sorrow well up inside him. His father
had tramped out into the night with the bewildered notion that
he was on his way to Italy.

"Calm down, Dad," he said. "I just thought I'd drive you down
to the station. Then you won't have to walk."

His father gave him a skeptical look. "I don't believe you,"
he said.

"Of course I'd drive my own dad to the station if he's going
on a trip."

Wallander picked up the suitcase, closed the lid, and started for the car. He put the bag in the trunk and stood waiting. His father looked like a wild animal caught in the headlights out in the field. An animal that has been chased to exhaustion and was now merely waiting for the fatal shot.

Then he started to walk toward the car. Wallander couldn't decide whether what he saw was an expression of dignity or humiliation. He opened the rear door and his father crawled in. Wallander had taken a blanket from the trunk, and now he wrapped it around his father's shoulders.

He gave a start when a man suddenly stepped out of the shadows. An old man, dressed in dirty overalls.

"I'm the one who called," said the man. "How's it going?"

"Everything's fine," replied Wallander. "Thanks for calling."

"It was pure chance that I saw him at all."

"I understand. Thanks again."

He got behind the wheel. When he turned his head he could see that his father was so cold he was shaking underneath the blanket.

"Now I'll take you to the station, Dad," he said. "It won't take long."

He drove straight to the emergency entrance of the hospital. He was lucky enough to run into the young doctor he had met earlier by Maria Lövgren's death bed. He explained what had happened.

"We'll admit him overnight for observation," said the doctor. "He may be suffering from exposure tonight. Tomorrow the social worker will try to find a place for him."

"Thank you," said Wallander. "I'll stay with him a while."

His father had been dried off and was lying on a gurney.

"Sleeping car to Italy," he said. "I'm finally on my way."

Wallander sat on a chair next to the gurney.

"That's right," he said. "Now you'll get to Italy."

It was past two o'clock in the morning when he left the hospital. He drove the short distance to the police station. Everyone except Hanson had gone home for the night. He was watching the taped discussion program with the chief of the National Police.

"Anything going on?" asked Wallander.

"Not a thing," said Hanson. "A few tips, of course. But nothing earthshaking. I took the liberty of sending people home to get a few hours' sleep."

"That's good. Funny that nobody has called about the car."

"I was just thinking about that. Maybe he just drove out E14 a little way and then took off on one of the back roads. I've looked at the maps. There's a whole maze of little roads in that area. Plus a big nature preserve for taking country walks, where no one goes in the winter. The patrols that check the camps are running a fine-tooth comb over those roads tonight."

Wallander nodded.

"We'll send in a helicopter when it gets light," he said. "The car might be hidden somewhere in that nature preserve."

He poured a cup of coffee.

"Svedberg told me about your dad," said Hanson. "How did it go?"

"It went all right. The old man is turning senile. He's at the hospital. But it went well."

"Go home and sleep for a few hours. You look beat."

"I've got some things to write up."

Hanson turned off the video.

"I'll stretch out on the sofa for a while," he said.

Wallander went into his office and sat down at the typewriter. His eyes stung with fatigue.

And yet the weariness brought with it an unexpected clarity. A double murder was committed, he thought. And the manhunt triggers another murder. Which we have to solve fast, so we won't be saddled with more murders.

All this had happened within the past five days.

Then he wrote his memo to Björk. He decided to make sure that it was delivered to him by hand at the airport.

He yawned. It was quarter to four. He was too tired to think about his father. He was just afraid that the social worker at the hospital wouldn't be able to come up with a good solution.

The note with his sister's name on it was still stuck to the telephone. In a few hours, when it was morning, he would have to call her.

He yawned again and sniffed his armpits. He stank. Just then Hanson appeared in the half-open door.

Wallander saw at once that something had happened.

"We've got something," said Hanson.

"What?"

"A guy from Malmö just called and said his car has been stolen."

"A Citroën?"

Hanson nodded.

"How come he discovers it at four in the morning?"

"He said he was on his way to some trade fair in Göteborg."

"Did he report it to our colleagues in Malmö?"

Hanson nodded. Wallander grabbed the phone.

"Then let's get moving," he said.

The police in Malmö promised to hurry their interrogation of the man. The license number of the stolen car, the model, year, and color were already being sent all over the country.

"BBM 160," said Hanson. "A dove-blue turtle with a white roof. How many of those can there be in this country? A hundred?"

"If the car isn't buried, we'll find it," said Wallander. "When does the sun come up?"

"Around eight or nine o'clock," replied Hanson.

"As soon as it gets light we need a chopper over the preserve. You take care of that."

Hanson nodded. He was just leaving the room when he remembered something he had forgotten to say because he was so tired.

"Damn it! There was one more thing."

"Yes?"

"The guy who called and said that his car was stolen. He was a cop."

Wallander gave Hanson a puzzled look.

"A cop? What do you mean by that?"

"I mean he was a cop. Like you and me."

Chapter Eleven

Kurt Wallander went into one of the holding cells in the police station and lay down for a nap. After a great deal of effort, he managed to set the alarm function on his watch. He was going to allow himself two hours of sleep. When the beeping sound on his wrist woke him up, he had a slight headache. The first thing he thought about was his father. He took a few headache tablets out of the first-aid kit he found in a cupboard and washed them down with a cup of lukewarm coffee. Then he stood there for a long time, trying to decide whether he should take a shower first or call his sister in Stockholm. Finally he went down to the officers' locker room and got into the shower. His headache slowly faded. But he felt weighed down with weariness as he sank onto the chair behind his desk. It was seven fifteen. He knew that his sister was always up early. And she picked up the phone almost as soon as it started ringing. As gently as possible he told her about what had happened.

"Why didn't you call me before?" she asked indignantly. "You must have noticed what was going on."

"I guess I noticed too late," he replied evasively.

They agreed that she would wait to hear about his talk with the hospital social worker before she decided when to come to Skåne.

"How are Mona and Linda?" she asked as the conversation was drawing to a close.

He realized that she didn't know about the separation.

"Fine," he said. "I'll call you back later."

Then he drove over to the hospital. The temperature had dropped below freezing again. An icy wind was blowing through the town from the southwest.

A nurse, who had just received a report from the night staff, told Wallander that his father had slept fitfully during the night. But apparently he had not suffered any physical harm from his nighttime promenade through the fields.

Wallander decided to put off facing his father until he had met with the social worker.

Wallander mistrusted social workers. All too often in his experience he had seen various social-welfare people who were called in when the police had caught juvenile offenders and who had misguided views about what should actually be done. Social workers were too soft and yielding when, in his opinion, they ought to make specific demands instead. More than once he had raged at the welfare authorities because he felt that their lax attitude encouraged young criminals to continue their activities.

But maybe the hospital social worker is different, he thought.

After a short wait he met with a woman in her fifties. Wallander described his father's sudden decline. How unexpected it was, how helpless he felt.

"It might be temporary," said the social worker. "Sometimes elderly people suffer from periods of confusion. If it passes, it might be enough to see that he gets regular home care. If it turns out that he really is chronically senile, then we'll have to come up with some other solution."

They decided that his father should stay through the weekend. Then she would talk to the doctors about what to do next.

Wallander stood up. This woman seemed to know what she was talking about.

"It's hard to be sure what to do," he said.

She nodded.

"Nothing is as troublesome as when we're forced to become parents to our own parents," she said. "I know. My mother finally became so difficult that I couldn't keep her at home."

Kurt Wallander went to see his father, who was in a room with four beds. All of them were occupied. One man was in a cast, another was curled up as if he had severe stomach pains. Wallander's father was lying in bed staring at the ceiling.

"How are you doing, Dad?" he asked.

It took a moment before his father answered. "Leave me alone." He spoke in a low voice. There was no hint of ill-humored petulance. Wallander had the impression that his father's voice was full of sorrow.

He sat on the edge of the bed for a while. Then he left.

"I'll be back, Dad. And Kristina says hello."

Wallander hurried out of the hospital, filled with a sense of powerlessness. The icy wind bit into his face. He didn't feel like going back to the police station, so he called Hanson on the screechy car phone.

"I'm driving over to Malmö," he said. "Have we gotten a chopper in the air?"

"It's been searching for half an hour," replied Hanson. "Nothing yet. We have two canine patrols out too. If that damned car is anywhere in the preserve, we'll find it."

Wallander drove to Malmö. The morning traffic was fierce and intense.

He was constantly forced over toward the shoulder by drivers who were passing without enough room.

I should have taken a marked squad car, he thought. But maybe that doesn't make any difference these days.

It was nine fifteen when he entered the room in the Malmö police station where the man who had had his car stolen was waiting for him. Before Wallander went in to see the man, he talked to the officer who had taken the report of the theft.

"Is it true that he's a cop?" Wallander asked.

"He was," the officer replied. "But he took early retirement."

"Why was that?"

The officer shrugged. "Nerve problems. I don't really know."

"Do you know him?"

"He kept mostly to himself. Even though we worked together for ten years, I can't say that I really knew him. To be honest, I don't think anybody did."

"But surely someone knows him?"

The police officer shrugged again. "I'll find out," he said.

"But anybody could have his car stolen."

Wallander went into the room and said hello to the man, whose name was Rune Bergman. He was fifty-three years old and had been retired for four years. He was thin, with nervous, flitting eyes. Along one side of his nose he had a scar from a knife wound.

Wallander immediately sensed that the man sitting in front of him was on guard. He couldn't say why. But the feeling was quite clear, and it grew stronger as the conversation progressed.

"Tell me what happened," he said. "At four in the morning you discovered your car was missing."

"I was going to drive to Göteborg. I like to start out before dawn when I'm taking a long drive. When I went outside, the car was gone."

"From the garage or from a parking spot?"

"From the street outside my house. I have a garage. But there's so much junk in it that there's no room for the car."

"Where do you live?"

"In a row-house neighborhood near Jägersrö."

"Do you think any of your neighbors saw anything?"

"I asked them. But no one heard or saw anything."

"When did you last see your car?"

"I stayed inside all day. But the car was there the night before."

"Locked?"

"Of course it was locked."

"Did it have a lock on the steering wheel?"

"Unfortunately, no. It was broken."

His answers came easily. But Wallander couldn't rid himself of the notion that the man was on guard.

"What kind of trade show were you going to?" he asked.

The man sitting across from him looked surprised. "What does that have to do with the case?"

"Nothing. I just wondered."

"An air show, if you want to know."

"An air show?"

"I'm interested in old planes. I build a lot of model planes myself."

"Is it true that you took early retirement?"

"What the hell does that have to do with my stolen car?"

"Nothing."

"Why don't you start looking for my car instead of poking around in my personal life?"

"We're already on it. As you know, we think that the person who stole your car may have committed a murder. Or maybe I should say an execution."

The man looked him straight in the eye. The nervous flitting had suddenly stopped.

"That's what I heard," he said.

Wallander had no more questions. "I thought we'd go over to your place. So I can see where the car was parked."

"I can't invite you in for coffee. The place is a mess."

"Are you married?"

"I'm divorced."

They took Wallander's car. The row-house neighborhood was an old one, located just beyond the trotting track at Jägersrö. They stopped outside a yellow brick house with a small front lawn.

"This is where the car was, right where you're parked," said the man. "Right here."

Wallander backed up a few meters and they got out. Wallander noticed that the car must have been parked between two streetlights.

"Are there a lot of cars parked on this street at night?" he asked.

"There's usually one parked in front of every house. A lot of people who live here have two cars. Their garages only hold one."

Wallander pointed at the streetlights. "Do they work?" he asked.

"Yes. I always notice if any of them are broken."

Wallander looked around, thinking. He had no further questions.

"I assume that we'll be talking to you again," he said.

"I want my car back," replied the man.

Wallander suddenly realized that he had one more question.

"Do you have a permit to carry a weapon?" he asked. "Do you own any weapons?"

The man stiffened.

At that instant a crazy idea flashed through Kurt Wallander's mind.

The car theft was completely made up.

The man standing beside him was one of the two men who had shot the Somali the day before.

"What the hell do you mean by that?" said the man. "A weapons permit? Don't tell me you're so fucking stupid that you think I had anything to do with that?"

"You've been a cop, so you should know that we have to ask all kinds of questions," said Wallander. "Do you have any weapons in your house?"

"I have weapons and a permit."

"What kind of weapons?"

"I like to hunt once in a while. I have a Mauser rifle for hunting moose."

"Anything else?"

"A shotgun. A Lanber Baron. It's a Spanish gun. For hunting rabbits."

"I'm thinking of sending someone over to pick up the weapons."

"Why is that?"

"Because the man who was killed yesterday was shot at close range with a shotgun."

The man gave him a disdainful look. "You're crazy," he said. "You're fucking out of your mind."

Wallander left. He drove straight back to the Malmö police station. He borrowed a phone and called Ystad. No car had been found yet. Then he asked to speak to the officer in charge of the department for homicide and violent crimes in Malmö. Wallander had met him once before and found him to be overbearing and self-important. That was on the same occasion when he met first Göran Boman.

Wallander explained the case he was working on.

"I want to have his weapons checked," he said. "I want his house searched. I want to know whether he has any connections with racist organizations."

The police officer gave him a long look. ' Do you have any reason whatsoever to believe that he made up the story about a stolen car? That he might be involved in the murder?"

"He owns guns. And we have to investigate everything."

"There are hundreds of thousands of shotguns in this country. And what makes you think I can get authorization to search his house when the case is about a stolen car?"

"This case has top priority," said Wallander, starting to get annoyed. "I'll call the county police chief. The chief of the *National Police*, if necessary."

"I'll do what I can," said the officer. "But it's never popular to mess around in the personal life of a colleague. And what do you think would happen if this got out to the press?"

"I don't give a shit," said Wallander. "I've got three murders on my hands. And somebody who's promised me a fourth one. Which I intend to prevent."

On his way to Ystad, Wallander stopped at Hageholm. The crime technicians were just wrapping up their investigation. At the scene he went over Rydberg's theory about how the murder most likely occurred, and he thought he was right. The car had probably been parked at the spot Rydberg had pointed out.

Suddenly he realized that he had forgotten to ask the policeman whose car was stolen whether he smoked. Or whether he ate apples.

He continued on to Ystad. It was noon. On his way in he ran into a temp who was on her way out to lunch. He asked her to pick up a pizza for him.

He stuck his head in Hanson's door; still no car.

"Meeting in my office in fifteen minutes," said Wallander. "Try to round everybody up. You should be able to reach anybody who isn't here by phone."

Without taking off his overcoat, Wallander sat down and called his sister again. They decided that he would pick her up at Sturup airport at ten o'clock the following morning.

Then he touched the lump on his forehead, which was now changing color, shifting to yellow and black and red.

Twenty minutes later everyone except Martinson and Svedberg had shown up.

"Svedberg is out digging around in a gravel pit," said Rydberg. "Somebody called and said they saw a mysterious car out there. Martinson is trying to track down someone in the Citroën club who supposedly knows everything about all the Citroëns on the road in Skåne. Some dermatologist from Lund."

"A dermatologist from Lund?" Wallander asked in surprise.

"There are hookers who collect stamps," said Rydberg. "Why shouldn't a dermatologist love Citroëns?"

Wallander reported on his meeting with the cop in Malmö.

He could hear how hollow it sounded when he said that he had ordered a thorough investigation of the man.

"That doesn't sound very likely," said Hanson. "A cop who wants to commit a murder wouldn't be dumb enough to report his own car stolen, would he?"

"Maybe not," said Wallander. "But we can't afford to ignore a single lead, no matter how unlikely it seems."

Then the discussion turned to the missing car.

"We aren't getting many tips from the public," said Hanson. "Which just reinforces my belief that the car never left the area."

Wallander unfolded the topographic map, and they leaned over it as if preparing for battle.

"The lakes," said Rydberg. "Krageholm Lake, Svaneholm Lake. Let's assume that they drove out there and ditched the car. There are little roads all over the place."

"It still sounds risky," objected Wallander. "Somebody could easily have seen them."

They decided at any rate to drag the lakes along the shore. And to send some men out to search through abandoned barns.

A canine patrol from Malmö had been out searching without finding a single trace. The helicopter search had produced no results either.

"Could your Arab have been mistaken?" wondered Hanson.

Wallander thought about this for a moment.

"We'll bring him in again," he said. "We'll test him on six

different kinds of cars. Including a Citroën."

Hanson promised to take care of the witness.

Then they moved on to a summary of the search for the perpetrators in Lenarp. Here too the car that the early-morning truck driver had seen still eluded them.

Wallander could see that the officers were tired. It was Saturday, and many of them had been working nonstop for a long time.

"We'll put Lenarp on hold until Monday morning," he said. "Right now we're going to concentrate on Hageholm. Whoever isn't needed at the moment should go home and get some rest. It looks like next week is going to be just as busy as this one."

Then he remembered that Björk would be back to work on Monday.

"Björk will be taking over," he said. "So I want to take this opportunity to thank everyone for their efforts so far."

"Did we pass?" asked Hanson sarcastically.

"You get the highest marks," replied Wallander.

After the meeting he asked Rydberg to stay behind for a moment. He realized that he needed to talk through the situation with somebody in peace and quiet. And Rydberg was, as usual, the one whose opinion he respected most. He told him about Göran Boman's efforts in Kristianstad. Rydberg nodded thoughtfully. Wallander saw that he was obviously hesitant.

"It might be a dud," said Rydberg. "This double murder is puzzling me more and more, the longer I think about it."

"In what way?" asked Wallander.

"I can't get away from what the woman said before she died. I have a feeling that deep inside her tormented and wounded consciousness, she must have realized that her husband was dead. And that she was going to die too. I think it's human instinct to offer a solution to a mystery if there's nothing else left. And she said only one word: 'foreign.' She repeated it. Four or five times. It has to mean something. And then we have that noose. The knot. You said it yourself. That murder smells of revenge and hatred. But we're still looking in a completely different direction."

"Svedberg has made a chart of all of Lövgren's relatives," said

Wallander. "There are no foreign connections. Only Swedish farmers and one or two craftsmen."

"Don't forget his double life," said Rydberg. "Nyström described the neighbor he had known for forty years as an ordinary man. With no assets. After two days we discovered that none of this was true. So what's to prevent us from finding other false bottoms to this story?"

"So what do you think we should do?"

"Exactly what we are doing. But be open to the possibility that we might be on the wrong track."

Then they switched over to talking about the murdered Somali. Ever since he left Malmö, Wallander had been carrying around an idea.

"Can you hang in there a little longer?" he asked.

"Sure," replied Rydberg, surprised. "Of course I can."

"There was something about that police officer," said Wallander. "I know it's mostly a hunch. An extremely dubious trait in a cop. But I thought we ought to keep an eye on that guy, you and I. Through the weekend, in any case. Then we can see whether we should keep it up and bring in more manpower. But if I'm right, that he might be involved himself, that his car wasn't stolen at all, then he should be feeling a little uneasy right now."

"I agree with Hanson when he said that no cop would be stupid enough to pretend his car had been stolen if he were planning to commit a murder," Rydberg objected.

"I think you're both wrong," replied Wallander. "The same way that he was wrong. Thinking that just because he had once been a cop, that fact alone would steer all suspicion away from him."

Rydberg rubbed his aching knee.

"We'll do as you say, then," he said. "What I believe or don't believe is irrelevant as long as you think it's important that we proceed."

"I want to put him under surveillance," said Wallander. "We'll split up the shifts until Monday morning. It'll be rough, but we can do it. I can take the night shifts, if you like."

It was noon. Rydberg said that he might as well handle the surveillance until midnight. Wallander gave him the address.

At that instant the temp came into the office with the pizza he had ordered.

"Have you eaten?" Wallander asked.

"Yes," replied Rydberg hesitantly.

"No you haven't. Take this one and I'll get another."

Rydberg ate the pizza while sitting at Wallander's desk. Then he wiped his mouth and stood up.

"Maybe you're right," he said.

"Maybe," replied Wallander.

Nothing happened the rest of the day.

The car continued to elude them. The fire department dragged the lakes without finding anything except parts of an old combine.

Only a few tips came in from the public.

Reporters from the newspapers, radio, and TV called incessantly, wanting updated status reports. Wallander repeated his appeal for tips about a pale blue Citroën. Nervous directors of the refugee camps called in, demanding increased police protection. Wallander answered as patiently as he could.

At four o'clock an old woman was hit by a car and killed in Bjäresjö. Svedberg, who had returned from the gravel pit, led the investigation, even though Wallander had promised him the afternoon off.

Näslund called at five o'clock, and Wallander could hear that he was tipsy. He wanted to know whether anything was happening, or whether he could go to a party in Skillinge. Wallander told him to go ahead.

He called the hospital twice to ask about his father. They told him that his father was tired and uncommunicative.

Right after his conversation with Näslund, he called up Sten Widén. A familiar voice answered the phone.

"I was the one who helped you with the ladder up to the loft," Wallander said. "The man you guessed was a cop. I'd like to talk to Sten, if he's there."

"He's in Denmark buying horses," replied the young woman, whose name was Louise.

"When will he be back?"

"Maybe tomorrow."

"Would you ask him to call me?"

"I'll do that."

He hung up. Wallander had the distinct impression that Sten Widén was not in Denmark at all. Maybe he was even standing right next to the young woman and listening in.

Maybe they were together in the unmade bed when he called.

There was no word from Rydberg.

He gave his memo to one of the patrol officers, who promised to hand it to Björk the minute he stepped off the plane at Sturup airport later that evening.

Then Wallander went through his bills, which he had forgotten to pay on the first of the month. He filled out a bunch of postal banking forms and enclosed a check in the manila envelope. He realized that he wasn't going to be able to afford either a VCR or a stereo this month.

Then he answered an inquiry about whether he intended to participate in a tour to the Royal Opera in Copenhagen at the end of February. He said yes. *Woyzeck* was one of the operas he had never seen staged.

At eight o'clock he read through Svedberg's report on the fatal accident in Bjäresjö. He could see at once that there was no question of any kind of criminal proceedings. The woman had stepped right out into the road in front of a car traveling at a low speed. The farmer who was driving the car was not at fault. All the eyewitness accounts agreed. He made a note to see to it that Anette Brolin read through the investigation report after the autopsy on the woman was done.

At eight thirty two men started slugging each other in an apartment building on the outskirts of Ystad. Peters and Norén quickly managed to separate the combatants. They were two brothers who were well known to the police. They got into a fight about three times a year.

A greyhound was reported lost in Marsvinsholm. Since the dog had been seen heading west, he passed the report on to his colleagues in Skurup.

At ten o'clock he left the police station. It was cold and the wind was blowing in gusts. The sky was clear and filled with stars. Still no snow. He went home and put on heavy long underwear and a woolen cap. Absentmindedly he also watered the drooping plants in the kitchen window. Then he drove to Malmö.

Norén was on duty that night. Wallander had promised to call in regularly. But presumably Norén would have his hands full with Björk, who would be coming home to discover that his vacation was definitely over.

Wallander stopped at a motel restaurant in Svedala. He hesitated for a long time before deciding on only a salad. He doubted that this was the proper time to change his eating habits. But he knew that he might fall asleep if he ate too much before an all-night shift.

He drank several cups of strong coffee after he finished eating. An elderly woman came over to his table and wanted to sell him *The Watch Tower*. He bought a copy, thinking that it would be sufficiently dull reading to last all night.

Just after eleven he pulled out onto E14 again and drove the last stretch to Malmö. He suddenly started to doubt the value of the assignment he had given Rydberg and himself. How justified was he in trusting his intuition? Shouldn't Hanson's and Rydberg's objections have been enough for him to drop the idea of this night-time stakeout?

He felt unsure of himself. Irresolute.

And the salad had not filled him up.

It was a few minutes past eleven thirty when he turned onto a cross street near the yellow row house where Rune Bergman lived. He pulled his cap over his ears as he stepped out into the cold night. All around him were dark houses. In the distance he heard the screech of car tires. He kept to the shadows as much as possible and turned down the street called Rosenallé.

Almost at once he caught sight of Rydberg, who was standing next to a tall chestnut tree. The trunk was so thick that it hid him entirely. Wallander discovered him only because it was the only conceivable hiding place that allowed a view of the yellow row house.

Wallander slipped into the shadow of the mighty tree trunk. Rydberg was freezing. He was rubbing his hands together and stamping his feet.

"Anything going on?" asked Wallander.

"Not much in twelve hours," replied Rydberg. "At four o'clock he went over to a local store to buy groceries. Two hours later he came out to close the gate, which had blown open. But he's definitely on guard. I think you may be right after all."

Rydberg pointed at the house next to the one where Rune Bergman lived.

"That one's empty," he said. "From the yard you can see both the street and his back door. In case he takes it into his head to slip out that way. There's a bench where you can sit. If your clothes are warm enough."

Wallander had noticed a phone booth on his way over to Bergman's house. He asked Rydberg to go over and call Norén. If nothing urgent was happening, Rydberg could get in his car and drive home.

"I'll be back around seven," said Rydberg. "Don't freeze to death."

He vanished without a sound. Wallander stood still for a moment, looking at the yellow house. Lights were on in two of the windows, one on the lower floor and one upstairs. The curtains were drawn. He looked at his watch. Three minutes past midnight. Rydberg had not returned. So everything must be quiet at the police station in Ystad.

He hurried across the street and opened the gate to the yard of the empty house. He fumbled his way in the dark and found the bench that Rydberg had mentioned. From there he had a good view. To keep warm, he started pacing, five steps forward and five steps back.

The next time he looked at his watch, it was only ten minutes to one. It was going to be a long night. He was already feeling cold. He tried to make the time pass by studying the starry sky. When his neck started to hurt, he resumed his pacing.

At one thirty the light on the ground floor went out. Wallander thought he could hear a radio on the second floor.

Rune Bergman keeps late hours, he thought.

Maybe that's what happens if you take early retirement.

At five minutes to two a car drove past. Immediately followed by another one. Then it was quiet again.

The light was on upstairs. Wallander was freezing.

At five minutes to three the light was turned off. Wallander listened for the radio. But everything was quiet. He flapped his arms to keep warm.

In his head he was humming the melody of a Strauss waltz.

The sound was so slight that he almost missed it.

The click of a door latch. That was all. Wallander stopped flapping his arms at once and listened.

Then he noticed the shadow.

The man must have been moving very quietly. Even so, Wallander caught a glimpse of Rune Bergman as he silently disappeared through the backyard of the yellow house. Wallander waited a few seconds. Then he cautiously climbed over the fence. It was hard to get his bearings in the dark, but he could vaguely make out a narrow passageway between a shed and the yard opposite Bergman's house. He moved quickly. Much too quickly, considering he could hardly see a thing.

Then he emerged onto the street running parallel to Rosenallé.

If he had arrived one second later, he would not have seen Rune Bergman vanish down a cross street on the right.

For a moment Wallander hesitated. His car was parked only fifty meters away. If he didn't get it now, and Bergman had a car parked somewhere in the vicinity, he would have no chance of following him.

He ran like a madman for his car. His frozen joints cracked and he was out of breath after only a few meters. He yanked open the door, fumbled with his keys, and swiftly decided to try to intercept Rune Bergman.

He turned down the street that he thought was the right one. Too late he realized that it was a dead end. He swore and backed up. Bergman probably had a lot of streets to choose from. There was also a park nearby.

Make up your mind, he thought furiously. Make up your mind, damn it.

He headed toward the big parking lot, which lay between the Jägersrö trotting track and some large department stores. He was just about to give up when he caught sight of Bergman. He was in a phone booth by a newly built hotel near the entrance to the track stables.

Wallander slammed on the brakes and turned off his engine and headlights.

The man in the phone booth hadn't noticed him.

Several minutes later a cab pulled up near the hotel. Rune Bergman got into the back seat, and Wallander turned on his engine.

The cab took the freeway heading toward Göteborg. Wallander had to let a semi go by before he took up the chase.

He glanced at the gas gauge. He wasn't going to be able to follow the cab farther than Halmstad.

Suddenly he noticed that the cab was blinking to turn right. He was going to take the exit for Lund. Wallander followed.

The cab stopped at the train station. As Wallander drove past, he saw Rune Bergman paying his fare. He turned onto a side street and carelessly parked in the middle of a crosswalk.

Bergman was walking fast. Wallander followed him in the shadows.

Rydberg had been right. The man was on his guard.

Suddenly he stopped short and looked around.

Wallander threw himself headlong into an entryway. He struck his forehead on the protruding edge of a step and could feel the lump above his eye split open. Blood ran down his face. He wiped it off with his glove, counted to ten, and continued his pursuit. The blood over his eye was sticky.

Bergman stopped outside a building covered with scaffolding and protective sacking. Again he looked around, and Wallander crouched down behind a parked car.

Then he was gone.

Wallander waited until he heard the door shut. Soon afterward the lights went on in a room on the third floor.

He ran across the street and pushed his way behind the sacking. Without hesitating, he climbed up onto the scaffold's first platform.

It creaked and groaned under his feet. He had to keep wiping away the blood trickling into his eye. Then he heaved himself up onto the second platform. The illuminated windows were now only a little more than a meter above his head. He took out his handkerchief and wrapped it around his head as an improvised bandage.

Then he cautiously hauled himself up onto the next platform. The effort left him so exhausted that he had to lie on the scaffolding for over a minute before he could go on. Carefully he crept forward along the cold planks, which were covered with scraped-off stucco. He didn't dare think about how far above the ground he was. He would just get dizzy instantly.

Cautiously he peeked over the window ledge outside the first lighted room. Through the thin curtains he could see a woman sleeping in a double bed. The covers next to her had been thrown back, as if someone had gotten out of bed in a hurry.

He crawled farther.

When he peeked over the next window ledge, he saw Rune Bergman talking to a man wearing a dark-brown bathrobe.

Wallander felt as if he had actually seen this man before. That's how well the young Romanian woman had described the man who was standing in a field eating an apple.

He felt his heart pounding.

So he had been right after all. It had to be the same man.

The two men were talking in low voices. Wallander couldn't hear what they were saying. Suddenly the man in the bathrobe disappeared through a door. At the same moment Rune Bergman looked straight at Wallander.

Caught, he thought, as he pulled back his head.

Those bastards won't hesitate to shoot me.

He was paralyzed with fear.

I'm going to die, he thought desperately. They're going to shoot my head off.

But no one came to shoot him in the head. Finally he got up the nerve to peek inside again.

The man in the bathrobe was standing there, eating an apple. Bergman was holding two shotguns. He put one of them down on a table. The other one he stuffed under his coat. Wallander realized that he had seen more than enough. He turned around and crept back the same way he had come.

How it happened, he would never know.

He lost his footing in the dark. When he reached for the scaffolding, his hand grabbed at empty space.

Then he fell.

It all happened so fast that he had barely enough time to think that he was going to die.

Right above the ground one of his legs got caught in a gap between two planks. The pain was horrendous when he jerked to a stop. But he was hanging upside down with his head barely a meter above the pavement.

He tried to wriggle loose. But his foot was wedged tight. He was hanging in midair, unable to do anything. The blood was pounding in his temples.

The pain was so bad that he had tears in his eyes.

At that moment he heard the door open.

Rune Bergman had left the apartment.

Wallander bit his knuckles to keep from screaming.

Through the sacking he saw the man stop suddenly. Right in front of him.

He saw a flash.

The shot, thought Wallander. Now I'm going to die.

Then he realized that Bergman had lit a cigarette.

The footsteps moved away.

Wallander was about to black out from the pressure of the blood in his head. The image of Linda flickered past.

With enormous effort he managed to grab hold of one of the uprights on the scaffolding. With one hand he pulled himself up far enough to get a grip on the planks where his foot was wedged tight. He gathered all his strength for one final attempt. Then he yanked hard. His foot came loose, and he landed on his back in a mound of gravel. He lay absolutely still, trying to feel if anything was broken.

Then he stood up, and he had to hold onto the wall so he wouldn't fall over from dizziness.

It took him almost twenty minutes to make his way back to the car. He saw the hands of the train station clock pointing to four thirty.

Wallander sank into the driver's seat and closed his eyes.

Then he drove back to Ystad.

I have to get some sleep, he thought. Tomorrow is another day. Then I'll have to do what has to be done.

He groaned when he looked at his face in the bathroom mirror. He rinsed his wounds with warm water.

It was almost six by the time he crawled between the sheets. He set the alarm clock for quarter to seven. He didn't dare sleep any later than that.

He tried to find the position that hurt the least.

Just as he was falling asleep, he was jerked awake by a bang on the front door.

The morning paper.

Then he stretched out again.

In his dreams Anette Brolin was coming toward him.

Somewhere a horse neighed.

It was Sunday, January fourteenth. The day arrived with increasing wind from the northeast.

Kurt Wallander slept.

Chapter Twelve

He thought he had slept for a long time. But when he woke up and looked at the clock on the nightstand, he realized that he had been asleep for only seven minutes. It was the telephone that woke him. Rydberg was calling from a phone booth in Malmö.

"Come on back," said Wallander. "You don't have to stand there freezing. Come here, to my place."

"What happened?"

"It's him."

"Are you sure?"

"Absolutely positive."

"I'm on my way."

Kurt Wallander climbed laboriously out of bed. His body ached and his temples were throbbing. While the coffee was brewing he sat at the kitchen table with a pocket mirror and a cotton ball. With great difficulty he succeeded in fastening a gauze pad over the wound on his forehead. He thought his whole face was nothing but shades of blue and purple.

Forty-three minutes later Rydberg stood in the doorway.

While they drank coffee, Wallander told him his story.

"Good," Rydberg said afterward. "Excellent footwork. Now we'll bring in those bastards. What was the name of the guy in Lund?"

"I forgot to look at the name in the entryway. And we're not the ones who'll bring them in. That's Björk's job."

"Is he back?"

"He was supposed to arrive last night."

"Then let's get him out of bed."

"The prosecutor too. And the action will probably have to be coordinated with our colleagues in Malmö and Lund, right?"

While Wallander was getting dressed, Rydberg was on the phone. With satisfaction Wallander could hear that he wasn't taking no for an answer.

He wondered whether Anette Brolin's husband was visiting this weekend.

Rydberg stood in the bedroom doorway and watched him knot his tie.

"You look like a boxer," he said, laughing. "A punch-drunk boxer."

"Did you get hold of Björk?"

"He seems to have spent the evening catching up with everything that's happened. He was relieved to hear that we had solved one of the murders, at least."

"The prosecutor?"

"She'll come right away."

"Was she the one who answered the phone?"

Rydberg looked at him in surprise. "Who else would have answered?"

"Her husband, for instance."

"What difference would that make?"

Wallander didn't feel like answering. "Goddamn, I feel like shit," he said instead. "Let's go."

They went out into the early dawn. A gusty wind was still blowing and the sky was overcast with dark clouds.

"You think it's going to snow?" asked Wallander.

"Not before February," said Rydberg. "I can feel it. But then it'll be a hard winter."

A Sunday calm prevailed at the police station. Norén had been relieved by Svedberg. Rydberg gave him a brief rundown of what had happened during the night.

"Well, I'll be damned," said Svedberg. "A cop?"

"An ex-cop."

"Where did he hide the car?"

"We don't know yet."

"Is the case airtight?"

"I think so."

Björk and Anette Brolin arrived at the police station simultaneously. Björk, who was fifty-four years old and originally from Västmanland, had a nice tan. Wallander had always imagined him to be the ideal chief for a medium-sized police district. He was friendly, not too intelligent, and at the same time extremely concerned with the good name and reputation of the police.

He gave Kurt Wallander a dismayed look. "You really look terrible."

"They beat me up," said Wallander.

"Beat you up? Who?"

"The cops. That's what happens when you're acting chief. They let you have it."

Björk laughed.

Anette Brolin looked at him with what seemed to be genuine sympathy.

"That must hurt," she said.

"I'll be all right," replied Wallander.

He turned his face away when he answered remembering that he had forgotten to brush his teeth.

They all went into Björk's office.

Since there was no written report, Wallander gave a verbal summary of the case. Both Björk and Anette Brolin asked a lot of questions.

"If it had been anyone but you who dragged me out of bed on Sunday morning with this kind of cops-and-robbers story, I wouldn't have believed it," said Björk.

Then he turned to Anette Brolin. "Do we have enough to detain them? Or should we just bring them in for questioning?"

"I'll get the detention order on them based on the interrogation results," said Anette Brolin. "Then, of course, it would be good if that Romanian woman could identify the man in Lund in a line-up."

"We'll need a court order for that," said Björk.

"Yes," said Anette Brolin. "But we could do a provisional identification."

Wallander and Rydberg gave her an interested look.

"We could bring in the woman from the refugee camp," she went on. "Then they could walk past each other by chance here in the hallway."

Wallander nodded in approval. Anette Brolin was a prosecutor who was Per Åkeson's equal when it came to taking a flexible view of the applicable rules.

"All right," said Björk. "I'll get in touch with our colleagues in Malmö and Lund. Then we'll pick up the suspects in two hours. At ten o'clock."

"What about the woman in the bed?" asked Kurt Wallander. "The one in Lund?"

"We'll bring her in too," said Björk. "How should we divide up the interrogations?"

"I want Rune Bergman," said Wallander. "Rydberg can talk to the man who munches on apples."

"At three o'clock we'll decide about the detention order," said Anette Brolin. "I'll be at home until then."

Wallander accompanied her out to the lobby. "I was thinking about asking you to dinner last night," he said. "But something came up."

"There'll be plenty more evenings," she said. "I think you've done a good job on this case. How did you figure out that he was the one?"

"I didn't. It was just a hunch."

He watched her as she headed toward town. He realized that he hadn't thought of Mona at all since the evening they had dinner together.

Then everything started to move very fast.

Hanson was wrenched out of his Sunday calm and ordered to bring in the Romanian woman and an interpreter.

"Our colleagues don't sound happy," Björk said with concern. "It's never popular to bring in someone from your own force. It's going to be a dismal winter because of this."

"What do you mean by dismal?" asked Wallander.

"New attacks on the police force."

"He was retired early, wasn't he?"

"Even so. The papers will be screaming about the fact that the murderer was a cop. There will be new persecution of the force."

At ten o'clock Wallander returned to the building that was covered in sacking and construction scaffolding. To assist him he had four plainclothes policemen from Lund.

"He has weapons," said Wallander while they were still sitting in the car. "And he has committed a cold-blooded execution. Still, I think we can take it easy. He's certainly not counting on the fact that we're on his tail. Two weapons drawn should be enough."

Wallander had brought along his service revolver from Ystad.

On the way to Lund he tried to remember when he had last taken it out. He decided it was over three years earlier, in conjunction with the capture of an escaped convict from Kumla prison who had barricaded himself in a summerhouse near Mossby beach.

Now they were sitting in a car outside the building in Lund. Wallander realized that he had climbed considerably higher than he had thought. If he had fallen all the way to the ground, he would have crushed his spine.

That morning the police in Lund had sent out an inspector disguised as a newspaper carrier to case the apartment.

"Let's review," said Wallander. "No back stairs?"

The officer sitting next to him in the front seat shook his head.

"No scaffolding on the rear side?"

"Nothing."

According to the officer, the apartment was occupied by a man named Valfrid Ström.

He wasn't listed in any police files. No one knew how he made his living either.

At ten o'clock on the dot they got out of the car and crossed the street. One officer stayed at the outside door of the building. There was an intercom system, but it was out of order. Wallander jimmied the door open with a screwdriver.

"One man stay in the stairwell," he said. "You and I will go upstairs. What was your name?"

"Enberg."

"You've got a first name, haven't you?"

"Kalle."

"Okay, let's go, Kalle."

They listened in the darkness outside the door.

Wallander drew his pistol and nodded to Kalle Enberg to do the same.

Then he rang the doorbell.

The door was opened by a woman wearing a housecoat. Wallander recognized her from the night before. It was the same woman who had been asleep in the double bed.

He hid his pistol behind his back.

"We're with the police," he said. "We're looking for your husband, Valfrid Ström."

The woman, who was in her forties and had a harried expression, looked scared.

Then she stepped aside and let the policemen in.

Suddenly Valfrid Ström was standing in front of them. He was dressed in a green jogging suit.

"Police," said Wallander. "We need to ask you to come with us."

The man with the half-moon-shaped bald spot looked at him tensely. "Why?"

"For questioning."

"About what?"

"You'll find out at the station."

Then Wallander turned to the woman. "You'd better come along too. Put on some clothes."

The man facing him seemed completely calm. "I'm not going anywhere if you don't tell me why," he said. "Perhaps you could start by showing me some ID?"

When Kurt Wallander put his right hand in his inside pocket, he couldn't hide the fact that he was carrying a pistol. He switched it over to his left hand and fumbled for his billfold, where he kept his ID.

At the same instant Ström leaped straight at him. He butted Wallander right in the forehead, smack in the middle of his swollen wound. Wallander went sailing backward, and the pistol flew

out of his hand. Kalle Enberg didn't have time to react before
the man in the green jogging suit had disappeared out the door.
The woman shrieked, and Wallander fumbled for his pistol. Then
he dashed down the stairs after the man, yelling a warning to the
two officers posted farther down.

Ström was fast. He gave the policeman standing inside the door
an elbow to the chin. The man outside was rammed by the front
door when Ström flung himself out into the street. Wallander, who
could hardly see with the blood streaming into his eyes, stumbled over the unconscious policeman lying in the stairwell. He
pulled at the safety on his pistol, which was stuck.

Then he was out on the street.

"Which way did he go?" he called to the bewildered policeman who had gotten entangled in the sacking.

"To the left."

Wallander ran. He could see Ström's green jogging suit just
as he ducked under a viaduct. He tore off his cap and wiped his
face. Several elderly women, who looked like they were on their
way to church, jumped aside in fright. He ran under the viaduct
just as a train rumbled by overhead.

When he reached the street level again, he saw how Ström
stopped a car, dragged out the driver, and drove off.

The only vehicle in the vicinity was a large horse van. The
driver was pulling a pack of condoms out of a vending machine
on the wall of the building. When Wallander came racing up, his
pistol drawn and blood running down his face, the man dropped
the condoms and ran off.

Wallander climbed into the driver's seat. Behind him he heard
a horse whinny. The engine was running, and he threw it into
first gear.

He thought he had lost sight of the car Valfrid Ström had stolen,
but then he saw it again. The car drove through a red light and
continued down a narrow street that led straight toward the cathe-
dral. Wallander was shifting gears fast, trying not to lose sight of
the car. Horses were whinnying behind him, and he smelled the
odor of warm manure.

In a tight curve he almost lost control of the van. He caromed off two cars parked by the curb, but finally managed to straighten out the van again.

The chase proceeded toward the hospital and then through an industrial area. Wallander suddenly discovered that the van was equipped with a cellular phone. He tried to dial the emergency number with one hand while struggling to keep the heavy vehicle on the road.

Just as the emergency operator answered, he had to negotiate a curve.

The phone fell out of his hand, and he realized that he wouldn't be able to reach it without stopping.

This is crazy, he thought in desperation. Totally nuts.

At the same time he remembered his sister. Right now he was supposed to be meeting her at Sturup airport.

In the roundabout by the entrance to Staffanstorp the chase ended.

Ström was forced to screech to a stop for a bus that had already entered the roundabout. He lost control of the car and ran straight into a cement column. Wallander, who was about a hundred meters behind him, saw the flames shooting out of the car. He braked so hard that the van slid into the ditch and tipped over. The back gates flew open and three horses jumped out and galloped away across the fields.

Ström was flung out of the car on impact. One foot was sliced off. His face had been gashed by shards of glass.

Even before Wallander reached him he could tell that he was dead.

People came running out of the nearby houses. Cars pulled over to the side of the road.

Suddenly he noticed that he was still holding his pistol.

A few minutes later the first squad car arrived. Then an ambulance. Kurt Wallander showed his ID and made a call from the squad car. He asked to talk to Björk.

"Did it go all right?" asked Björk. "Rune Bergman has been picked up and is on the way here. Everything went without a hitch.

And the Yugoslavian woman is waiting here with her interpreter."

"Send them over to the morgue at Lund General Hospital," said Wallander. "Now she'll have to identify a corpse. By the way, she's Romanian."

"What the hell do you mean by that?" said Björk.

"Just what I said," replied Wallander and hung up.

At that moment he saw one of the horses come galloping across the field. It was a beautiful white horse.

He didn't think he'd ever seen such a beautiful horse.

When he got back to Ystad the news of Valfrid Ström's death had already made the rounds. The woman who was his wife had collapsed, and a doctor refused to let the police interrogate her.

Rydberg told Wallander that Rune Bergman denied everything. He hadn't stolen his own car and then ditched it. He hadn't been at Hageholm. He hadn't visited Valfrid Ström the night before.

He demanded to be taken back to Malmö at once.

"What a goddamned weasel," said Wallander. "I'll crack him."

"Nobody is doing any cracking here," said Björk. "That ridiculous high-speed chase through Lund has caused enough trouble already. I don't understand why four full-grown policemen can't manage to bring in an unarmed man for questioning. By the way, do you know that one of those horses was run over? Its name was Super Nova, and its owner put a value of a hundred thousand kronor on it."

Wallander felt anger rise up inside him.

Why couldn't Björk grasp that it was support he needed? Not this officious whining.

"Now we're going to wait for the Romanian woman's identification," said Björk. "Nobody talks to the press or the media except me."

"Thank heaven for that," said Wallander.

He went back to his office with Rydberg and closed the door.

"Do you have any idea how you look?" Rydberg asked.

"Don't tell me, please."

"Your sister called. I asked Martinson to drive out and pick her up at the airport. I assumed that you had forgotten. He said he'd take care of her until you had time."

Wallander nodded gratefully.

A few minutes later, Björk stormed in.

"The ID is positive," he said. "We've got the murderer we were looking for."

"Did she recognize him?"

"Without a doubt. It was the same man who was eating the apple out in the field."

"Who was he?" asked Rydberg.

"Valfrid Ström called himself a businessman," replied Björk. "Forty-seven years old. But the Security Police in Stockholm didn't take long to answer our inquiry. Ström has been engaged in nationalist movements since the sixties. First in something called the Democratic Alliance, later in much more militant factions. But how he ended up a cold-blooded murderer—that's something Rune Bergman may be able to tell us. Or his wife."

Wallander stood up. "Now we'll tackle Bergman," he said.

All three of them went into the room where Rune Bergman sat smoking.

Kurt Wallander led the interrogation.

He went on the offensive at once.

"Do you know what I was doing last night?" he asked.

Bergman gave him a look of contempt. "How would I know that?"

"I tailed you to Lund."

Wallander thought he caught a fleeting shift in the man's face.

"I followed you to Lund," repeated Wallander. "And I climbed up on the scaffolding outside the building where Ström lived. I saw you exchange your shotgun for another one. Now Ström is dead. But a witness has identified him as the murderer at Hageholm. What do you have to say to all this?"

Bergman didn't say a word. He lit a new cigarette and stared into space.

"Okay, we'll take it from the top," said Wallander. "We know how everything happened. There are only two things we don't know. First, what did you do with your car? Second, why did you shoot the Somali?"

Rune Bergman wasn't talking.

Right after three that afternoon he was formally put under arrest and assigned a public defender. The charge was murder or accessory to murder.

At four o'clock Wallander questioned Valfrid Ström's wife briefly. She was still in shock, but she answered his questions. He found out that Ström dealt in importing exclusive automobiles.

She also told him that Ström hated the Swedish refugee policy.

She had only been married to him for a little over a year.

Wallander had the distinct impression that she would get over her loss quite soon.

After the interrogation he talked with Rydberg and Björk. Then they released the woman with a warning not to leave town, and she was taken back to Lund.

Just before they left, Wallander and Rydberg made another attempt to get Rune Bergman to talk. The public defender, who was young and ambitious, claimed that there were no grounds for submission of evidence, and he was of the opinion that the arrest was equivalent to a preliminary miscarriage of justice.

At about the same time Rydberg had an idea.

"Where was Ström trying to escape to?" he asked Wallander. He pointed at a map.

"The chase ended at Staffanstorp. Maybe he had a warehouse there or somewhere in the vicinity. It's not far from Hageholm, if you know all the back roads."

A conversation with Ström's wife confirmed that Rydberg was on the right track. The man did indeed have a warehouse between Staffanstorp and Veberöd where he kept his imported cars. Rydberg drove over there in a squad car and soon called Wallander back.

"Bingo," he said. "There's a pale-blue Citroën here."

"Maybe we ought to teach our children to identify cars by their sound," said Wallander.

He tackled Rune Bergman again. But the man said nothing.

Rydberg returned to Ystad after a preliminary examination of the Citroën. In the glove compartment he found a box of shotgun

HENNING MANKELL

shells. In the meantime the police in Malmö and Lund searched Bergman's and Ström's apartments.

"It seems as though these two gentlemen were members of some sort of Swedish Ku Klux Klan movement," said Björk. "I'm afraid we're going to have a knotty problem to untangle. There might be more people involved."

Rune Bergman still wasn't talking.

Wallander was greatly relieved that Björk was back and could take charge of dealing with the media. His face was stung and burned, and he was very tired. By six o'clock he finally had time to call Martinson and talk to his sister. Then he drove over and picked her up. She was startled when she saw his battered face.

"It might be best if Dad didn't see me," said Wallander. "I'll wait for you in the car."

His sister had already visited their father in the hospital that day. The old man was still tired, but he brightened up a little when he saw his daughter.

"I don't think he remembers much about that night," she said as they drove up to the hospital. "Maybe that's just as well."

Wallander sat in the car and waited while she visited their father again. He closed his eyes and listened to a Rossini opera. When she opened the car door, he jumped. He had fallen asleep.

Together they drove to the house in Löderup.

Wallander could see that his sister was shocked at their father's decline. They helped each other clean up the stinking garbage and filthy clothes.

"How could this happen?" she asked, and Wallander felt that she was blaming him.

Maybe she was right. Maybe he could have done more. At least discovered his father's decline in time.

They stopped and bought groceries and then returned to Mariagatan. At dinner they talked about what would happen to their father.

"He'll die if we put him in a retirement home," she said.

"What's the alternative?" asked Wallander. "He can't live here. He can't live with you. The house in Löderup won't work either.

What's left?"

They agreed that it would be best, all the same, if their father could keep on living in his own house, with regular home-care visits.

"He has never liked me," said Wallander as they were drinking coffee.

"Of course he does."

"Not since I decided to be a cop."

"You think maybe he had something else in mind for you?"

"Yes, but what? He never says anything."

Wallander made up the sofa for his sister.

When they had no more to say about their father, Wallander told her about everything that had happened. Suddenly he realized that the old sense of intimacy, which had always bound them before, was gone.

We haven't gotten together often enough, he thought. She doesn't even dare ask me why Mona and I went our separate ways.

He brought out a half-empty bottle of cognac. She shook her head, so he just filled his own glass.

The evening news was dominated by the story of Valfrid Ström. Rune Bergman's identity was not revealed. Wallander knew that it was because he had a past as a policeman. He assumed that the chief of the National Police was hard at work setting out the necessary smoke screens so they could keep Rune Bergman's identity a secret for as long as possible.

But sooner or later, of course, the truth would have to come out.

When the news broadcast was over, the telephone rang.

Wallander asked his sister to answer it. "Find out who it is and say you'll check to see if I'm home," he told her.

"It's someone named Brolin," she said when she came back from the hall.

He laboriously got up from his chair and took the telephone.

"I hope I didn't wake you," said Anette Brolin.

"Not at all. My sister is visiting."

"I just thought I'd call and say that I think all of you did an extraordinary job."

"Mostly we were lucky."

Why is she calling? he wondered. He made a quick decision.

"How about a drink?" he suggested.

"Great. Where?" He could hear that she was surprised.

"My sister is just going to bed. How about your place?"

"That's fine."

He hung up the phone and went back into the living room.

"I wasn't planning to go to bed at all," said his sister.

"I have to go out for a while. Don't wait up for me. I don't know how long I'll be."

The cool evening made it easy to breathe. He turned down Regementsgatan and felt a sudden sense of relief. They had solved the brutal murder in Hageholm within forty-eight hours. Now they had to turn their attention back to the double murder in Lenarp.

He knew that he'd done a good job.

He had trusted his intuition, acted without hesitation, and it had produced results.

The thought of the crazy chase with the horse van gave him the shakes. But the relief was still there.

He called up from the intercom and Anette Brolin answered. She lived on the third floor in a building from the turn of the century. The apartment was large but sparsely furnished. Leaning against one wall were several paintings still waiting to be hung up.

"Gin and tonic?" she asked. "I'm afraid I don't have much of a selection."

"Please," he said. "Right now anything is fine. Just so it's strong."

She sat down across from him on a sofa and pulled her legs up under her. He thought she was extremely beautiful.

"Do you have any idea how you look?" she asked with a laugh.

"Everybody asks me that," he replied.

Then he remembered Klas Månson. The man who robbed the store, whom Anette Brolin refused to detain. He really didn't think he could talk about work. Yet he couldn't help it.

"Klas Månson," he said. "Do you remember that name?"

She nodded.

"Hanson complained that you thought our investigation was poor. That you didn't intend to remand Månson into further custody unless the investigation was done more carefully."

"The investigation *was* poor. Sloppily written. Insufficient evidence. Vague testimony. I'd be committing dereliction of duty if I demanded further detention based on material like that."

"The investigation was no worse than most. Besides, you forgot one important fact."

"What was that?"

"That Klas Månson is guilty. He robbed stores before."

"Then you'll have to come up with better investigative work."

"I don't think there's anything wrong with the report. If we let that damned Månson loose, he'll just commit more crimes."

"You can't just put people in jail willy-nilly."

Wallander shrugged. "Will you hold off releasing him if I rustle up some more exhaustive testimony?" he asked.

"That depends on what the witness says."

"Why are you so stubborn? Månson is guilty. If we just hold him for a while, he'll confess. But if he has the slightest inkling that he can get out, he'll clam up."

"Prosecutors have to be stubborn. Otherwise what do you think would happen to law and order in this country?"

Wallander could feel that the liquor had made him rebellious.

"That question can also be asked by an insignificant, provincial police detective," he said. "Once I believed that being on the police force meant that you were involved in protecting the property and safety of ordinary people. I probably still believe it. But I've seen law and order being eroded away. I've seen young people who commit crimes being almost encouraged to continue. No one intervenes. No one cares about the victims of the increasing violence. It just keeps getting worse and worse."

"Now you sound like my father," she said. "He's a retired judge. A true old reactionary civil servant."

"Could be. Maybe I am conservative. But I mean what I say. I actually understand why people sometimes take matters into their own hands."

"So you probably also understand how some misguided individuals can fatally shoot an innocent asylum seeker?"

"Yes and no. The insecurity in this country is enormous. People are afraid. Especially in farming communities like this one. You'll soon find out that there's a big hero right now at this end of the country. A man who is applauded in silence behind drawn curtains. The man who saw to it that there was a municipal vote that said no to accepting refugees."

"So what happens if we put ourselves above the decisions of the parliament? We have a refugee policy in this country that must be followed."

"Wrong. It's precisely the lack of a refugee policy that creates chaos. Right now we're living in a country where anyone with any motive at all can come in anywhere in this country at any time and in any manner. Control of the borders has been eliminated. The customs service is paralyzed. There are plenty of unguarded airstrips where the dope and the illegal immigrants are unloaded every night."

He noticed that he was starting to get excited. The murder of the Somali was a crime with many layers.

"Rune Bergman, of course, must be locked up with the most severe possible punishment," he went on. "But the Immigration Service and the government have to take their share of the blame."

"That's nonsense."

"Is it? People who belonged to the fascist secret police in Romania are starting to show up here in Sweden. They're seeking asylum. Should they get it?"

"The principle has to apply equally."

"Does it really? Always? Even when it's wrong?"

She got up from the sofa and refilled their glasses.

Kurt Wallander was starting to feel depressed.

We're too different, he thought.

After talking for ten minutes, a chasm opens.

The liquor made him aggressive. He looked at her and could feel himself getting aroused.

How long was it since the last time he and Mona had made love?

Almost a year ago. A whole year with no sex.

He groaned at the thought.

"Are you in pain?" she asked.

He nodded. It wasn't true at all. But he yielded to his dark need for sympathy.

"Maybe it would be best if you went home," she said.

That was the last thing he wanted to do. He didn't feel that he even had a home since Mona moved out.

He finished his drink and held out his glass for a refill. Now he was so intoxicated that he was starting to shed his inhibitions.

"One more," he said. "I've earned it."

"Then you have to go," she said.

Her voice had suddenly turned cool. But he didn't let it bother him. When she brought his glass, he grabbed her and pulled her down in the chair.

"Sit here by me," he said, laying his hand on her thigh.

She pulled herself free and slapped him. She hit him with the hand with the wedding ring, and he could feel it tear his cheek.

"Go home now," she said.

He put his glass down on the table. "Or you'll do what?" he asked. "Call the police?"

She didn't answer. But he could see that she was furious.

He stumbled when he stood up.

Suddenly he realized what he had tried to do.

"Forgive me," he said. "I'm exhausted."

"We'll forget all about this," she replied. "But now you have to go home."

"I don't know what came over me," he said, putting out his hand.

She took it.

"We'll just forget it," she said. "Good night."

He tried to think of something more to say. Somewhere in his muddled consciousness the thought gnawed at him that he had done something that was both unforgivable and dangerous. Just as he had driven his car home from the meeting with Mona when he was drunk.

He left and heard the door close behind him.

I've got to stop drinking, he thought angrily. I can't handle it.

Down on the street he sucked the cool air deep into his lungs.

How the hell can anyone act so stupid? he thought. Like some drunken kid who doesn't know a thing about himself, women, or the world.

He went home to Mariagatan.

The next day he would have to resume the hunt for the Lenarp killers.

Chapter Thirteen

On Monday morning, January fifteenth, Kurt Wallander drove out to the shopping center on the road to Malmö and bought two bouquets of flowers. He recalled that eight days ago he had driven the same road, toward Lenarp and the crime scene, which was still demanding all his attention. He thought that the past week had been the most intense he had ever experienced in all his years as a cop. When he looked at his face in the rearview mirror, he thought that every scratch, every lump, every discoloration from purple to black was a reminder of the past week.

The temperature was several degrees below freezing. There was no wind. The white ferry from Poland was making its way into the harbor.

When Wallander arrived at the police station a little after eight, he gave one of the bouquets to Ebba. At first she refused to take it, but he could see that she was pleased with the attention. He took the other bouquet along with him to his office. He got a card from his desk drawer and pondered for a long time what to write to Anette Brolin. Too long a time. By the time he finally wrote a few lines, he had given up any attempt to find the perfect phrasing. Now he simply apologized for his rash behavior the night before. He blamed his actions on fatigue.

"I'm actually quite shy by nature," he wrote. Which was not exactly true.

But he thought it would give Anette Brolin the opportunity to turn the other cheek.

He was just about to go over to the prosecutor's office when Björk came through the door. As usual, he had knocked so softly that Wallander hadn't heard him. "Somebody sent you flowers?" said Björk. "You deserve them, as a matter of fact. I'm impressed how quickly you solved the murder of the Negro."

Wallander didn't like the way Björk referred to the Somali as the Negro. There had been a dead man lying in the mud under the tarp, nothing more. But of course he had no intention of getting into a discussion about it.

Björk was wearing a flowered shirt that he had bought in Spain. He sat down on the rickety spindle-backed chair near the window.

"I thought we ought to go over the murders at Lenarp," he said. "I've looked through the investigative material. There seem to be a lot of gaps. I've been thinking that Rydberg should take over the main responsibility for the investigation while you concentrate on getting Rune Bergman to talk. What do you think about that?"

Wallander countered with a question. "What does Rydberg say?"

"I haven't talked to him yet."

"I think we should do it the other way around. Rydberg has a bad leg, and there's still a lot of footwork to be done in that investigation."

What Wallander said was true enough. But it wasn't concern for Rydberg's rheumatism that made him suggest reversing the responsibilities.

He didn't want to give up the hunt for the Lenarp killers.

Even though police work was a team effort, he thought of the murderers as belonging to him.

"There's a third option," said Björk. "We could let Svedberg and Hanson handle Rune Bergman."

Wallander nodded. He agreed with Björk.

Björk got up out of the rickety chair.

"We need new furniture," he said.

"We need more manpower," replied Wallander.

After Björk had left, Wallander sat down at his typewriter and typed up a comprehensive report about the capture of Rune

Bergman and Valfrid Ström. He made a special effort to compile a report that Anette Brolin would not object to. It took him over two hours. At ten fifteen he pulled the last page out of the typewriter, signed it, and took the report over to Rydberg.

Rydberg was sitting at his desk; he looked tired. When Wallander came into his office, he was just finishing a phone conversation.

"I hear that Björk wants to split us up," he said. "I'm glad I got out of dealing with Bergman."

Wallander put his report on the desk. "Read through it," he said. "If you don't have any objections, give it to Hanson."

"Svedberg had a go at Bergman this morning," said Rydberg. "But he still refuses to talk. Even though the cigarettes match. The same brand that was lying in the mud next to the car."

"I wonder what's going to turn up," said Wallander. "What's behind this whole thing? Neo-Nazis? Racists with connections all over Europe? Why would someone commit a crime like this anyway? Jump out into the road and shoot a complete stranger? Just because he happened to be black?"

"I don't know," said Rydberg. "But it's something we're going to have to learn to live with."

They agreed to meet again in half an hour, after Rydberg had read the report. Then they would start on the Lenarp investigation in earnest.

Wallander went over to the prosecutor's office. Anette Brolin was in district court. He left the bouquet of flowers with the young woman at the reception desk.

"Is it her birthday?" asked the receptionist.

"Sort of," said Wallander.

When he got back to his office, his sister Kristina was sitting there waiting for him. She had already left the apartment by the time he woke up that morning.

She told him that she had talked to both a doctor and a social worker.

"Dad seems better," she said. "They don't think he's slipping into chronic senility. Maybe it was just a temporary period of confusion. We agreed to try regular home care. I was thinking about asking you to drive us out there around noon today. If you can't do it, maybe I could borrow your car."

"Of course I can drive you. Who's going to do the home care?"

"I'm supposed to meet with a woman who doesn't live far from Dad."

Wallander nodded. "I'm glad you're here. I couldn't have handled this alone."

They agreed that he would come over to the hospital right after twelve. After his sister left, Wallander straightened up his desk and placed the thick folder of investigative material pertaining to Johannes and Maria Lövgren in front of him. It was time to get started.

Björk had told him that for the time being, there would be four people on the investigative team. Since Näslund was at home with the flu, only three of them attended the meeting in Rydberg's office. Martinson was silent and seemed to have a hangover. But Wallander remembered his decisive manner when he had taken care of the hysterical widow at Hageholm.

They began with a thorough review of all the investigative material.

Martinson was able to add information produced by his work with the central criminal records. Wallander felt a great sense of security in this methodical and careful scrutiny of numerous details. To an outside observer such work would probably seem unbearably tedious and dull. But that was not the case for the three police officers. The solution and the truth might be found under the most inconsequential combination of details.

They isolated the loose ends that had to be dealt with first.

"You take Johannes Lövgren's trip to Ystad," Wallander said to Martinson. "We need to know how he got to town and how he got back home. Does he have other safe-deposit boxes that we don't know about? What did he do during the hour between his appearances at the two banks? Did he go into a store and buy something? Who saw him?"

"I think Näslund has already started calling around to the banks," said Martinson.

"Call him at home and find out," said Wallander. "This can't wait until he's feeling better."

Rydberg was going to pay a visit to Lars Herdin, while Wallander again drove over to Malmö to talk to the man named Erik Magnusson, the one Göran Boman thought might be Johannes Lövgren's secret son.

"All the other details will have to wait," said Wallander. "We'll start with these and meet again at five o'clock."

Before he left for the hospital, Wallander called Göran Boman in Kristianstad and talked to him about Erik Magnusson.

"He works for the county council," said Boman. "Unfortunately, I don't know exactly what he does. We've had an unusually rowdy weekend up here with a lot of fights and drunkenness. I haven't had time for much besides hauling people in."

"No problem. I'll find him," said Wallander. "I'll call you tomorrow morning at the latest."

At a few minutes past twelve he set off for the hospital. His sister was waiting in the lobby, and together they took the elevator up to the ward where their father had been moved after the first twenty-four hours of observation.

By the time they arrived, he had already been discharged and was sitting on a chair in the hall, waiting for them. He had his hat on his head, and the suitcase with the dirty underwear and tubes of paint stood by his side. Wallander didn't recognize the suit he was wearing.

"I bought it for him," his sister said. "It must be thirty years since he bought himself a new suit."

"How are you feeling, Dad?" asked Wallander.

His father looked him in the eye. Wallander could see that he had recovered.

"It'll be nice to get back home," he said curtly and stood up.

Wallander picked up the suitcase as his father leaned on Kristina's arm. She sat next to him in the back seat during the drive to Löderup.

Wallander, who was in a hurry to get to Malmö, promised to come back around six. His sister was going to stay the night, and she asked him to buy food for dinner.

His father immediately changed out of his suit and into his painting overalls. He was already at his easel, working on the unfinished painting.

"Do you think he'll be able to get by with home care?" asked Wallander.

"We'll have to wait and see," replied his sister.

It was almost two in the afternoon when Wallander pulled up in front of the county council's main building in Malmö. On the way he had stopped at the motel restaurant in Svedala for a quick lunch. He parked his car and went into the large lobby.

"I'm looking for Erik Magnusson," he told the woman who shoved the glass window open.

"We have at least three Erik Magnussons working here," she said. "Which one are you looking for?"

Wallander took out his police ID and showed it to her.

"I don't know," he said. "But he was born in the late fifties."

The woman behind the glass knew at once who it was.

"Then it must be Erik Magnusson in central supply," she said. "The two other Erik Magnussons are much older. What did he do?"

Wallander smiled at her undisguised curiosity.

"Nothing," he said. "I just want to ask him some routine questions."

She told him how to get to central supply. He thanked her and returned to his car.

The county council's supply warehouse was located on the northern outskirts of Malmö, near the Oil Harbor. Wallander wandered around for a long time before he found the right place.

He went through a door marked *Office*. Through a big glass window he could see yellow forklift trucks driving back and forth between endless rows of shelves.

The office was empty. He went down a stairway and entered the enormous warehouse. A young man with hair down to his shoulders was piling up big plastic bags of toilet paper. Wallander went over to him.

"I'm looking for Erik Magnusson," he said.

The young man pointed to a yellow forklift which had stopped next to a loading dock where a semi was being unloaded.

The man sitting in the cab of the yellow truck had blond hair.

Wallander thought it unlikely that Maria Lövgren would have thought about foreigners if this blond man was the one who put the noose around her neck.

Then he pushed the thought away with annoyance. He was getting ahead of himself again.

"Erik Magnusson!" he shouted over the engine noise from the forklift.

The man gave him an inquiring look before he turned off the engine and jumped down.

"Erik Magnusson?" asked Wallander.

"Yes?"

"I'm from the police. I'd like to have a word with you for a moment."

Wallander scrutinized his face.

There was nothing unexpected about his reaction. He merely looked surprised. Quite naturally surprised.

"Why is that?" he asked.

Wallander looked around. "Is there someplace we can sit down?" he asked.

Erik Magnusson led the way to a corner with a coffee vending machine. There was a dirty wooden table and several rickety benches. Wallander fed two one-krona coins into the machine and got a cup of coffee. Erik Magnusson settled for a pinch of snuff.

"I'm from the police in Ystad," he began. "I have a few questions for you regarding a brutal murder in a town called Lenarp. Maybe you read about it in the papers?"

"I think so. But what does that have to do with me?"

Wallander was beginning to wonder the same thing. The man named Erik Magnusson seemed completely unruffled by a visit from the police at his workplace.

"I have to ask you for the name of your father."

The man frowned.

"My dad?" he said. "I don't have any dad."

"Everybody has a father."

"Not one that I know about, at any rate."

"How can that be?"

"Mom wasn't married when I was born."

"And she never told you who your father was?"

"No."

"Did you ever ask her?"

"Of course I've asked her. I bugged her about it my whole childhood. Then I gave up."

"What did she say when you asked her about it?"

Erik Magnusson stood up and pressed the button for a cup of coffee. "Why are you asking about my dad? Does he have something to do with the murder?"

"I'll get to that in a minute," said Wallander. "What did your mother say when you asked her about your father?"

"It varied."

"It varied?"

"Sometimes she would say that she didn't really know. Sometimes that it was a salesman she never saw again. Sometimes something else."

"And you were satisfied with that?"

"What the hell was I supposed to do? If she won't tell me, she won't tell me."

Wallander thought about the answers he was getting. Was it really possible to be so uninterested in who your father was?

"Do you get along well with your mother?" he asked.

"What do you mean by that?"

"Do you see each other often?"

"She calls me now and then. I drive over to Kristianstad once in a while. I got along better with my stepfather."

Wallander gave a start. Göran Boman had said nothing about a stepfather.

"Is your mother remarried?"

"She lived with a man while I was growing up. They probably weren't ever married. But I still called him my dad. Then they split up when I was about fifteen. I moved to Malmö a year later."

"What's his name?"

"*Was* his name. He's dead. He was killed in a car crash."

"And you're sure that he wasn't your real father?"

"You'd have to look hard to find two people as unlike each other as we were."

Wallander tried a different tack. "The man who was murdered at Lenarp was named Johannes Lövgren," he said. "Isn't it possible that he might have been your father?"

The man sitting across from Wallander gave him a look of surprise.

"How the hell would I know? You'll have to ask my mother."

"We've already done that. But she denies it."

"So ask her again. I'd like to know who my father is. Murdered or not."

Kurt Wallander believed him. He wrote down Erik Magnusson's address and personal ID number and then stood up.

"You may hear from us again," he said.

The man climbed back into the cab of the forklift.

"That's fine with me," he said. "Say hello to my mom if you see her."

Wallander returned to Ystad. He parked near the square and headed down the pedestrian street to buy some gauze bandages at the pharmacy. The clerk gazed sympathetically at his battered face. He bought food for dinner in the supermarket on the square. On his way back to the car he changed his mind and retraced his steps to the state liquor store. There he bought a bottle of whiskey. Even though he couldn't really afford it, he chose malt whiskey.

By four thirty Wallander was back at the station. Neither Rydberg nor Martinson was around. He went over to the prosecutor's office. The girl at the reception desk smiled.

"She loved the flowers," she said.

"Is she in her office?"

"She's in district court until five o'clock."

Wallander headed back. In the corridor he ran into Svedberg.

"How's it going with Bergman?" asked Wallander.

"He's still not talking," said Svedberg. "But he'll soften up eventually. The evidence is piling up. The crime lab technicians think they can connect the weapon to the crime."

"What else have we got on this?"

"It looks as if both Ström and Bergman were active in various anti-immigrant groups. But we don't know whether they were operating on their own or as entrepreneurs working for some organization."

"In other words, everybody is perfectly happy?"

"I'd hardly say that. Björk's talking about how he was so anxious to catch the murderer, but then it turned out to be a cop. I suspect they're going to play down Bergman's importance and dump it all on Valfrid Ström, who has nothing more to say about it. Personally, I think Bergman was just as involved in the whole thing."

"I wonder whether Ström was the one who called me at home," said Wallander. "I never heard him say enough to tell for sure."

Svedberg gave him a searching look. "Which means?"

"That in the worst case, there are others who are prepared to take over the killing from Bergman and Ström."

"I'll tell Björk that we have to continue our patrols of the camps," said Svedberg. "By the way, we've gotten a lot of tips indicating that it was a gang of kids who set the fire here in Ystad."

"Don't forget the old man who got a sack of turnips in the head," said Wallander.

"How's it going with Lenarp?"

Wallander hesitated with his answer. "I'm not really sure," he said. "But we're doing some serious work on it again."

At ten minutes past five Martinson and Rydberg were in Wallander's office. He thought that Rydberg still looked tired and worn-out. Martinson was in a bad mood.

"It's a mystery how Lövgren got to Ystad and back again on Friday, January fifth," he said. "I talked to the bus driver on that route. He said that Johannes and Maria used to ride with him whenever they went into town. Either together or separately. He was absolutely certain that Johannes Lövgren did not ride his bus any time after New Year's. And no cab had a fare to Lenarp. According to Nyström, they took the bus when they had to go anywhere. And we know that Lövgren was tight-fisted."

"They always drank coffee together," said Wallander. "In the afternoon. The Nyströms must have noticed if Lövgren went off to Ystad or not."

"That's exactly what's such a mystery," said Martinson. "Both of them claim that he didn't go into town that day. And yet we know that he went to two different banks between eleven thirty and one fifteen. He must have been away from home at least three or four hours that day."

"Strange," said Wallander. "You'll have to keep working on it."

Martinson referred to his notes. "At any rate, he doesn't have any other safe-deposit boxes in town."

"Good," said Wallander. "At least we know that much."

"But he might have one in Simrishamn," Martinson objected. "Or Trelleborg. Or Malmö."

"Let's concentrate on his trip to Ystad first," said Wallander, turning to Rydberg.

"Lars Herdin stands by his story," he said after glancing at his worn notebook. "By coincidence he ran into Lövgren and that woman in Kristianstad in the spring of 1979. And he claims that it was from an anonymous letter that he found out they had a child together."

"Could he describe the woman?"

"Vaguely. In the worst case we could line up all the ladies and have him point out the right one. If she's one of them, that is," he added.

"You sound like you have some doubt."

Rydberg closed his notebook with an irritable snap.

"I can't get anything to fit," he said. "You know that. Obviously we have to follow up the leads we have. But I'm not at all sure that we're on the right track. What bothers me is that I can't figure out any alternative path to take."

Wallander told them about his meeting with Erik Magnusson.

"Why didn't you ask him for an alibi for the night of the murder?" wondered Martinson in surprise when he was done.

Wallander felt himself starting to blush behind his black and blue marks.

It had slipped his mind.

But he didn't tell them that.

"I decided to wait," he said. "I wanted to have an excuse to visit him again."

He could hear how lame that sounded. But neither Rydberg nor Martinson seemed to react to his explanation.

The conversation came to a halt. Each was wrapped up in his own thoughts.

Wallander wondered how many times he had found himself in exactly this same situation. When an investigation suddenly ceases to breathe. Like a horse that refuses to budge. Now they would be forced to tug and pull at the horse until it started to move.

"How should we continue?" asked Wallander at last, when the silence became too oppressive.

He answered his own question. "For your part, Martinson, it's a matter of finding out how Lövgren could go to Ystad and back without anyone noticing. We have to figure that out as soon as possible."

"There was a jar full of receipts in one of the kitchen cupboards," said Rydberg. "He might have bought something in a shop on that Friday. Maybe some clerk would remember seeing him."

"Or maybe he had a flying carpet," said Martinson. "I'll keep working on it."

"His relatives," said Wallander. "We have to go through all of them."

He pulled out a list of names and addresses from the thick folder and handed it to Rydberg.

"The funeral is on Wednesday," said Rydberg. "In Villie Church. I don't care much for funerals. But I think I'll go to this one."

"I'm going back to Kristianstad tomorrow," said Wallander. "Göran Boman was suspicious about Ellen Magnusson. He didn't think she was telling the truth."

It was a few minutes before six when they finished their meeting. They decided to meet again on the following afternoon.

"If Näslund is feeling better, he can work on the stolen rental car," said Wallander. "By the way, did we ever find out what that Polish family is doing in Lenarp?"

"The husband works at the sugar refinery in Jordberga," said Rydberg. "All his papers are in order. Even though he wasn't fully aware of it himself."

Wallander sat in his office for a while after Rydberg and Martinson left. There was a stack of papers on his desk that he was supposed to go through, including all the investigative material from the assault case he had been working on over New Year's. There were also countless reports pertaining to everything from missing bull calves to trucks that had tipped over during the last stormy night. At the bottom of the stack he found a paper informing him that he had been given a raise. He swiftly calculated that he would be taking home an extra 39 kronor per month.

By the time he had made his way through the pile of papers, it was almost half past seven. He called Löderup and told his sister that he was on his way.

"We're starving," she said. "Do you always work late?"

Wallander selected a cassette tape of a Puccini opera and went out to his car. He had wanted to make sure that Anette Brolin had really forgotten all about what had happened the night before. But he put it out of his mind. It would have to wait.

Kristina told him that the home-care help for their father had turned out to be a resolute woman in her fifties who would have no trouble taking care of him.

"He couldn't ask for anyone better," she said when she came out to the driveway and met him in the dark.

"What's Dad doing?"

"He's painting," she said.

While his sister made dinner, Wallander sat on the sled in the studio and watched the autumn motif emerge. His father seemed to have completely forgotten about what had happened a few days before.

I have to visit him more regularly, thought Wallander. At least three times a week, and preferably at specific times.

After dinner they played cards with their father for a couple of hours. At eleven o'clock he went to bed.

"I'm going home tomorrow," said Kristina. "I can't be away any longer."

"Thanks for coming," said Wallander.

They decided that he would pick her up at eight o'clock the next morning and drive her to the airport.

"The plane was full out of Sturup airport," she said. "I'm leaving from Everöd."

That suited Wallander just fine, since he had to drive to Kristianstad anyway.

Just after midnight he walked into his apartment on Mariagatan. He poured himself a big glass of whiskey and took it with him into the bathroom. He lay in the tub for a long time, thawing out his limbs in the hot water.

Even though he tried to push them out of his mind, Rune Bergman and Valfrid Ström kept popping into his thoughts. He was trying to understand. But the only thing he came up with was the same idea he had had so many times before. A new world had emerged, and he hadn't even noticed it. As a cop, he still lived in another, older world. How was he going to learn to live in this new time? How would he deal with the great uncertainty he felt about the great changes, which were happening much too fast?

The murder of the Somali had been a new kind of murder.

The double murder in Lenarp, however, was an old-fashioned crime.

Or was it really? He thought about the brutality and the noose. He wasn't sure.

It was one-thirty when he finally crawled between the cool sheets. His loneliness in bed felt worse than ever.

For the next three days nothing happened.

Näslund came back to work and succeeded in solving the problem of the stolen car.

A man and a woman went on a robbery spree and then left the car in Halmstad. On the night of the murder they had been staying in a boarding house in Båstad. The owner vouched for their alibi.

Wallander talked to Ellen Magnusson. She firmly denied that Johannes Lövgren was the father of her son Erik.

He also visited Erik Magnusson again and asked for the alibi he had forgotten to get during their first encounter.

Erik Magnusson had been with his fiancée. There was no reason to doubt his statement.

Martinson got nowhere with Lövgren's trip to Ystad.

The Nyströms were quite sure about their story, as were the bus drivers and cab owners.

Rydberg went to the funeral, and he talked to nineteen different relatives of the Lövgrens.

Nothing came up that gave them any leads.

The temperature hovered around the freezing point. One day there was no wind, the next day it was gusty.

Wallander ran into Anette Brolin in the hall. She thanked him for the flowers. But he was still uncertain whether she had really decided to forget about what had happened that night.

Rune Bergman still refused to talk, even though the evidence against him was overwhelming. Various nationalist extremist movements tried to take credit for the crime. The press and the rest of the media became engulfed in a violent debate about Sweden's immigration policy. Although it was calm in Skåne, crosses burned in the night outside various refugee camps in other parts of the country.

Wallander and his colleagues on the investigative team trying to solve the double murder in Lenarp shielded themselves from all of this. Only rarely were any opinions expressed that were not directly related to the deadlocked investigation. But Wallander realized that he was not alone in his feelings of uncertainty and confusion about the new society that was emerging.

We're living as if we were in mourning for a lost paradise, he thought. As if we longed for the car thieves and safecrackers of the old days, who doffed their caps and behaved like gentlemen when we came to take them in. But those days have irretrievably vanished, and it's questionable whether they were ever as idyllic as we remember them.

On Friday, January nineteenth, everything happened at once. The day did not start off well for Kurt Wallander. At seven thirty he had his Peugeot checked out and barely managed to avoid having his car declared unfit to drive. When he went through the inspection report, he saw that his car needed repairs that would cost thousands of kronor.

Despondent, he drove to the police station.

He hadn't even taken off his overcoat when Martinson came storming into his office.

"Goddamn," he said. "Now I know how Johannes Lövgren got to Ystad and back home again."

Wallander forgot all about his misery over his car and felt himself instantly seized with excitement.

"It wasn't a flying carpet, after all," continued Martinson. "The chimney sweep drove him."

Wallander sat down in his desk chair.

"What chimney sweep?"

"Master chimney sweep Arthur Lundin from Slimminge. Hanna Nyström suddenly remembered that the chimney sweep had been there on Friday, January fifth. He cleaned the chimneys at both properties and then took off. When she told me that he cleaned Lövgren's flues last and that he left around ten thirty, bells started to go off in my head. I just talked to him. I got hold of him while he was cleaning the hospital chimney in Rydsgård. It turned out that he never listens to the radio or watches TV or reads the papers. He cleans chimneys and spends the rest of his time drinking aquavit and taking care of several caged rabbits. He had no idea that the Lövgrens had been murdered. But he told me that Johannes Lövgren rode with him to Ystad. Since he has a van and Lövgren was sitting in the windowless back seat, it's not so strange that nobody saw him."

"But didn't the Nyströms see the car coming back?"

"No," replied Martinson triumphantly. "That's just it. Lövgren asked Lundin to stop on Veberödsvägen. From there you can walk along a dirt road right up to the back of Lövgren's house. It's about a kilometer. If the Nyströms were sitting in the window, it would have looked as if Lövgren were coming in from the stable."

Wallander frowned. "It still seems odd."

"Lundin was very frank. He said that Johannes Lövgren promised him a bottle of vodka if he would drive him back home. He let Lövgren out in Ystad and then continued on to a couple of houses north of town. Later he picked up Lövgren at the appointed time, dropped him off on Veberödsvägen, and got his bottle of vodka."

"Good," said Wallander. "Do the times match up?"

"It all fits perfectly."

"Did you ask him about the briefcase?"

"Lundin seemed to remember that he had a briefcase with him."

"Did he have anything else?"

"Lundin didn't think so."

"Did Lundin see whether Lövgren met anybody in Ystad?"

"No."

"Did Lövgren say anything about what he was going to do in town?"

"No, nothing."

"And you don't think that this chimney sweep knew about Lövgren having twenty-seven thousand kronor in his briefcase?"

"Hardly. He seemed the least likely person to be a robber. I think he's just a solitary chimney sweep who lives contentedly with his rabbits and his aquavit. That's all."

Wallander thought for a moment. "Do you think Lövgren could have arranged a meeting with someone on that dirt road? Since the briefcase is gone."

"Maybe. I was thinking of taking a canine patrol out to finecomb the road."

"Do it right away," said Wallander. "Maybe we're finally getting somewhere."

Martinson left the office. He almost collided with Hanson, who was on his way in.

"Do you have a minute?" he asked.

Wallander nodded. "How's it going with Bergman?"

"He's not talking. But he's been linked to the crime. That bitch Brolin is going to remand him today."

Wallander didn't feel like commenting on Hanson's contemptuous attitude toward Anette Brolin.

"What do you want?" he merely asked.

Hanson sat down on the spindle-backed chair near the window, looking ill at ease.

"You probably know that I play the horses a bit," he began. "By the way, the horse you recommended ran dead last. Who gave you that tip?"

Wallander vaguely recalled a remark he had let drop one time in Hanson's office. "It was just a joke," he said. "Go on."

"I heard that you were interested in an Erik Magnusson, who works in central supply for the county council in Malmö," he said. "It just so happens that there's a guy named Erik Magnusson who often shows up at Jägersrö. He bets big time, loses a bundle, and I happen to know that he works for the county council."

Wallander was immediately interested.

"How old is he? What does he look like?"

Hanson described him. Wallander realized at once that he was the same man he had met twice.

"There are rumors that he's in debt," said Hanson. "And gambling debts can be dangerous."

"Good," said Wallander. "That's exactly the kind of information we need."

Hanson stood up. "You never know," he said. "Gambling and drugs can sometimes have the same effect. Unless you're like me and just gamble for the fun of it."

Wallander thought about something Rydberg had said. About people who, because of a drug dependency, were capable of unlimited brutality.

"Good," he said to Hanson. "Excellent."

Hanson left the office. Wallander thought for a moment and then called Göran Boman in Kristianstad. He was in luck and got hold of him at once.

"What do you want me to do?" he asked after Wallander told him about Hanson's story.

"Run the vacuum cleaner over him," said Wallander. "And

keep an eye on her."

Boman promised to put Ellen Magnusson under surveillance.

Wallander got hold of Hanson just as he was on his way out of the station.

"Gambling debts," he said. "Who would he owe the money to?"

Hanson knew the answer. "There's a hardware dealer from Tågarp who lends money," he said. "If Erik Magnusson owes money to anybody, it would be him. He's a loan shark for a lot of the high rollers at Jägersrö. And as far as I know, he's got some real unpleasant types working for him that he sends out with reminders to people who are lax with their payments."

"Where can I get hold of him?"

"He's got a hardware store in Tågarp. A short, hefty guy in his sixties."

"What's his name?"

"Larson. But people call him the Junkman."

Wallander went back to his office. He looked for Rydberg but couldn't find him. Ebba, who was at the switchboard, knew where he was. Rydberg wasn't due in until ten, because he was over at the hospital.

"Is he sick?" wondered Wallander.

"It's probably his rheumatism," said Ebba. "Haven't you noticed how he's been limping this winter?"

Wallander decided not to wait for Rydberg. He put on his coat, went out to his car, and drove to Tågarp.

The hardware store was in the middle of town.

At the moment there was a sale on wheelbarrows.

The man who came out of the back room when the doorbell rang was indeed short and hefty. Wallander was the only one in the store, and he decided to get right to the point. He took out his police ID. The man called the Junkman studied it carefully but seemed totally unaffected.

"Ystad," he said. "What can the police from Ystad want with me?"

"Do you know a man named Erik Magnusson?"

The man behind the counter was much too experienced to lie.

"Could be. Why?"

"When did you first meet him?"

Wrong question, thought Wallander. It gives him the chance to retreat.

"I don't remember."

"But you do know him?"

"We have a few common interests."

"Such as the sport of harness racing and tote betting?"

"That's possible."

Wallander felt provoked by the man's overbearing self-confidence.

"Now you listen to me," he said. "I know that you lend money to people who can't control their gambling. Right now I'm not thinking of asking about the interest rates you charge on your loans. I don't give a damn about your involvement in an illegal money-lending operation. I want to know something else entirely."

The man called the Junkman looked at him with curiosity.

"I want to know whether Erik Magnusson owes you money," he said. "And I want to know how much."

"Nothing," replied the man.

"Nothing?"

"Not a single öre."

A dead end, thought Wallander. Hanson's lead was a dead end.

The next second he realized that he was wrong. They were finally on the right track.

"But if you want to know, he did owe me money," said the man.

"How much?"

"A lot. But he paid up. Twenty-five thousand kronor."

"When?"

The man made a swift calculation. "A little over a week ago. The Thursday before last."

Thursday, January eleventh, thought Wallander.

Three days after the murder in Lenarp.

"How did he pay you?"

"He came over here."

"In what denominations?"

"Thousands. Five hundreds."

"Where did he have the money?"

"What do you mean?"

"In a bag? A briefcase?"

"In a plastic grocery bag. From ICA, I think."

"Was he late with the payment?"

"A little."

"What would have happened if he hadn't paid?"

"I would have been forced to send him a reminder."

"Do you know how he got hold of the money?"

The man called the Junkman shrugged. At that moment a customer came into the store.

"That's none of my business," he said. "Will there be anything else?"

"No, thanks. Not at the moment. But you may hear from me again."

Wallander went out to his car.

The wind had picked up.

Okay, he thought. Now we've got him.

Who would have thought that something good would come out of Hanson's lousy gambling?

Wallander drove back to Ystad, feeling as if he had drawn a winning number in the lottery.

He was on the scent of the solution.

Erik Magnusson, he thought.

Here we come.

Chapter Fourteen

After intensive work that dragged on until late into the night on Friday, January nineteenth, Kurt Wallander and his colleagues were ready for battle. Björk had sat in on the long meeting of the investigative team, and at Wallander's request he had let Hanson put aside work on the murder in Hageholm so he could join the Lenarp group, as they now called themselves. Näslund was still sick, but he called in and said he'd be there the next day.

In spite of the weekend, the work had to continue with undiminished effort. Martinson had returned with a canine patrol from a detailed inspection of the dirt road that led from Veberödsvägen to the rear of Lövgren's stable. He had made a meticulous examination of the road, which ran for 1.912 kilometers through a couple of patches of woods, divided two pieces of pasture land as the boundary line, and then ran parallel to an almost dry creek bed. He hadn't found anything unusual, even though he returned to the police station with a plastic bag full of objects. Among other things, there was a rusty wheel from a doll's baby buggy, a greasy sheet of plastic, and an empty cigarette pack of a foreign brand. The objects would be examined, but Wallander didn't think they would produce anything of use to the investigation.

The most important decision during the meeting was that Erik Magnusson would be placed under round-the-clock surveillance. He lived in a rented house in the old Rosengård area. Since Hanson reported that there were harness races at Jägersrö on Sunday, he was assigned the surveillance during the races.

"But I'm not authorizing any tote receipts," said Björk, in a dubious attempt at a joke.

"I propose that we all go in on a regular v5 ticket," replied Hanson. "There's a unique possibility that this murder investigation could pay off."

But it was a serious mood that dominated the group in Björk's office. There was a feeling that a decisive moment was approaching.

The question that aroused the longest discussion concerned whether Erik Magnusson should be told that a fire had been lit under his feet. Both Rydberg and Björk were skeptical. But Wallander thought that they had nothing to lose if Magnusson discovered that he was the object of police interest. The surveillance would be discreet, of course. But beyond that, no measures would be taken to hide the fact that the police had mobilized.

"Let him get nervous," said Wallander. "If he has anything to be nervous about, then I hope we discover what it is."

It took three hours to go through all the investigative material to look for threads that indirectly could be tied to Erik Magnusson. They found nothing, but they also found nothing to contradict the idea that it could have been Magnusson who was in Lenarp that night, despite the alibi his fiancée gave him. Now and then Wallander felt a vague uneasiness that they were traipsing around in yet another blind alley after all.

It was mostly Rydberg who showed signs of doubt. Time after time he asked himself whether a lone individual could have carried out the double murder.

"There was something that hinted at teamwork in that slaughterhouse," he said. "I can't get it out of my mind."

"Nothing is preventing Erik Magnusson from having an accomplice," replied Wallander. "We have to take one thing at a time."

"If he committed the murder to cover up a gambling debt, he wouldn't want an accomplice," Rydberg objected.

"I know," said Wallander. "But we have to keep at it."

Thanks to some quick work by Martinson, they obtained a photograph of Erik Magnusson, which was dug up from the county council's archives. It was taken from a brochure in which the county council presented its comprehensive activities for a populace that was assumed to be ignorant. Björk was of the opinion that all national and municipal governmental institutions needed their own ministries of defense, which when necessary could drum into the uninformed public the colossal significance of precisely that institution. He thought the brochure was excellent. In any case, Erik Magnusson was standing next to his yellow forklift truck, dressed in dazzling white overalls. He was smiling.

The police officers looked at his face and compared it with some black-and-white photos of Johannes Lövgren. One of the pictures showed Lövgren standing next to a tractor in a newly plowed field.

Could they be father and son? The tractor driver and the forklift operator?

Wallander had a hard time focusing on the pictures and making them blend together.

The only thing he thought he saw was the bloody face of an old man with his nose cut off.

By eleven o'clock on Friday night they had completed their plan of attack. By that time Björk had left them to go to a dinner organized by the local country club.

Wallander and Rydberg were going to spend Saturday paying another visit to Ellen Magnusson in Kristianstad. Martinson, Näslund, and Hanson would split up the surveillance of Erik Magnusson and also confront his fiancée with his alibi. Sunday would be devoted to surveillance and an additional run-through of all the investigative material. On Monday Martinson, who had been appointed computer expert in spite of his lack of any real interest in the subject, would examine Erik Magnusson's business dealings. Did he have other debts? Had he ever been mixed up in any kind of criminal activity before?

Wallander asked Rydberg to go through everything personally. He wanted Rydberg to do what they called a crusade. He would try to match up events and individuals who outwardly had nothing in common. Were there actually points of contact that they had previously missed? That was what Rydberg would examine.

Rydberg and Wallander walked out of the police station together. Wallander was suddenly aware of Rydberg's fatigue and remembered that he had paid a visit to the hospital.

"How's it going?" he asked.

Rydberg shrugged his shoulders and mumbled something unintelligible in reply.

"With your leg, I mean," said Wallander.

"Same old thing," replied Rydberg, obviously not wanting to talk any more about his ailments.

Wallander drove home and poured himself a glass of whiskey. But he left it untouched on the coffee table and went into the bedroom to lie down. His exhaustion got the upper hand. He fell asleep at once and escaped all the thoughts that were whirling around in his head.

That night he dreamed about Sten Widén.

Together they were attending an opera in which the performers were singing in an unfamiliar language.

Later, when he awoke, Wallander couldn't remember which opera they had seen.

On the other hand, as soon as he woke up the next day he remembered something they had talked about the day before.

Johannes Lövgren's will. The will that didn't exist.

Rydberg had spoken with the estate administrator who had been engaged by the two surviving daughters, a lawyer who was often called on by the farmers' organizations in the area. No will existed. That meant that the two daughters would inherit all of Johannes Lövgren's unexpected fortune.

Could Erik Magnusson have known that Lövgren had huge assets? Or had Lövgren been just as reticent with him as he had been with his wife?

Wallander got out of bed intending not to let this day pass before he knew definitively whether Ellen Magnusson had given birth to her son Erik with Johannes Lövgren as the unknown father.

He ate a hasty breakfast and met Rydberg at the police station just after nine o'clock. Martinson, who had spent the night in a car outside Erik Magnusson's apartment in Rosengård and had been relieved by Näslund, had turned in a report which said that absolutely nothing had happened during the night. Magnusson was in his apartment. The night had been quiet.

The January day was hazy. Hoarfrost covered the brown fields. Rydberg sat tired and uncommunicative in the front seat next to Wallander. They didn't say a word to each other until they were approaching Kristianstad.

At ten thirty they met Göran Boman at the police station in Kristianstad.

Together they went through the transcript of the woman's interrogation, which Boman had conducted earlier.

"We've got nothing on her," said Boman. "We ran a vacuum over her and the people she knows. Not a thing. Her whole story fits on one sheet of paper. She has worked at the same pharmacy for thirty years. She belonged to a choral group for a few years but finally quit. She takes out a lot of books from the library. She spends her vacations with a sister in Vemmenhög, never travels abroad, never buys new clothes. She's a person who, at least on the surface, lives a completely undramatic life. Her habits are regular almost to the point of pedantry. The most surprising thing is that she can stand to live this way."

Wallander thanked him for his work.

"Now we'll take over," he said.

They drove to Ellen Magnusson's apartment building.

When she opened the door, Wallander thought that the son looked a lot like his mother. He couldn't tell whether she had been expecting them. The look in her eyes seemed remote, as if she were actually somewhere else.

Wallander looked around the living room of the apartment. She asked if they wanted a cup of coffee. Rydberg declined, but Wallander said yes.

Every time Wallander stepped into a strange apartment, he felt as though he were looking at the covers of a book he had just bought. The apartment, the furniture, the pictures on the walls, and the smells were the title. Now he had to start reading. But Ellen Magnusson's apartment was odorless. As if Wallander were

in an uninhabited apartment. He breathed in the smell of hopelessness. A gray resignation. Against a background of pale wallpaper hung colored prints with indefinable abstract motifs. The
furniture that filled the room was heavy and old-fashioned. Doilies
lay decoratively arranged on several mahogany drop-leaf tables.
On a little shelf stood a photograph of a child sitting in front of a
rose bush. Wallander noticed that the only picture of her son she
had on display was one from his childhood. As a grown man he
was not present at all.

Next to the living room was a small dining room. Wallander
nudged the half-open door with his foot. To his undisguised amazement, one of his father's paintings hung on the wall.

It was the autumn landscape without the grouse.

He stood looking at the picture until he heard the rattle of a
tray behind him.

It was as if he were looking at his father's motif for the first
time.

Rydberg had sat down on a chair by the window. Wallander
thought that someday he would have to ask him why he always
sat by a window.

Where do our habits come from? he thought. What secret
factory produces our habits, both good and bad?

Ellen Magnusson served him coffee.

He figured he'd better begin.

"Göran Boman from the Kristianstad police was here and asked
you a number of questions," he said. "Please don't be surprised if
we ask you some of the same questions."

"Just don't be surprised if you get the same answers," said Ellen
Magnusson.

At that moment Wallander realized that the woman sitting
across from him was the mystery woman with whom Johannes
Lövgren had had a child.

Wallander knew it without knowing how he knew.

In a rash moment he decided to lie his way to the truth. If he
wasn't mistaken, Ellen Magnusson was a woman who had very
little experience with the police. She no doubt assumed that they

searched for the truth by using the truth themselves. She was the one who would be lying, not the police.

"Mrs. Magnusson," said Wallander. "We know that Johannes Lövgren is the father of your son Erik. There's no use denying it."

She looked at him, terrified. The absent look in her eyes was suddenly gone. Now she was fully present in the room again.

"It's not true," she said.

A lie begs for mercy, thought Wallander. She's going to break soon.

"Of course it's true," he said. "You and I both know it's true. If Johannes Lövgren hadn't been murdered, we would never have had to worry about asking these questions. But now we have to know. And if we don't find out now, you'll be forced to answer these questions under oath in court."

It went more quickly than he thought.

Suddenly she broke.

"Why do you want to know?" she shrieked. "I haven't done anything. Why can't a person be allowed to keep her secrets?"

"No one is forbidding secrets," said Wallander deliberately. "But as long as people are murdered, we have to search for the perpetrators. This means we have to ask questions. And we have to get answers."

Rydberg sat motionless on his chair by the window. His tired eyes stared at the woman.

Together they listened to her story. Wallander thought it inexpressibly dreary. Her life, as it was laid out before him, was just as hopeless as the frosty landscape he had driven through that same morning.

She had been born the daughter of an elderly farming couple in Yngsjö. She had torn herself free from the land and had eventually become a clerk in a pharmacy. Johannes Lövgren had come into her life as a customer at the pharmacy. She told Wallander and Rydberg that they first met when he was buying bicarbonate of soda. Then he had returned and started to court her.

His story was that of the lonely farmer. Not until the baby was born did she find out that he was married. Her feelings had been resigned, never spiteful. He had bought her silence with money, which was paid several times a year.

But she had raised the son alone. He was hers.

"What did you think when you found out that he had been murdered?" asked Wallander when she fell silent.

"I believe in God," she said. "I believe in righteous vengeance."

"Vengeance?"

"How many people did Johannes betray?" she asked. "He betrayed me, his son, his wife, and his daughters. He betrayed everyone."

And now she will soon learn that her son is a murderer, thought Wallander. Will she imagine that he was an archangel who was carrying out a divine decree for vengeance? Will she be able to stand it?

He continued asking his questions. Rydberg shifted his position on the chair by the window. A bell went off in the kitchen.

When they finally left, Wallander felt that he had gotten the answers to all his questions.

He knew who the mystery woman was. The secret son. He knew that she was expecting money from Johannes Lövgren. But Lövgren had never shown up.

Another question, however, proved to have an unexpected answer.

Ellen Magnusson never gave any of Lövgren's money to her son. She put it into a savings account. He wouldn't inherit the money until she was gone. Maybe she was afraid he would gamble it away.

But Erik Magnusson knew that Johannes Lövgren was his father. On that point he had lied. And did he also know that Lövgren, who was his father, had vast financial assets?

Rydberg was silent during the entire interrogation. Just as they were about to leave, he had asked her how often she saw her son. Whether they got along well with each other. Did she know about his fiancée?

Her reply was evasive. "He's grown now," she said. "He lives his own life. But he's good about coming to visit. And of course I know that he has a fiancée."

Now she's lying again, thought Wallander. She didn't know about the fiancée.

They stopped at the inn at Degeberga and ate. Rydberg seemed to have revived.

"Your interrogation was perfect," he said. "It should be used as a training exercise at the police academy."

"Still, I did lie," said Wallander. "And that's not considered kosher."

During the meal they took stock of their strategy. Both of them agreed that they should wait for the background investigation of Erik Magnusson. Not until that was compiled and ready would they pick him up for questioning.

"Do you think he's the one?" asked Rydberg.

"Of course he is," replied Wallander. "Alone or with an accomplice. What do you think?"

"I hope you're right."

They arrived back at the police station in Ystad at quarter past three. Näslund was sitting in his office, sneezing. He had been relieved by Hanson at noon.

Erik Magnusson had spent the morning buying new shoes and turning in some betting coupons at a tobacco shop. Then he had returned home.

"Does he seem on guard?" asked Wallander.

"I don't know," said Näslund. "Sometimes I think so. Sometimes I think I'm imagining things."

Rydberg drove home, and Wallander locked himself in his office.

He leafed absentmindedly through a new stack of papers that someone had put on his desk.

He was having a hard time concentrating.

Ellen Magnusson's story had made him uneasy.

He imagined that his own life wasn't that far from her reality. His own dubious life.

I'm going to take some time off when this is over, he thought. With all my overtime I could probably be gone for a week. I'm going to devote seven whole days to myself. Seven days like seven lean years. Then I'll emerge a new man.

He pondered whether he ought to go to some health spa where he could get help losing some weight. But he found the thought disgusting. He would rather get in his car and drive south. Maybe to Paris or Amsterdam. In Arnhem he knew a cop he had met once at a narcotics seminar. Maybe he could visit him.

But first we've got to solve the murder in Lenarp, he thought. We'll do that next week.

Then I'll decide where I'm going to go.

On Thursday, January twenty-fifth, Erik Magnusson was picked up by the police for questioning. They nabbed him right outside the building where he lived. Rydberg and Hanson took care of it while Wallander sat in the car and watched. Erik Magnusson went along to the squad car without protest. They had scheduled it for morning, when he was on his way to work. Since Kurt Wallander was anxious for the first interrogations with the man to take place without arousing any attention, he let Magnusson call his workplace and explain why he wasn't coming in. Björk, Wallander, and Rydberg were present in the room when Magnusson was interrogated. Björk and Rydberg stayed in the background while Wallander asked the questions.

During the days before Erik Magnusson was taken to Ystad for the first interrogations, the police grew even more certain that he was guilty of the double murder in Lenarp. Various investigations had shown that Magnusson was a man with heavy debts. On several occasions he had barely managed to avoid being physically beaten because he had not paid off his gambling debts. In a visit to Jägersrö, Hanson had seen Magnusson wagering large sums. His financial situation was catastrophic.

The year before, he had been the object of attention by the Eslöv police for some time as the suspect in a bank robbery. It was never possible to connect him to the crime, however. It did seem conceivable, on the other hand, that Magnusson was mixed up in narcotics smuggling. His fiancée, who was now unemployed, had on several occasions been sentenced for various narcotics violations, and in one instance for postal fraud. So Erik Magnusson had large debts. At times, however, he had amazing amounts of money. In comparison, his salary from the county council was insignificant.

This Thursday morning in January would mean the final breakthrough in the investigation. Now the double murder in Lenarp would be cleared up. Kurt Wallander had awakened early this morning with a great sense of tension in his body.

The next day, Friday, January twenty-sixth, he realized that he was wrong.

The assumption that Erik Magnusson was the guilty party, or at least one of the guilty parties, was completely obliterated. The track they had been following was a blind alley. On Friday afternoon they realized that Magnusson could never be tied to the double murder, for the simple reason that he was innocent.

His alibi for the night of the murder had been corroborated by his fiancée's mother, who was visiting. Her credibility was beyond reproach. She was an elderly lady who suffered from insomnia. Erik Magnusson had snored all night long the night that Johannes and Maria Lövgren were so brutally murdered.

The money with which he had paid his debt to the hardware store owner in Tågarp came from the sale of a car. Magnusson was able to produce a receipt for the Chrysler he had sold. And the buyer, a cabinetmaker in Lomma, told them that he had paid cash, with thousand-krona and five-hundred-krona bills.

Magnusson was also able to give a believable explanation for the fact that he lied about Johannes Lövgren being his father. He had done it for his mother's sake, since he thought she would want it that way. When Wallander told him that Lövgren was a wealthy man, he had looked truly astonished.

In the end there was nothing left.

When Björk asked whether anyone was opposed to sending Erik Magnusson home and dropping him from the case until further notice, no one had any objections. Wallander felt a crushing guilt over having steered the entire investigation in the wrong direction. Only Rydberg seemed unaffected. He was also the one who had been the most skeptical from the beginning.

The investigation had run aground. All that was left was a wreck. There was nothing to do but start over again.

At the same time the snow arrived.

In the wee hours of Saturday, January twenty-seventh, a violent snowstorm came in from the southwest. After a few hours, E14 was blocked. The snow fell steadily for six hours. The heavy wind made the efforts of the snowplows futile. As fast as they scraped the snow off the roads, it would collect in drifts again.

For twenty-four hours the police were busy preventing the mess from developing into chaos. Then the storm moved off, as quickly as it had come.

January thirtieth was Kurt Wallander's forty-third birthday. He celebrated by reforming his eating habits and starting to smoke again. To his great delight, his daughter Linda called him that evening. She was in Malmö and had decided to enroll at a college outside Stockholm. She promised to come and see him before she left.

Wallander arranged his schedule so that he could visit his father at least three times a week. He wrote a letter to his sister in Stockholm, telling her that the new home-care worker had done wonders with their father. The confusion that had driven him out on that desolate nighttime promenade toward Italy had dissipated. Having a woman come regularly to his house had been his salvation.

One evening several days after his birthday, Wallander called up Anette Brolin and offered to show her around wintry Skåne. He again apologized for the night at her apartment. She thanked him and said yes, and the following Sunday, February fourth, he took her out to see the ancient stones at Ales Stenar and the medieval castle of Glimmingehus. They ate dinner in Hammenhög at the inn, and Wallander started to think that she really had decided that he was someone other than the man who had pulled her down on his knee.

The weeks passed with no new breakthrough in their investigation. Martinson and Näslund were transferred to new assignments. Wallander and Rydberg, however, were allowed to concentrate exclusively on the double murder for the time being.

One cold, clear day in the middle of February, a day with absolutely no wind, Wallander was visited in his office by the Lövgrens' daughter, who lived and worked in Göteborg.

She had returned to Skåne to oversee the placement of a headstone on her parents' grave in Villie cemetery. Wallander told her the truth — that the police were still fumbling around for some definite clue. The day after her visit, he drove out to the cemetery and stood there for a while, meditating by the black stone with the gold inscription.

The month of February was spent in broadening and deepening the investigation.

Rydberg, who was silent and uncommunicative and was suffering greatly from the pain in his leg, did most of his work by phone, while Wallander was often out in the field. They checked out every single bank in Skåne, but found no additional safe-deposit boxes. Wallander talked with over two hundred people who were either relatives or acquaintances of Johannes and Maria Lövgren. He made numerous return forays into the bulging investigative material, went back to points he had covered long ago, and ripped up the floorboards in old, played-out reports and scrutinized them anew. But he found no opening anywhere.

One icy and windy February day he picked up Sten Widén at his farm and they visited Lenarp. Together they inspected the horse that might be concealing a secret and watched the mare eat an armload of hay. Old Nyström was at their heels wherever they went. Nyström had been given the mare by the two daughters.

But the property itself, which stood silent and closed up, had been turned over to a real estate agent in Skurup for sale. Kurt Wallander stood in the wind looking at the broken kitchen window, which had never been fixed, just boarded up with a piece of masonite. He tried to reestablish the contact with Sten Widén that had been lost for the past ten years, but the racehorse trainer and former friend appeared uninterested. After Wallander had driven him home, he realized that their contact was broken permanently.

The preliminary investigation of the murder of the Somali refugee was concluded, and Rune Bergman was brought before the district court in Ystad. The court building was filled with a large crowd from the media. By now it had been established that it was Valfrid Ström who had fired the fatal shots. But Rune Bergman was indicted for complicity in the murder, and the psychiatric evaluation declared him fit to stand trial.

Kurt Wallander testified in court, and on several occasions he sat in and listened to Anette Brolin's appeals and cross-examinations. Rune Bergman didn't say much, even though his silence was no longer unbroken. The court proceedings revealed a racist underground landscape in which political views similar to those of the Ku Klux Klan were prevalent. Bergman and Ström had acted on their own at the same time as they were connected to various racist organizations.

The thought again occurred to Wallander that something decisive was about to happen in Sweden. For brief moments he could also detect contradictory sympathies in himself for some of the anti-immigrant arguments that came up in discussions and the press while the trial was in progress. Did the government and the Immigration Service have any real control over which individuals sought to enter Sweden? Who was a refugee and who was an opportunist? Was it possible to differentiate at all?

How long would the principle of the generous refugee policy be able to hold without leading to chaos? Was there any upper limit?

Kurt Wallander had made halfhearted attempts to study the questions thoroughly. He realized that he harbored the same vague apprehension that so many other people did. Anxiety about the unknown, about the future.

At the end of February the sentence was pronounced, giving Rune Bergman a long prison term. To everyone's undisguised astonishment, he did not appeal the verdict, which took effect immediately.

No more snow fell on Skåne that winter. One early morning at the beginning of March, Anette Brolin and Kurt Wallander took a long walk along Falsterbo Spit. Together they watched the early flocks of birds returning from the distant lands of the Southern Cross. Wallander suddenly took her hand, and she didn't pull it away, at least not at once.

He managed to lose four kilos, but he realized that he would never get back to what he had weighed when Mona had suddenly left him.

Occasionally their voices would meet on the telephone. Wallander noticed that his jealousy was gradually crumbling away. The black woman who used to visit him in his dreams no longer showed up either.

March began with Svedberg repeating his desire to move back to Stockholm. At the same time Rydberg was admitted to the hospital for two weeks. At first everyone thought it was for his bad leg. But one day Ebba told Wallander in confidence that Rydberg was apparently suffering from cancer. She didn't say how she knew, or what type of cancer it was. When Wallander visited Rydberg at the hospital, he told him it was only a routine check of his stomach. A spot on an X-ray plate had revealed a possible lesion on his large intestine.

Wallander felt a burning pain inside at the thought that Rydberg might be seriously ill. With a growing sense of hopelessness he trudged on with his investigation. One day, in a fit of rage, he threw the thick folders at the wall. The floor was covered with paper. For a long time he sat looking at the havoc. Then he crawled around sorting the material again and started from the beginning.

Somewhere there's something I'm not seeing, he thought.

A connection, a detail, which is exactly the key I have to turn. But should I turn it to the right or the left?

He often called Göran Boman in Kristianstad to complain about his plight.

On his own authority, Boman had carried out intensive investigations of Nils Velander and other conceivable suspects. Nowhere did the rock crack. For two whole days Wallander sat with Lars Herdin without advancing a single meter.

He still didn't want to believe that the crime would never be solved.

In the middle of March he managed to entice Anette Brolin to make an opera trip with him to Copenhagen. During the night she embraced his desolation. But when he told her that he loved her, she shied away.

It was what it was. Nothing more.

On the weekend of March seventeenth and eighteenth his daughter came to visit. She came alone, without the Kenyan medical student, and Wallander met her at the train station. Ebba had sent a friend of hers over the day before to give his apartment on Mariagatan a major cleaning. And he finally felt that he had his daughter back. They took a long walk along the beach by Österleden, ate lunch at Lilla Vik, and then stayed up talking till five in the morning. They visited Wallander's father, and he surprised them both by telling funny stories about Kurt as a child.

On Monday morning he took her to the train.

He seemed to have regained some of her trust.

When he was back in his office, poring over the investigative material, Rydberg suddenly came in. He sat down on the spindle-backed chair by the window and told Wallander straight out that he had been diagnosed with prostate cancer. Now he was going in for cytotoxin and radiation therapy, which could last a long time and might not do any good. He wouldn't permit any sympathy. He had merely come to remind Wallander about Maria Lövgren's last words. And the noose. Then he stood up, shook Wallander's hand, and left.

Wallander was left alone with his pain and his investigation. Björk thought that for the time being he ought to work alone, since the police were swamped.

Nothing happened in March. Or in April either.

The reports on the status of Rydberg's health varied. Ebba was the unflagging messenger.

On one of the first days in May, Wallander went into Björk's office and suggested that someone else take over the investigation. But Björk refused. Wallander would have to continue at least until the summer and vacation period were over. Then they would reevaluate the situation.

Time after time Wallander started over. Retreated, prying and twisting at the material, trying to make it come alive. But the stones he was walking on remained cold.

At the beginning of June he traded in his Peugeot on a Nissan. On June eighth he went on vacation and drove up to Stockholm to see his daughter.

Together they drove all the way to the North Cape. Herman Mboya was in Kenya but would be coming back in August.

On Monday, July ninth, Wallander was back on duty.

A memo from Björk informed him that he was to continue with his investigation until Björk returned in early August. Then they would decide what to do next.

He also received a message from Ebba that Rydberg was doing much better. The doctors might be able to control his cancer after all.

Tuesday, July tenth, was a beautiful day in Ystad. At lunchtime Wallander went downtown and strolled around. He went into the store by the square and decided to buy a new stereo.

Then he remembered that he had some Norwegian bills in his wallet that he had forgotten to exchange. He had been carrying them around since the trip to the North Cape. He went down to the Union Bank and got in line for the only window that was open.

He didn't recognize the woman behind the counter. It wasn't Britta-Lena Bodén, the young woman with the good memory, or any of the other tellers he had met before. He thought it must be a summer temp.

The man in front of him in line made a large withdrawal. Distractedly, Wallander wondered what he was going to use such a large amount of cash for. While the man counted up his bills, Wallander absentmindedly read his name on the driver's license he had placed on the counter.

Then it was his turn, and he exchanged his Norwegian money. Behind him in the line he heard a summer tourist speaking Italian or Spanish.

As he emerged onto the street, an idea suddenly occurred to him.

He stood there motionless, as if he were frozen solid in his inspiration.

Then he went back inside the bank. He waited until the tourists had exchanged their money.

He showed his police id to the teller.

"Britta-Lena Bodén," he said, smiling. "Is she on vacation?"

"She's probably with her parents in Simrishamn," said the teller.
"She has two weeks of vacation left."

"Bodén," he said. "Is that her parents' name too?"

"Her father runs a gas station in Simrishamn. I think it's the
one called Statoil nowadays."

"Thank you," said Wallander. "I just have some routine questions to ask her."

"I recognize you," said the teller. "So you haven't been able to
solve that awful crime yet?"

"No," said Wallander. "It's terrible, isn't it?"

He practically ran back to the police station, jumped into his
car, and drove to Simrishamn. From Britta-Lena Bodén's father
he learned that she was spending the day with friends at the beach
at Sandhammaren. He searched a long time before he found her,
well hidden behind a sand dune. She was playing backgammon
with her friends, and all of them gave Wallander an astonished
look as he came tramping through the sand.

"I wouldn't bother you if it weren't important," he said.

Britta-Lena Bodén seemed to grasp his serious mood and stood
up. She was dressed in a minuscule bathing suit, and Wallander
averted his eyes. They sat down a little way from the others, so
they wouldn't be disturbed.

"That day in January," said Wallander. "I wanted to ask you
about it again. I'd like you to think back to that day. And I want
you to try and remember whether there was anyone else in the
bank when Johannes Lövgren made his big withdrawal."

Her memory was still excellent.

"No," she said. "He was alone."

He knew that what she said was true.

"Keep going," he continued. "Lövgren went out the door. The
door closed behind him. What happened then?"

Her reply was quick and firm. "The door didn't close."

"Another customer came in?"

"Two of them."

"Did you know them?"

"No."

The next question was crucial.

"Because they were foreigners?"

She looked at him in astonishment.

"Yes. How did you know?"

"I didn't know until now. Keep thinking."

"There were two men. Quite young."

"What did they want?"

"They wanted to exchange money."

"Do you remember what currency?"

"Dollars."

"Did they speak English? Were they Americans?"

She shook her head. "Not English. I don't know what language they were speaking."

"Then what happened? Try to picture it in your mind."

"They came up to the window."

"Both of them?"

She thought carefully before she answered. The warm wind was ruffling her hair.

"One of them came up and put the money on the counter. I think it was a hundred dollars. I asked him if he wanted to exchange it. He nodded."

"What was the other man doing?"

She thought again.

"He dropped something on the floor, which he bent over and picked up. A mitten, I think."

He backed up a step with his questions.

"Johannes Lövgren had just left," he said. "He had received a large amount of cash which he put into his briefcase. Did he receive anything else?"

"He got a receipt for his money."

"Which he put in the briefcase?"

For the first time she was hesitant.

"I think so."

"If he didn't put the receipt in his briefcase, then what happened to it?"

She thought again.

"There was nothing lying on the counter. I'm sure of that. Otherwise I would have picked it up."

"Could it have slipped off onto the floor?"

"Possibly."

"And the man who bent over for the mitten could have picked it up?"

"Maybe."

"What was on the receipt?"

"The amount. His name and address."

Wallander held his breath.

"All that was on it? Are you sure?"

"He filled out his withdrawal slip in big letters. I know that he wrote down his address too, even though it wasn't required."

Wallander backtracked again. "Lövgren takes his money and leaves. In the doorway he runs into two unknown men. One of them bends down and picks up a mitten, and maybe the withdrawal slip too. It says that Johannes Lövgren has just withdrawn twenty-seven thousand kronor. Is that correct?"

Suddenly she understood. "Are they the ones that did it?"

"I don't know. Think back again."

"I exchanged their money. He put the bills in his pocket. They left."

"How long did it take?"

"Three, four minutes. No more."

"The bank has a copy of their exchange receipt, I suppose?"

She nodded.

"I exchanged money at the bank today. I had to give my name. Did they give any address?"

"Maybe. I don't remember."

Kurt Wallander nodded. Now something was starting to burn.

"Your memory is phenomenal," he said. "Did you ever see those two men again?"

"No. Never."

"Would you recognize them?"

"I think so. Maybe."

Wallander thought for a few moments.

"You might have to interrupt your vacation for a few days," he said.

"We're supposed to drive to Öland tomorrow!"

Wallander made a decision on the spot. "I'm sorry, you can't," he said. "Maybe the next day. But not before then."

He stood up and brushed off the sand.

"Be sure to tell your parents where we can reach you," he said.

She stood up and got ready to rejoin her friends.

"Can I tell them?" she asked.

"Make up something," he replied. "I'm sure you can do that."

Just after four o'clock that afternoon they found the exchange receipt in the Union Bank's files.

The signature was illegible. No address was given.

To his surprise, Wallander was not disappointed. He thought this was because now at least he understood how the whole thing might have happened.

From the bank he drove straight to Rydberg's place, where he was convalescing.

Rydberg was sitting on his balcony when Wallander rang the doorbell. He had grown thin and was very pale.

Together they sat on the balcony, and Wallander told him about his discovery.

Rydberg nodded thoughtfully.

"You're probably right," he said when Wallander finished. "That's probably how it happened."

"The question now is how to find them," said Wallander. "Some tourists who happened to be visiting Sweden more than six months ago."

"Maybe they're still here," said Rydberg. "As refugees, asylum seekers, immigrants."

"Where do I start?" asked Wallander.

"I don't know," said Rydberg. "But you'll figure out something."

They sat for a couple of hours on Rydberg's balcony.

Just before seven o'clock Wallander went back to his car.

The stones were no longer as cold under his feet.

Chapter Fifteen

urt Wallander would always remember the following days as the time when the chart was drawn. He started with what Britta-Lena Bodén remembered and an illegible signature. A conceivable scenario existed, and the last word Maria Lövgren spoke before she died was a puzzle piece that had finally fallen into place. He also had the oddly knotted noose to take into account. Then he drew the chart. On the same day he had talked with Britta-Lena Bodén in the warm sand dunes at Sandhammaren he had gone over to Björk's house, pulled him away from the dinner table, and extracted an immediate promise to assign Hanson and Martinson full-time to the investigation, which was once again given top priority and put into high gear.

On Wednesday, July eleventh, before the bank opened for business, they reconstructed the scene. Britta-Lena Bodén took her place behind the teller's window, Hanson assumed the role of Johannes Lövgren, and Martinson and Björk played the two men who came in to exchange their dollars. Wallander insisted that everything should be exactly as it was on that day six months earlier. The anxious bank manager finally agreed to allow Britta-Lena Bodén to hand over 27,000 kronor in bills of mixed but large denominations to Hanson, who had borrowed an old briefcase from Ebba.

Wallander stood to one side, watching everything. Twice he ordered them to start over when Britta-Lena Bodén remembered some detail that didn't seem right.

Wallander carried out this reconstruction in order to spark her memory. He hoped that she might be able to open a door to yet another room in her extraordinarily clear memory.

Afterwards she shook her head. She had told him everything she could remember. She had nothing to add. Wallander asked her to postpone her trip to Öland another couple of days and then left her alone in an office where she could look through photographs of foreign criminals who, for one reason or another, had been caught in the net of the Swedish police. When this search produced no results either, she was put on a plane to Norrköping to go through the extensive photo archives at the Immigration Service. After eighteen hours of staring at countless pictures, she returned to Sturup airport, where Wallander himself went to meet her. The results were negative.

The next step was to link up with Interpol. The scenario of how the crime might have occurred was fed into their computers, which then made comparative studies at European headquarters. Still, nothing turned up to change the situation in any significant way.

While Britta-Lena Bodén was sitting and sweating over the endless rows of photographs, Wallander carried out three long interviews with Arthur Lundin, the master chimney sweep from Slimminge. His trips between Lenarp and Ystad were reconstructed, clocked, and repeated. Wallander continued drawing up his chart. Now and then he went to see Rydberg, who sat on his balcony, weak and pale, and went over the investigation with him. Rydberg insisted that Wallander was not bothering him and that these sessions did not tire him. But Wallander left his balcony each time with a nagging feeling of guilt.

Anette Brolin returned from her vacation, which she had spent with her husband and children in a summer house in Grebbestad on the west coast. She brought her family back to Ystad with her, and Wallander assumed his most formal tone of voice when he called her to report on his breakthrough in the practically lifeless investigation.

After the first intensive week everything came to a standstill. Wallander stared at his chart. They were stuck again.

"We'll just have to wait," said Björk. "Interpol's dough rises slowly."

Wallander groaned inwardly at the strained metaphor.

At the same time he realized that Björk was right.

When Britta-Lena Bodén came back from Öland and was about to start work at the bank again, Wallander asked the bank management to give her a few more days off. Then he took her out to the refugee camps around Ystad. They also made a trip to the floating camps on ships in Malmö's Oil Harbor. But nowhere did she recognize any faces.

Wallander arranged for a police artist to fly down from Stockholm.

In spite of working with the artist on countless sketches, Britta-Lena Bodén was not satisfied with any of the faces the artist produced.

Wallander began to have doubts. Björk forced him to give up Martinson and make do with Hanson, as his closest and only colleague in the investigative work.

On Friday, July twentieth, Wallander was again ready to give up.

Late in the evening he sat down and wrote a memo suggesting that the investigation be put on hold for the time being because of a lack of pertinent material that could move the case forward in any meaningful way.

He put the paper on his desk and decided to leave the decision to Björk and Anette Brolin on Monday morning.

He spent Saturday and Sunday on the Danish island of Bornholm. It was windy and rainy, and he got sick from something he ate on the ferry. He spent Sunday night in bed. At regular intervals he had to get up and vomit.

When he woke up on Monday morning, he was feeling better. But he was still undecided about whether to stay in bed or not.

At last he got up and left the apartment. A few minutes before nine he was in his office. Since it was Ebba's birthday, they all had cake in the lunchroom. It was almost ten o'clock when Wallander finally had a chance to read through his memo to Björk. He was just about to deliver it when the phone rang.

It was Britta-Lena Bodén.

Her voice was barely a whisper.

"They've come back. Get over here in a hurry!"

"Who's come back?" asked Wallander.

"The men who changed the money. Don't you understand?"

Out in the hall he ran into Norén, who had just come back from a traffic shift.

"Come with me!" shouted Wallander.

"What the hell's going on?" said Norén as he bit into a sandwich.

"Don't ask. Come on!"

When they arrived at the bank Norén was still holding the half-eaten sandwich. On the way over, Wallander had gone through a red light and driven over a dividing strip. He left the car in the midst of some market stalls in the square by the city hall. But they still got there too late. The men had already disappeared. Britta-Lena Bodén had been so shocked at seeing them again that she hadn't thought to ask anyone to follow them.

On the other hand she did have the presence of mind to press the button for the alarm camera.

Wallander studied the signature on the exchange receipt. The name was again illegible. But the signature was the same. No address was given this time either.

"Good," said Wallander to Britta-Lena Bodén, who was standing in the bank manager's office, shaking. "What did you say when you left to call me?"

"That I had to go get a stamp."

"Do you think the two men suspected anything?"

She shook her head.

"Good," Wallander repeated. "You did exactly the right thing."

"Do you think you'll catch them now?" she asked.

"Yes," said Wallander. "This time we're going to get them."

The videotape from the bank's camera showed two men who did not look particularly Mediterranean. One of them had short blond hair, the other was balding. In police jargon the first was at once dubbed Lucia and the other Baldy.

Britta-Lena Bodén listened to samples of various languages and finally decided that the men had exchanged several words in Czech or Bulgarian. The fifty-dollar bill they had exchanged was immediately sent to the crime lab for examination.

Björk called a meeting in his office.

"After six months they turn up again," said Wallander. "Why did they go back to the same small bank? First, because they live somewhere in the vicinity, of course. Second, because they once made a lucky catch after one of their bank visits. This time they weren't so lucky. The man ahead of them in line was depositing money, not making a withdrawal. But it was an elderly man like Johannes Lövgren. Maybe they think that elderly men who look like farmers always make large cash withdrawals."

"Czechs?" asked Björk. "Or Bulgarians?"

"That's not absolutely positive," said Wallander. "The girl might have been mistaken. But it fits with their appearance."

They watched the video four times and decided which pictures should be copied and enlarged.

"Every Eastern European who lives in town or the surrounding area will have to be investigated," said Björk. "It's not going to be pleasant, and it will be regarded as unjustified discrimination. But we'll have to say the hell with that. They've got to be around here somewhere. I'll have a talk with the county police chiefs in Malmö and Kristianstad to find out what they think we should do on the county level."

"Show the video to all the patrol officers," said Hanson. "They might turn up on the streets."

Wallander was reminded of the slaughterhouse.

"After what they did in Lenarp, we have to consider them dangerous," he said.

"If they were the ones," corrected Björk. "We don't know that yet."

"That's true," said Wallander. "But even so."

"We're going to move into high gear now," said Björk. "Kurt is in charge and will divide up the work as he sees fit. Anything that doesn't have to be done right away should be put aside. I'll call the prosecutor; she'll be glad to hear that something's happening."

But nothing happened.

In spite of a massive police effort and the small size of the town, the men had vanished.

Tuesday and Wednesday passed without results. The two county police chiefs gave the go-ahead to implement special measures
in their regions. The videotape was copied and distributed.
Wallander had last-minute doubts about whether the pictures
should be released to the press. He was afraid that the men would
make themselves even scarcer if their description was issued. He
asked for advice from Rydberg, who did not agree with him.

"You have to drive foxes out into the open," he said. "Wait a
few days. But then release the pictures."

For a long time he sat staring at the copies that Wallander
had brought along.

"There's no such thing as a murderer's face," he said. "You
imagine something: a profile, a hairline, a set of the jaw. But it
never matches up."

Tuesday, July twenty-fourth, was a windy day in Skåne. Ragged
clouds raced across the sky, and the wind was gusting up to gale
force. After waking at dawn, Wallander lay in bed for a long
time and listened to the wind. When he stepped on the scale in
the bathroom, he saw that he had lost another two pounds. This
cheered him up so much that when he pulled into the parking
lot at the police station he did not have the sense of despondency
he'd been feeling lately.

This crime investigation is turning into a personal defeat, he
had been thinking. I'm driving my colleagues hard, but in the
end we're stuck in a vacuum again.

But those two men had to be somewhere, he thought angrily
as he slammed the car door. Somewhere — but where?

In the lobby he stopped to exchange a few words with Ebba.
He noticed that there was an old-fashioned music box sitting
next to the switchboard.

"I haven't seen one of those in ages," he said. "Where did you
get it?"

"I bought it at a stall in the Sjöbo marketplace," she replied.
"Sometimes you can actually find something great in the midst
of all the junk."

Wallander smiled and moved on. On the way to his office he

dropped by to see Hanson and Martinson and asked them to come along with him.

There was still no trace of Baldy or Lucia.

"Two more days," said Wallander. "If we don't come up with something by Thursday, we'll call a press conference and release the pictures."

"We should have done that right from the start," said Hanson. Wallander said nothing.

They went over the chart again. Martinson would continue to organize a search of various campgrounds where the two men might be hiding out.

"Check the youth hostels," said Wallander. "And all the rooms that are for rent in private homes in the summer."

"It was easier before," said Martinson. "People used to stay put in the summer. Now they run all over the place."

Hanson would continue to look into a number of smaller, less particular construction companies that were known to hire undocumented workers from various Eastern European countries.

Wallander would go out to the strawberry fields. He couldn't overlook the possibility that the two men might be hiding out at one of the big berry farms.

But all their efforts turned up nothing.

When they met again late that afternoon, the reports were negative.

"I found an Algerian pipelayer," said Hanson, "two Kurdish bricklayers, and a huge number of Polish manual laborers. I feel like writing a note to Björk. If we hadn't had this damn double homicide, we could have cleaned up that crap. They're making the same wages as kids with summer jobs. They don't have any insurance. If there's an accident, the contractors will say that the workers were living illegally at the sites."

Martinson didn't have any good news either.

"I found a bald Bulgarian," he said. "With a little luck he could have been Baldy. But he's a doctor at the clinic in Mariestad and would have no trouble producing an alibi."

The room was stuffy. Wallander got up and opened the window.

All of a sudden he thought of Ebba's music box. Even though he hadn't heard its melody, the music box had been playing in his subconscious all day.

"The marketplaces," he said, turning around. "We should take a look at them. Which market is open next?"

Both Hanson and Martinson knew the answer.

The one in Kivik.

"It opens today," said Hanson. "And closes tomorrow."

"I'll go out there tomorrow," said Wallander.

"It's a big one," said Hanson. "You should take somebody with you."

"I can go," said Martinson.

Hanson looked happy to get out of the trip. Wallander thought that there were probably harness races on Wednesday nights.

They concluded their meeting, said goodbye to each other, and Hanson and Martinson left. Wallander stayed at his desk and sorted through a stack of phone messages. He arranged them by priority for the following day and got ready to leave. Suddenly he caught sight of a note that had fallen under his desk. He bent down to pick it up and saw that the message was about a call from the director of a refugee camp.

He tried the number. He let it ring ten times and was just about to hang up when someone answered.

"This is Wallander at the Ystad police. I'm looking for someone named Modin."

"Speaking."

"I'm returning your call."

"I think I have something important to tell you."

Kurt Wallander held his breath.

"It's about the two men you're looking for. I came back from vacation today. The photographs the police sent were on my desk. I recognize those two men. They lived at this camp for a while."

"I'm on my way," said Wallander. "Don't leave your office before I get there."

The refugee camp was located outside of Skurup. The drive took him nineteen minutes. The camp was housed in an empty parsonage and was used only as a temporary shelter when all the permanent camps were full.

Modin, the director, was a short man close to sixty. He was waiting in the courtyard when Wallander's car skidded to a stop.

"The camp is empty right now," said Modin. "But we're expecting a number of Romanians next week."

They went into his small office.

"Start at the beginning," Wallander said.

"They lived here between December of last year and the middle of February," said Modin, leafing through some papers. "Then they were transferred to Malmö. To Celsius Estate, to be exact."

Modin pointed to the photo of Baldy. "His name is Lothar Kraftczyk. He's a Czech citizen seeking political asylum because he claims that he was persecuted for being a member of an ethnic minority in his own country."

"Are there minorities in Czechoslovakia?" wondered Wallander.

"I think he regarded himself as a gypsy."

"Regarded himself?"

Modin shrugged. "I don't believe he is. Refugees who know they have insufficient reason for staying in Sweden learn quickly that one excellent way to improve their chances is to claim that they're gypsies."

Modin picked up the photo of Lucia. "Andreas Haas. Also a Czech. I don't really know what his reason was for seeking asylum. The paperwork went with them to Celsius Estate."

"And you're positive that they're the men in the photographs?"

"Yes. I'm sure of it."

"Go on," said Wallander. "Tell me more."

"About what?"

"What were they like? Did anything special happen while they were living here? Did they have plenty of money? Anything you can recall."

"I've been trying to remember," said Modin. "They mostly kept to themselves. You should know that life in a refugee camp is probably the most stressful thing anyone can be subjected to. They played chess. Day in and day out."

"Did they have any money?"

"Not that I can recall."

"What were they like?"

"Very reserved. But not unfriendly."

"Anything else?"

Wallander noticed that Modin hesitated.

"What are you thinking about?" he asked.

"This is a small camp," said Modin. "I don't stay here at night, and neither does anyone else. On certain days it was also unstaffed. Except for a cook who prepared the meals. We usually keep a car here. The keys are locked in my office. But sometimes when I arrived in the morning, I had the feeling that someone had been using the car. Somebody had been in my office, taken the keys, and driven off in the car."

"And you suspected these two men?"

Modin nodded. "I don't know why. It was just a feeling I had."

Wallander pondered this.

"So at night no one was here," he said. "Or on certain days either. Is that right?"

"Yes."

"Friday, January fifth," said Wallander. "That's over six months ago. Can you remember whether there were any staff here that day?"

Modin paged through his desk calendar.

"I was at an emergency meeting in Malmö," he said. "There was such a backlog of refugees that we had to find more temporary camps."

The stones were starting to burn under Kurt Wallander's feet.

The chart had come alive. Now it was speaking to him.

"So nobody was here that day?"

"Only the cook. But the kitchen is in the back. She might not have noticed if anyone had used the car."

"None of the refugees said anything?"

"Refugees don't get involved. They're scared. Even of each other."

Wallander stood up.

He was suddenly in a big hurry.

"Call up your colleague at Celsius Estate and tell him I'm on my way," he said. "But don't mention anything about these two men. Just make sure that the director is available."

Modin stared at him.

"Why are you looking for them?" he asked.

"They may have committed a crime. A serious crime."

"The murders in Lenarp? Is that what you mean?"

Wallander suddenly saw no reason not to answer. "Yes. I think they're the ones."

He reached Celsius Estate in central Malmö at a few minutes past seven PM. He parked on a side street and went up to the main entrance, which was protected by a security guard. After several minutes a man came to get him. His name was Larson, a former seaman, and he was emanating the unmistakable odor of beer.

"Haas and Kraftczyk," said Wallander after they sat down in Larson's office. "Two Czech asylum seekers."

The man who smelled like beer answered at once.

"The chess players," he said. "Yes, they live here."

Goddamn, thought Wallander. We've finally got them.

"Are they here in the building?"

"Yes," said Larson. "I mean, no."

"No?"

"They live here. But they're not here."

"What do you mean?"

"I mean they're not here."

"Where the hell are they then?"

"I don't really know."

"But they do live here?"

"They ran away."

"Ran away?"

"It happens all the time — people run away from here."

"But aren't they seeking asylum?"

"They still run away."

"What do you do then?"

"We report them, of course."

"And then what happens?"

"Usually nothing."

"Nothing? People run away who are waiting to hear whether they can stay in this country or whether they're going to be deported? And nobody cares?"

"I guess the police are supposed to look for them."

"This is completely idiotic. When did they disappear?"

"They left in May. They both probably suspected that their applications for asylum would be turned down."

"Where do you think they went?"

Larson threw his hands wide. "If you only knew how many people live in this country without residency permits. More than you can imagine. They live together, falsify their papers, trade names with each other, work illegally. You can live all your life in Sweden without anyone asking about you. No one wants to believe it. But that's the way it is."

Wallander was speechless.

"This is crazy," he said. "This is fucking crazy."

"I agree. But that's the way things are."

Wallander groaned.

"I need all the documents you have on these two men."

"I can't give those out to just anybody."

Wallander exploded. "These two men have committed murder," he shouted. "A double murder."

"I still can't release the papers."

Wallander stood up.

"Tomorrow you're going to hand over those papers. Even if I have to get the chief of the National Police to come and get them himself."

"That's just the way things are. I can't change the regulations."

Wallander drove back to Ystad. At quarter to nine he rang Björk's doorbell. Quickly he told him what had happened.

"Tomorrow we put out an APB on them," he said.

Björk nodded. "I'll call a press conference for two o'clock. In the morning I have a consultation with the police chiefs. But I'll see to it that we get the papers from that camp."

Wallander went over to see Rydberg. He was sitting in the dark on his balcony.

All of a sudden he saw that Rydberg was in pain.

Rydberg, who seemed to read his thoughts, said bluntly, "I don't think I'm going to make it through this. I might live past Christmas; I might not."

Wallander didn't know what to say.

"One has to endure," said Rydberg. "But tell me why you're here."

Wallander told him. He could dimly make out Rydberg's face in the darkness.

Then they sat in silence.

The night was cool. But Rydberg didn't seem to notice as he sat there in his old bathrobe with slippers on his feet.

"Maybe they've skipped the country," said Wallander. "Maybe we'll never catch them."

"In that case, we'll have to live with the fact that at least we know the truth," said Rydberg. "Justice doesn't only mean that the people who commit crimes are punished. It also means that we can never give up."

With great effort he stood up and got a bottle of cognac. With shaking hands he filled two glasses.

"Some old police officers die worrying about ancient, unsolved puzzles," he said. "I guess I'm one of them."

"Have you ever regretted becoming a cop?" asked Wallander.

"Never. Not a single day."

They drank cognac. Talked some, or sat in silence. Not until midnight did Wallander get up to leave. He promised to come back the following evening. After he left, Rydberg stayed where he was, sitting on the balcony in the dark.

On Wednesday morning, July twenty-fifth, Wallander told Hanson and Martinson what had happened after the meeting the day before. Since the press conference was set for that afternoon, they decided to pay a visit to the Kivik market after all. Hanson took on the task of writing the press release along with Björk. Wallander figured that he and Martinson would be back no later than noon.

They drove by way of Tomelilla and joined a long line of cars just south of Kivik. They pulled in and parked in a field where a greedy landowner demanded a fee of twenty kronor.

Just as they reached the market area, which stretched before them with a view of the sea, it started to rain. In dismay they stared at the throngs of stalls and people. Loudspeakers were screeching, drunken youths were bellowing, and they were shoved back and forth by the crowd.

"Let's try to meet somewhere in the middle," said Wallander.

"We should have brought walkie-talkies in case something happens," said Martinson.

"Nothing's going to happen," said Wallander. "Let's meet in an hour."

He watched Martinson shamble off and vanish into the crowd. He turned up the collar of his jacket and headed off in the opposite direction.

After a little more than an hour they met up again. Both of them were soaked and feeling annoyed with the throngs of people and the jostling.

"To hell with this," said Martinson. "Let's go someplace and get some coffee."

Wallander pointed at a cabaret tent in front of them.

"Have you been in there?" he asked.

Martinson grimaced. "Some tub of lard doing a striptease. The audience roared like it was some kind of sexual revival meeting. Jesus."

"Let's walk around the tent," said Wallander. "I think there are a few stalls over there too. Then we can go."

They trudged through the mud, pushing their way between a house trailer and rusty tent stakes.

A few stalls were selling various goods. They all looked the same, their awnings pitched above red-painted metal poles.

Wallander and Martinson saw the two men at exactly the same moment.

They were standing inside a stall, its counter covered with leather jackets. A sign showed the price, and Wallander had time to think that the jackets were unbelievably cheap.

The two men were behind the counter.

They stared at the two police officers.

Much too late Wallander realized that they recognized him. His face had appeared so often in pictures in the papers and on television. Kurt Wallander's description had been spread all over the country.

Then everything happened very fast.

One of the men, the one they had started calling Lucia, stuck his hand under the leather jackets on the counter and pulled out a gun. Both Martinson and Wallander dove to the side. Martinson got tangled up in the ropes of the cabaret tent, while Wallander hit his head on the back end of the house trailer. The man behind the counter fired at Wallander. The shot could hardly be heard amid the commotion from the tent where the "death riders" were tearing around on their roaring motorcycles. The bullet struck the trailer, just a few inches from Wallander's head. In the next instant he saw that Martinson was holding a pistol. Even though Wallander was unarmed, Martinson had brought along his service revolver.

Martinson fired. Wallander saw Lucia jerk back and put his hand up to his shoulder. The gun flew out of his hand and landed outside the counter. With a bellow Martinson yanked himself free from the tent ropes and threw himself at the counter, straight at the wounded man. The counter broke in two, and Martinson landed in a jumble of leather jackets. By this time Wallander had lunged forward and grabbed the gun, which was lying in the mud. At the same time he saw Baldy dash away and vanish in the throng. No one seemed to have noticed the exchange of gunfire. The vendors in the surrounding stalls had watched in amazement as Martinson made his furious tiger pounce.

"Go after the other guy," shrieked Martinson from the heap of leather jackets. "I'll take care of this one."

Wallander ran with the pistol in his hand. Baldy was somewhere in the crowd. Terrified people pulled away as Wallander came running with mud on his face and the gun in his hand. He thought he had lost the man when suddenly he caught sight of him again, in wild and reckless flight through the market crowds. He shoved aside an elderly woman who stepped in front of him and crashed into a stall selling cakes. Wallander stumbled over the mess, knocked over a candy cart, and then took off after him.

Suddenly the man disappeared.

Shit, thought Wallander. Shit.

Then he saw him again. He was running toward the outskirts of the market area, on his way down to the steep cliff. Wallander raced after him. A couple of security guards came running toward him, but they leaped aside when he waved the gun and yelled at them to stay away. One of the guards crashed into a tent serving beer, while the other one knocked over a stall selling homemade candlesticks.

Kurt Wallander ran. His heart was pounding like a piston in his chest.

Suddenly the man vanished over the steep cliff. Wallander was about thirty meters behind him. When he reached the edge he stumbled and fell headlong down the slope. He lost his grip on the gun in his hand. For a moment he hesitated, wondering whether he should stop and search for the weapon. Then he saw Baldy running along the shore, and he took off after him.

The chase ended when neither of them had any energy left to keep running. Baldy leaned against a black-tarred rowboat that lay turned over on the shore. Wallander stood ten meters away, so out of breath that he thought he was going to fall over.

Then he noticed that Baldy had drawn a knife and was coming toward him.

That's the knife he cut off Johannes Lövgren's nose with, he thought. That's the knife he used to force Lövgren to tell him where the money was hidden.

He looked around for a weapon. A broken oar was the only thing he could find.

Baldy made a lunge with the knife. Wallander parried with the heavy oar.

The next time the man jabbed with the knife, Wallander hit him. The oar struck the man on the collarbone. Wallander could

hear the bone crack. The man stumbled, and Wallander let go of
the oar and slammed his right fist into the man's chin. His knuckles hurt like hell.

But the man fell.

Wallander collapsed onto the wet sand

A second later Martinson came running.

The rain was suddenly pouring down.

"We got them," said Martinson.

"Yes," said Wallander. "I guess we did."

He walked over to the edge of the water and rinsed off his face.
In the distance he saw a freighter heading south.

He thought about how glad he was to be able to give Rydberg
some good news in the midst of his misery.

Two days later the man named Andreas Haas confessed that
they had committed the murders. He confessed but blamed it all
on the other man. When Lothar Kraftczyk was confronted with
the confession, he gave up too. But he blamed the violence on
Andreas Haas.

Everything had happened just as Wallander had imagined. On
several occasions the two men had gone into various banks to
exchange money and to try to find a customer who was with-
drawing a large sum. They had followed Johannes Lövgren when
Lundin, the chimney sweep, had driven him home. They had tailed
him along the dirt road, and two nights later they had returned
in the car from the refugee camp.

"There's one thing that puzzles me," said Wallander, who was
heading the interrogation of Lothar Kraftczyk. "Why did you give
hay to the horse?"

The man looked at him in surprise.

"The money was hidden in the hay," he said. "Maybe we threw
some of the hay over to the horse when we were looking for the
briefcase."

Wallander nodded. The solution to the mystery of feeding
the horse was that simple.

"One more thing," said Wallander. "Why the noose?"

He got no answer. Neither of the two men wanted to admit

to being the one behind the insane violence. He repeated his question but never got an answer.

The Czech police informed them, however, that both Haas and Kraftczyk had done time for assault in their native country.

After fleeing from the refugee camp, the two men had rented a little dilapidated house outside of Höör. The leather jackets they were selling came from the burglary of a leather-goods shop in Tranås.

The detention hearing was over in a matter of minutes.

No one doubted that the evidence would be airtight, even though the two men were still accusing each other.

Kurt Wallander sat in the courtroom and stared at the two men he had been tracking for such a long time. He remembered that early morning in January when he stepped inside the house in Lenarp. Even though the double murder had now been solved and the criminals would receive their punishment, he still wasn't satisfied. Why had they put a noose around Maria Lövgren's neck? Why so much violence for its own sake?

He shuddered. He had no answers. And that made him uneasy.

Late in the evening on Saturday, August fourth, Wallander took a bottle of whiskey and went over to see Rydberg. On the following day Anette Brolin was going to go with him to visit his father.

Wallander thought about the question he had asked her.

Whether she would consider getting a divorce for his sake.

Of course she had said no.

But he knew that she hadn't been offended by the question.

As he drove over to Rydberg's place, he listened to Maria Callas on the tape deck. He was taking the next week off, as comp time for the extra hours he had worked. He was going to go to Lund to visit Herman Mboya, who had come back from Kenya. He was planning to spend the rest of the time repainting his apartment.

Maybe he would even treat himself to a new stereo.

He parked outside the building where Rydberg lived.

He caught a glimpse of the yellow moon overhead. He could feel that autumn was on the way.

As usual, Rydberg was sitting in the dark on the balcony.
Wallander filled two glasses with whiskey.

"Do you remember when we sat around worrying about what
Maria Lövgren had whispered?" said Rydberg. "That we would be
forced to search for some foreigners? Then, when Erik Magnusson
came into the picture, he was the most sought-after murderer imag-
inable. But he wasn't the one. Now we've got a couple of foreigners after all. And a poor Somali who died needlessly."

"You knew all along," said Wallander. "Didn't you? You were
sure the whole time that it was foreigners."

"I wasn't positive," said Rydberg. "But I thought so."

Slowly they went over the investigation, as if it were already
a distant memory.

"We made lots of mistakes," said Wallander thoughtfully. "I
made lots of mistakes."

"You're a good cop," said Rydberg emphatically. "Maybe I
never told you that. But I think you're a damned fine cop."

"I made too many mistakes," replied Wallander.

"You kept at it," said Rydberg. "You never gave up. You wanted to catch whoever committed those murders in Lenarp. That's
the important thing."

The conversation gradually petered out.

I'm sitting here with a dying man, thought Kurt Wallander
in confusion. I don't think I ever realized that Rydberg is actually going to die.

He remembered the time in his youth when he was stabbed.

He also thought about the fact that a little less than six months
ago he had driven his car while intoxicated. In reality he should
have been dismissed from the police force.

Why don't I tell Rydberg about that? he wondered. Why don't
I say anything? Or does he already know?

The incantation flashed through his mind.

A time to live, a time to die.

"How are you doing?" he asked cautiously.

Rydberg's face was invisible in the darkness.

"Right now I don't have any pain," he said. "But tomorrow

it'll be back. Or the next day."

It was almost two in the morning when Wallander left Rydberg, who stubbornly remained sitting on his balcony.

Wallander left his car where it was and walked home.

The moon had disappeared behind a cloud.

Now and then he took a little hop.

The voice of Maria Callas resounded in his head.

Before he went to sleep, he lay in bed for a while in the dark of his apartment with his eyes open.

Again he thought about the senseless violence. The new times, which might demand a different kind of cop.

We're living in the time of the noose, he thought. Fear will be on the rise.

Then he forced himself to push these thoughts aside and started looking for the black woman in his dreams.

The investigation was over.

Now he could finally get some rest.